ON GUARD

Caroline was sure she at last had Lord Andrew where she wanted him. The handsome earl had sustained a painful injury when thrown from his horse, and Caroline had been assigned the task of nursing him back to health.

At last she would have a chance to make him notice her. At last she could reveal her disguised beauty and breeding to his eyes only.

The she returned to his sickroom to find Lady Phoebe Rutherford sitting by his bedside. They were laughing together, and Lord Andrew clearly had eyes only for this creature who was as captivating as she was treacherous.

Caroline knew she had to take bold measures if she was to save this all-too susceptible male from himself . . . and for herself. . . .

Honor's Way

by

Katherine Kingsley

A SIGNET BOOK

NEW AMERICAN LIBRARY

NAL BOOKS ARE AVAILABLE AT QUANTITY DISCOUNTS WHEN USED TO
PROMOTE PRODUCTS OR SERVICES. FOR INFORMATION PLEASE WRITE
TO PREMIUM MARKETING DIVISION, NEW AMERICAN LIBRARY, 1633
BROADWAY, NEW YORK, NEW YORK 10019.

 SIGNET TRADEMARK REG. U.S. PAT. OFF. AND FOREIGN
COUNTRIES
REGISTERED TRADEMARK—MARCA REGISTRADA
HECHO EN CHICAGO, U.S.A.

SIGNET, SIGNET CLASSIC, MENTOR, ONYX, PLUME,
MERIDIAN and NAL BOOKS are published by NAL PENGUIN
INC., 1633 Broadway, New York, New York 10019

First Printing, August, 1988

1 2 3 4 5 6 7 8 9

PRINTED IN THE UNITED STATES OF AMERICA

Prologue

Soft you; a word or two before you go.
I have done the state some service and they know't.

—William Shakespeare, *Othello*, V, ii

The Marquess of Hambledon stood at the window looking out at the windswept afternoon, but without seeing the last of the leaves that swirled around, red and yellow, in a mad dance before their final fall to earth. His heart was heavy not only with his own grief but also with pity for the girl he had never met and for whom he felt a certain responsibility. It seemed no one else did, and he wanted to be very sure she had made the decision to enter a convent quite freely, and not from desperation because she thought she had nowhere else to turn. He could only hope that she would allow him to speak with her. A rustle came at the door and he turned to see the mother superior, who now smiled at him for the first time since his arrival.

"Lady Caroline awaits you in the garden, my lord. Please, come this way. It is good that she has agreed to see you. The child has had enough of seclusion."

Julian followed her down a series of corridors. Nuns passed him in the other direction, their eyes lowered, their hands clasped together, the swishing of their long black habits the only sound in the deep silence, save for the distant ringing of a bell. The convent emanated a sense of peace; he hoped that Caroline had found it for herself here. The mother superior gestured at a high vaulted archway, and then she melted away. He stepped through the arch. Standing in the garden, her back to him, was a tall slim figure dressed, not in the habit of a novice, which he had ex-

5

pected, but in the plain black of mourning. Her fair hair was cut short, almost as a boy's might be, but as she turned, sensing his presence, he saw that her face had an unusual and solemn beauty, highlighted by large gray eyes, a sweet and generous mouth, and a fine bone structure.

"Lady Caroline," he said as he approached.

"Lord Hambledon." Caroline reached out a slender hand and Julian took it lightly and bowed over it.

"Thank you for seeing me. I did not wish to disturb you in your time of grief, but your father was a close friend, and I felt compelled to offer my condolences on his unexpected death. It saddened me deeply. He shall be sorely missed, not only by his friends but also by his country."

"Thank you, my lord. I know how highly my father regarded you, and your words mean a great deal. It was kind of you to think of me. But shall we sit down? I doubt you are at your most comfortable in convents, and I should like to ease the experience as much as possible."

She smiled, a smile which touched her clear eyes, and Julian suddenly found himself relaxing. This was no fool, easily led, as he had feared. There was something of her father in her, a sense of steadiness and gentle humor, coupled with the same quiet intelligence. General Lord Alexander Peninghurst had been Wellington's right arm and responsible for many of the brilliant strategies of the Peninsular campaign. He had only returned to England on Wellington's insistence, for his health had suffered from the long years in the Peninsula. And now he was dead, not due to any physical collapse, but because he had been attacked and killed by highwaymen whilst journeying to London, a horrible, freak twist of fate which had left Caroline an orphan and England bereft of one of her finest soldiers.

Julian regarded Caroline curiously as she led him to a bench. He knew little of her save that she was Lord Peninghurst's only and much-loved child, and had traveled at her father's side throughout the years of war. He also knew that she had made a rather unusual name for herself: "the little soldier of the Peninsula," they had called her, known not for bearing arms but for her skills in healing. He found that he wanted to know a great deal more.

He sat down and turned to face her. "Tell me, Lady Caroline. What plans have you made for your future? I should like to help you in any way that I can, but I must confess, I had been under the impression that you had converted to the Catholic religion and intended to take vows. By your dress, I assume that is not the case.''

"Please, my lord, call me Caroline; it is what I am accustomed to. As for converting and taking vows, I am afraid that I would not make a very good Catholic, let alone a nun. It is not why I came here. The nuns helped to bring me up after my mother's death in Constantinople. They gave me an education, and taught me how to nurse. And so when my father died, I turned to the same order for solace and for solitude, to try to think things through.'' She made a little face. "The awful truth of the matter is that I'm not a very religious person in the strictest sense of the word. The nuns have done their best, but humility and unquestioning obedience seem to escape me no matter how hard I try.''

Julian smiled. "I see. They were never my strongest suit either.'' His heart was touched by her simple and honest explanation. "What will you do now? Will you stay at the convent and continue your nursing?''

"No. I have had my time here.''

"Ah. Then will you go back to Manleigh House to live with your cousin?''

Caroline frowned. "No. It was never really home to me, given that we left for the Continent when I was only three. Now that my cousin has inherited the title and the land, he will want to live there with his family, without being saddled with a peculiar relation. He is very staid and proper, my cousin, and I fear I should worry at him dreadfully. He would want to give me a Season, despite my advanced age of twenty-two, and see me safely married away to someone as respectable as himself, and I'm afraid that wouldn't suit me at all.''

Julian laughed. "I know him, as it happens; Manleigh is not so very far from Hambledon Abbey. 'Pompous and dull' would be a better description, and I think I should feel exactly as you do about living with him, let alone having to marry one of his friends! Thank goodness that's not a dilemma for me. Well, then. Perhaps you might consider coming to live with my wife and me at the Abbey,'' he said, surprising even himself. "I assure you, my wife prides herself on being unconventional, and we live very simply. It needn't be a permanent arrangement, but it might give you some time to decide what you would like to do with yourself, now that you've made up your mind to leave the convent. I gather, then, that you're not interested in having a Season."

Caroline smiled broadly. "I cannot dance, nor hold polite conversation, although I can converse at great length on religion, campaign strategy, and the treatment of mentionable and unmentionable diseases. I can only ride astride, for there were no sidesaddles in the Peninsula, and that would never do. However, I can sew, for I learned to stitch wounds, and needlepoint was good practice, and I can shoot extremely well, although I doubt that is a skill that is required in a female. In short, I don't think that I am prepared for a Season, my lord. In fact, the only qualification I have is the money my father left me, but I doubt that even five thousand pounds a year would be worth any man's while, considering what would come with it. And I thank you very much for your own offer, which is very kind, but I have my heart set on something quite different. If you really wish to help me, my lord, perhaps you might help me arrange it."

"And what might that be?" asked Julian, amused. His amusement vanished as Caroline looked him straight in the eyes and spoke perfectly calmly.

"I want to expose the traitor who had my father murdered."

It took Julian a moment to collect himself. "I . . . I beg your pardon?"

Caroline stood and turned to face him. "My lord, when I heard you had arrived today, I realized that you might be the answer to my prayers. I knew that you were my father's friend, for he spoke of you as such, and that recommended you highly to me. I also knew that you worked for the Foreign Office, which was also important, for I haven't known where to turn, or to whom. But I needed to judge you for myself before trusting you with this information. I am usually a good judge of character, and you have reassured me as to yours. I don't mean to sound self-inflated, but you see, it's not just a matter of my own feelings. It is truly a matter of national security.''

Julian examined Caroline's face very carefully as she spoke. "What, exactly, do you mean?'' he finally said.

Caroline took a deep breath. "I know it was believed that my father returned to England because of poor health. That was an outright lie; my father was as fit as a horse. Lord Wellington sent him home six months ago because someone in England, someone in a position of power, has been leaking secrets to the French. Our troop movements have been consistently compromised and maneuvers have been sabotaged at an early stage. My father's job was to discover who was responsible for the leak. I believe he did his job too well.''

Julian drew in a sharp little breath. "You think he was murdered for what he knew?''

"I do, my lord.''

Julian thought carefully, balancing his intrinsic liking for Caroline against his habitual caution. "I saw your father shortly after he returned from the Peninsula. He said nothing of the matter to me. Why should he not have enlisted my help if that was the case?'' He paused, then spoke again, measuring his words. "Could you not have somehow misunderstood? Your father surely would have mentioned something of that importance to the Foreign Office or the War Office?''

"I'm sorry, my lord. But he said he couldn't trust anyone.''

"I take no offense,'' said Julian, inwardly relieved at her honesty, and finally prepared to trust her in turn. "I suspected something like this myself. But your father's reticence tells me a great deal right there of the severity of this case. It also tells me much about you, or he never would have confided in you to the degree he did, although it may seem little enough to you. But tell me: does anyone else know about this—anyone at all?''

"My father spoke to only one other person, Captain Jake Renard, his aide-de-camp in the Peninsula, who returned to England with us. But he is completely trustworthy. As for myself, I have spoken only to Mother Superior and to you, my lord. And I assure you, the secret is quite safe with Mother Superior.''

"And, as it happens, with me. You've done well to confide in me, Caroline, and I will return your confidence by telling you something which few people know. It is true that I work with the Foreign Office. But for years I have also been doing very sensitive work for the government, which has often taken me to the Continent. Your father knew of this. If he could not trust me, then he truly could not trust anyone.''

Caroline breathed a sigh of relief. "Then you do believe me? You'll help me to bring this man to justice?''

"Do you mean to say you *know* the identity of this man?''

Caroline hesitated. "I know that my father had a meeting at Manleigh with a certain member of Parliament, and the very next day, my father left for London. He told me that he was going to bring the matter to a close, that he had his evidence. And then he was killed by highwaymen before he could reach London. I believe that he must have confronted this man with his crime, and rather than be exposed, the man arranged for my father's murder. I realize that the evidence is purely circumstantial, and I don't want to implicate a possibly innocent person on that alone, but I've been through it and through it, and it's the only thing that makes sense.''

"It sounds plausible enough," said Julian. "In which case," he continued, gently prompting, "you might now tell me the name of this man. I shan't jump to any conclusions, but I need a starting point, and I can go on from there.''

"His name is Sir Henry Rutherford.''

"Dear heaven.'' Julian put his forehead in his hands for a moment, then looked up. "Caroline. Are you quite sure?''

"Yes. Although I didn't actually see him, I heard the butler announcing him in the library. My father believed me to be away for the day, you see, but I returned early and was working on some papers in the drawing room, which is directly adjacent. I don't think he meant for me to know of the meeting. Do you know Sir Henry, my lord?''

"Yes, I'm afraid I do. I've always found him a distasteful character, although he's well-enough-respected. I wonder what his motive could be for selling out his country . . . Ah, well, aside from the obvious difficulties of smoking out and then exposing a member of Parliament as a traitor and a murderer, the problem becomes a touch more personal. Sir Henry is a close connection of my dearest friend; his brother-in-law, to be exact. This is not going to be easy." He rubbed his forehead and sighed. "But it is no longer your problem, my dear. I thank you for telling me of this, and I shall take it from here. But we still have not resolved the question of your future. I wish you would reconsider my offer—"

Caroline shook her head impatiently and quickly sat down again. "Wait—please, wait. You said Sir Henry is related to your closest friend—that means you have an inside contact! I think I can help, and it will solve the question of where I am to live and what I am to do."

Julian smiled. "And how do you think you're going to help, my dear girl? You don't travel in the right government circles to begin with; you're not even out in society. And even if you were, it would be far too dangerous to involve yourself. Don't you think that as your father's daughter you might be somewhat suspect if you start to ask questions?"

"Of course, but I wouldn't *be* my father's daughter. It's quite simple, really. All you have to do is arrange for me to be hired as . . . as a parlormaid or some such thing in Sir Henry's household. I could watch and listen, and no one would think twice. You could arrange it all through your friend."

Julian opened his mouth to explain why such a wild scheme couldn't possibly work, and then shut it again. "Do you know," he said slowly, "there might be something in this. . . . You couldn't possibly be a parlormaid, for you're too well-spoken, and you wouldn't have the right access to Sir Henry in any case, but you could certainly pass as a governess. There would be very little danger, and you might well overhear something which could be useful to me—if there is anything to this."

"Where else would you begin, my lord? You said you have suspected something wrong yourself, but you obviously have found nothing, and you do travel in the right circles. My presence in Sir Henry's house could not be suspect and might either confirm his treachery or clear him.''

"Yes, it is a point. An impoverished governess, straight from a convent—young, innocent . . . I imagine with a little ingenuity it could be arranged. I would only need to dispense of the present governess. And I would have to find someone trustworthy to place as a stablehand to keep an eye on you, who would have the freedom to pass any necessary information between us. Still, I don't know. It would be asking a great deal of you. You'd have to give up your position in life, temporarily at least. You'd have to be able to think on your feet, be alert, able to deal with any contingency. You're not trained—"

"I could do it, my lord," said Caroline calmly. "After all, virtually no one in England knows me. I am not accustomed to position, for as I have explained, I have spent most of the last six years in a convent or on a battlefield, and there's no room in either for that sort of thing. I was brought up to be independent and to think quickly under pressure, and I have nerves of steel. Please, my lord. It's a question of honor—my own and my father's, and that of my country."

"Honor," mused Julian. "Yes, indeed. One can hardly argue with that; in the end, honor always wins me over. Hmm. Honor. How would you like that for a new name, Caroline Manleigh?"

"It will do perfectly, my lord. It is succinct and to the point, and will constantly remind me of my purpose," she said, and reaching out her hand, she shook his firmly.

Julian threw back his head and laughed. "I think I like you, Caroline Manleigh. I think I like you very much. And I think you had better call me Julian if we are to work together. Now shall we discuss details?"

1

Well, honor is the subject of my story.

—William Shakespeare, *Julius Caesar*, I, ii

"My lord, the Marquess of Hambledon has arrived," intoned Hobson from the bedroom door to his Most Honorable the Earl of Chesney, who was engaged at that moment in arranging his starched cravat, much to Hobson's dismay, whose fingers had been itching to do it himself, and far more elaborately.

"Thank you, Hobson," Andrew said without looking up, thinking to himself that he really must find a less difficult valet. "Have Nugent show him into the study and I'll be down directly." He turned his attention back to the snowy white neckcloth, pulling it into the proper folds, ran a brush through his thick dark hair, flicked a piece of lint from his fawn-colored pantaloons, which stretched without a crease over long muscular legs, then buttoned his white waistcoat and allowed Hobson to help him into his blue swallow-tailed evening coat.

"Ah, my lord," said Hobson with satisfaction. "Exactly the color of your eyes, that dark blue. I thought as much when it was delivered. Mr. Weston once again outdid himself. But I do think you really must wear the heavier benjamin this evening when you go out. We don't want to have you catching cold in this inclement weather—"

"Thank you, Hobson," said Andrew with a sigh. "I shan't be needing you again this evening."

"Very good, my lord," said Hobson with a bow, no expression passing over his long, thin face, but Andrew knew perfectly well what he was thinking, and also knew that the benjamin would be waiting for him downstairs, no doubt along with warm bricks for his feet.

He descended the long staircase and crossed the vast expanse of marble hallway broken only by tall columns rising to support a frescoed ceiling, which was painted improbably with rosy-cheeked cherubs. The thought brought a grin to Andrew's face, which faded as Nugent murmured, "Good

13

evening, your lordship,'' bowing very low and majestically throwing open the double doors to the study.

That room was Andrew's refuge; he had decorated it according to his own tastes, a complete departure from the rest of the house, which overflowed with delicate French furniture. The study was paneled in rich oak, and on one wall was hung sporting and hunting prints, the only visible legacy from his brother. The other wall was lined with overflowing bookcases, holding Andrew's sizable legal collection as well as an eclectic assortment of literature. A large mahogany desk sat in front of the long windows, whose cranberry velvet draperies were pulled against the night. The leather sofa and chairs grouped in front of the wood-paneled fireplace were large and pleasantly well-worn. The room exuded a distinctly masculine atmosphere.

"Good evening, your worship," said Julian, who had patiently been waiting inside, and flashed him a wicked smile. "And how is your oh-so-delicate health?"

"By God, it's good to see you again, my friend!" exclaimed Andrew with pleasure, clapping him on the shoulder. "How long has it been—three months?"

They might have been brothers, so close was the resemblance. Both were tall and well-built, with full heads of waving black hair. But where Julian Ramsay's eyes were a clear gray, Andrew's were a sapphire blue, and where Julian's mouth was hard and determined, Andrew's curved up as if ever ready to laugh.

They had been the best of friends for more than twelve years now, since their time up at Oxford, and had been in many scrapes together, not the least of which included rescuing Julian's ward Bryonny from a difficult and dangerous situation. Julian and Bryonny had been married now for a year and a half, and were as happy as any married couple that Andrew had ever known. His reward for his part in the piece was to have their child named after him, and he spent as much time with the three of them as he could manage.

But he had to admit there was something missing in his own life. Since his brother George had died the year before, leaving him the earldom, his previously comfortable life as a younger son with his own competency had been completely disrupted, and all of the crushing responsibilities which his elder brother had cheerfully managed to neglect had been brought heavily to bear upon him. Not only were there the pressing concerns of the various estates, many of which George had allowed to fall into decay from sheer lack of interest in anything other than his horses, but there was also the family George had left behind, consisting of a helpless widow (despite the fact that she had married again shortly after) and her two young daughters, whose dilemma Andrew had been wrestling with all day. His heart had lightened at the sight of Julian, and he stepped back and regarded him with a broad smile.

"My health continues to be excellent, but you, on the other hand, look exhausted." Julian did appear tired; fine lines were drawn under his eyes, and he looked as if he hadn't had much sleep recently.

"Tactless, but observant as ever," Julian said with a wry smile. "I confess, it's been a difficult few days."

"What is it, Julian?" asked Andrew with concern.

"A touch of trouble at the Foreign Office. You know how it is."

"I see," said Andrew, knowing that he would discover no more. Julian's work was too sensitive to be discussed. "So how goes the rest, my friend?"

"Well enough. And how is it with you? Are your sycophantic nursemaids keeping you safe and sound?"

"Laugh away all you want, but you have no idea how wretched it is—like having a houseful of adoring watchdogs following me around to make sure I don't catch a chill and lose the earldom for them, and this time for good!" He poured them both a generous measure of the good French cognac Julian had brought on his last trip to town.

"What you need to do is marry quickly and get yourself with heirs. Then they'll all stop worrying about the succession and leave you in peace. Believe me, I do know, having been a confirmed bachelor for more years than I care to remember!"

"So you were," said Andrew glumly. It wasn't the first time that his responsibility to marry to ensure the succession had occurred to him. But that was the last thing he wanted to discuss, and he quickly changed the subject.

"Speaking of your wedded bliss, how are Bryonny and

my godson? Have you brought them with you? I haven't seen them since the summer, you know.''

"They're both very well, thank you, safely tucked away at the Abbey, where they belong. Bryonny sent her love.''

"And is she managing to stay out of trouble?''

Julian laughed. "Bryonny and trouble were whelped together, as you well know, but she is keeping clear more or less, I suppose. I have to take care not to stay too long away from home or all hell is likely to break loose. Which reminds me, how is your dear sister-in-law?''

"Well enough—only in a fearful flap, as usual. I've just had a letter from her this morning. I'll have to get up there directly, I suppose. My God, my dear brother was inconsiderate enough to depart this world with no notice and leave me saddled with the blasted earldom, but to throw in Arabella in the bargain was really too unfair.''

"Ah, well, at least he left you rich as Golden Ball for your troubles, despite his efforts to the contrary. What is it this time?''

"Here, see for yourself," said Andrew, picking up the letter from his desk and handing it to Julian, who attempted to decipher the crossed and recrossed sheet.

"What on earth . . . ?'' Julian said with a smothered laugh, beginning to read aloud. " ' . . . And dear Phoebe, Sir Henry's daughter, you'll remember, is due home from her ladies' seminary any day, and of course will need a Season come spring, but I'm sure I don't know how I'm going to cope, not knowing anything about being a mama to a girl of seventeen, so much older than my own two darling little girls, although of course I shall do my very best, for Sir Henry's sake. But far worse, the governess, Miss Torch, has picked up and left this very day with no notice, leaving me alone with the children and goodness only knows what else. I cannot be sad that we have lost Miss Torch, for she had me quite cowed, but the girls must have a governess and I have no idea how to acquire one in a hurry. What am I to do and Sir Henry not at home? Please help me, Andrew dearest. You know how I count on you since my darling George caught that dreadful chill on the hunting field and left us.'

"My goodness, Andrew," said Julian with not an ounce

of sympathy. "You do have a serious problem on your hands." He handed the letter back, then walked over to the window, pulling the heavy curtains back, and looked out onto the square. The gas lamps had been lit, and his carriage stood outside, his groom sitting patiently on the box. He smiled with satisfaction, then turned back to the room again, letting the curtains fall closed.

Andrew leaned one broad shoulder against the mantlepiece. "You would think her husband would be the person she applied to when she's in trouble."

"I'm sure Henry Rutherford is far too busy attending to his business concerns to worry about the hiring of governesses," said Julian. "His seat is up for reelection this year, which will keep him on his toes. But tell me, how do you think the marriage is going? I can't help but think it an odd match."

" 'Odd' is certainly the word; aside from the large difference in their ages, their temperaments couldn't be more different, but it's a clear-cut case of Henry marrying Arabella for her money, and Arabella marrying Henry from sheer loneliness. Henry was right there at Croftsfield, only five miles away, just waiting to comfort her in her time of need. My God, he didn't even have the decency to wait a year! He pounced the minute I went to attend to the property in Scotland, where he knew I would be unable to interfere, and by the time I returned, the deed was done, poor George not dead six months! And now it seems that he's not often at home, so Arabella is as lonely as before."

"I know, my friend, but there you are. At least your nieces have a father again."

"That's the shame of it: from what I've seen, he pays them no more attention than one would kennel dogs, poor things, and Jocie's become so strange since George died—worse than strange. According to Arabella's last letter, she shows all signs of turning into a religious fanatic, and little Minerva now doesn't speak at all. I must confess to special concern about the child." He shook his head. "I've done my best to see them when I can, but I've been so busy this last year that I've hardly managed to be around. Still, once I have this last piece of business completed, I intend to retire to Chesney and make it up to them. You'd think the man might make the effort to be kind to his new stepdaughters. He's not exactly a fountain of warmth, but it will be interesting to see if he is any different with his own daughter.''

"Ah, then you haven't met the young Phoebe yet. I heard from some quarter or other that she has all the makings of an Incomparable. If it's the case, Arabella might well have her hands fuller this Season than she realizes—and you, if you have to trot her all over town,'' he added with amusement, and Andrew shot him a look of annoyance.

"Someone has to help Arabella out of this quake she's in over the girl's Season. You know Arabella—she's as dear as can be, but absolutely helpless and as timid as a rabbit. George adored her, of course, and married her straight out of the schoolroom, but he left her no more prepared to go out on her own in the world than an infant. I'm sure that's why Henry snapped her up so easily; all he had to do was be kind to her and take away all her troubles, and I, blast it, was so busy untangling my brother's affairs that I didn't even notice what was happening. Oh, well, it's done now, and I suppose I shall have to pay the price for not watching Arabella more closely. Now, where the deuce am I to find a governess?'' He ran a hand through his hair in distraction. "God knows the girls could use somebody warm and kind, unlike that demon Miss Torch that Henry hired, but what do I know of finding that sort of woman? And the devil of it is that I really can't leave London for at least a month, not while I'm in the middle of handing over my legal practice.''

"Hmm,'' said Julian. "Don't raise your hopes too high, but something just occurred to me.''

"Well, good God, man, what is it!''

"She's really fairly young, but I suppose it might do.''

"*Who's* fairly young?'' said Andrew impatiently.

"A certain Miss Winslow. She's an orphan with the nuns at St. Mary's Convent, quite close to Hambledon Abbey. I had a letter from her recently, requesting employment, but I had nothing to offer. I gather after all these years she's decided that the convent is not for her, but she is educated. She's only twenty-two. Would that be acceptable, do you think?''

"I certainly wouldn't quibble! It's a gift from heaven, Julian—literally, perhaps," he said with a grin. "What an enormous relief! When can it be arranged?"

"I suppose I could stop in tomorrow on my way home. If she agrees to take the position, I can arrange to have her sent directly to Croftsfield. Can Arabella survive for a few more days?"

"She'll have to," said Andrew, cheerfully dismissing Arabella and her problems with a wave of his hand. "Now, what about that supper? I'm famished, and I'm sure you must be as well. Shall we take your carriage or mine?"

"Mine, I think. It's standing outside with nothing to do but let the horses grow cold. Which reminds me, I must tell you about Stafford nearly succumbing to apoplexy when Derby told him he was a pompous fool with no more idea of how to manage a team then a nursling. . . ."

They collected their cloaks and hats—Andrew declining the heavy drab benjamin—and went out into the cool October evening, chatting amiably, two gentlemen who appeared to have not a care in the world.

Honor Winslow alighted from the carriage that Julian had been kind enough to supply, thanked the groom, pressing a shilling into his hand, and received her portmanteau from the footman, who unstrapped it from the back of the chaise and placed it on the ground by her feet. He pulled the steps up, mounted his seat, and the carriage departed with a clatter of hooves and wheels. And then it was completely silent. She looked down at her battered case as if it might offer some friendly comfort; she had never felt so alone in all her life.

She had a strong urge to go running after the carriage and have it take her back to Hambledon Abbey, where life for the last week had been peaceful and secure. She had found Julian's wife, Bryonny, absolutely charming, and as unconventional as Julian had promised, which suited her absolutely. They had prepared her for her new role as best they could and had discussed together all of the possible problems that might occur, and Julian had questioned her time and time again to be certain that she truly wanted to go ahead. She had not wavered in her determination, and so yesterday he had given her her new wardrobe, appropriate for Honor Winslow, an impoverished governess. They had all called her Honor, to accustom her to the name, and she had become used to hearing it. But she hadn't really put Caroline Manleigh behind her until this morning when she had put on the first of the governess dresses. She felt as if she had shed her skin, leaving Caroline behind, consigned to some distant future when Honor Winslow had successfully completed her job. And here she was, for however long it would take to bring Sir Henry Rutherford to justice.

Her gaze traveled to the house. Croftsfield was a large square, three stories high, large enough to need a big staff of servants—and she was about to become one of their order. The thought made her smile, for she had no idea how one went about becoming a servant. But she had played enough different roles in her life to be able to adjust, and she had agreed to fill the position of governess, so fill it she would. Wondering just what she had let herself in for, she reminded herself of her purpose, squared her shoulders, and marched to the front door. The door knocker felt cold and heavy in her hand, but she resolutely let it fall three times and heard it echo in the recesses of the house. No one appeared, and after three minutes she knocked again, then drew her shabby brown cloak more closely around her, warding off the autumn chill, trying to suppress a shiver that had less to do with the weather than her own apprehension.

And then the door finally opened to reveal an elderly butler who looked her up and down with a chilly regard, taking in her worn bonnet and cloak.

"Good afternoon, miss," he finally said with a questioning air, his disdain unmistakable.

"Good afternoon, sir," she said, wondering if she had woken him from his afternoon nap, given how put-out he looked. "I am Miss Honor Winslow, come to interview with Lady Rutherford for the position of governess. I believe Lady Rutherford is expecting me."

Once again the butler looked her up and down, and then, with an almost imperceptible shrug that was not lost on her, he stepped aside. "This way, miss." She left the portmanteau sitting on the ground and followed.

He led her through the great hall to a pair of double doors, and knocked, then drew the doors open. It was a drawing room. The afternoon light streamed in through the windows. Lady Arabella Rutherford sat at a tambour frame, her head bent over her work. She was no more than thirty and very fair, her hair arranged *à la grecque*, with soft curls tumbling down around her face. She wore a dress of rose muslin sprigged with dainty violets, with full sleeves buttoned tightly at the wrist, and a knot of white ribbons fell from the high waist to the floor, where the hem was deeply flounced. That was all Honor could see from her limited view behind the butler's back.

"My lady, Miss Winslow is here," said the man. "Will you see her now?" His voice held a doubtful note.

Arabella's blue eyes flew to the door. "Oh, yes, Spencer, do show her in!" She jumped to her feet, her hands clasped together in anticipation.

He stepped aside and Honor entered the room. "My lady." She swept her a little curtsy.

"Miss Winslow—how happy I am that you have finally come! We must see you settled in directly and have you meet the children; they do so need some guidance! Here, now, take off your bonnet and let me look at you."

Honor untied the ribbons of her deep poke bonnet and removed it, trying to smooth down her short curls. Was it possible that Julian had been so efficient that there was to be no question about the position? But then, he had created the difficulty in the first place by having the formidable Miss Torch receive a more attractive offer for a governess position.

"Why, you're so young!" exclaimed Arabella, and Honor found herself blushing to be put under such close inspection. "I had expected someone much older. And such a pleasant face! Somehow one always thinks of religious people . . ." She trailed off uncertainly, then brightened again. "But how very pleasant it will be to have another young person about the house. Now, do sit down and tell me all about yourself. I know absolutely nothing about you at all!" She took Honor's arm and led her to a little sofa covered in pale blue silk and pulled her down onto it.

Honor relaxed immediately. She felt like a venerated guest who had been kind enough to pay a call, most certainly not like the impoverished gentlewoman she was supposed to be, in desperate need of work, and she had to resist an impulse to laugh. "I'm afraid I haven't any references, my lady. I only just left the convent, and this is my first position."

"References! La, child, what more reference do I need than my dear brother-in-law Lord Chesney saying you were just the thing!"

"I know I may appear young for the position, although I am fully twenty-two, but I believe I can be a good governess: I had a well-rounded education at the convent, I can sew, I was trained in nursing, and I love children. I hope you will find me suitable, my lady."

"Of course I will! I could immediately see that you love children just from looking at your face. And Jocelyn and Minerva do so need to be loved. Their last governess had to leave very suddenly, and we've been lost ever since. And with Sir Henry gone from home—well, you know how it is. My husband is often away from Croftsfield, you see. He is a member of Parliament and must constantly travel." Arabella's brow seemed to cloud over.

Honor considered all of this, but said only, "Perhaps you might tell me about the children, my lady?"

"Oh, of course, how silly of me. Jocelyn is eleven—I know her name seems a touch masculine, but her dear father, may he rest in peace, was so hoping for a boy, and the name stayed. She's very clever, but rather serious. Minerva is six and . . . quiet. She doesn't talk, you see. It's shyness, I suppose, although Miss Torch said she was only being willful—but she won't be any trouble, I assure you. She's always been so good. Jocie might be a little more difficult; she can be very rude and recalcitrant, which Sir Henry won't tolerate. That's why he hired Miss Torch, hoping her firmness would teach the girls manners. But it didn't seem to help, despite everything."

"I understood there was an older girl."

"Oh! Oh, yes, that would be Phoebe, but she won't be one of your charges. Phoebe is Sir Henry's daughter. But I only met her briefly last spring, before Sir Henry and I were married, so I cannot tell you very much about her. She returns home in a month's time from her ladies' seminary, in preparation for a Season." Arabella gave a little twist to her handkerchief. "Now, what else? The housekeeper, Mrs. Lipp, can see to any of your needs; she knows everything, far more than I do, but she often has to keep to her bed with the rheumatism. It makes it so dreadfully difficult to keep things running smoothly. When we were at Chesney it was so much easier, with a full staff. But it can't be helped," she said, stopping herself abruptly. "So that is the situation. Is there anything else you desire to know?"

"Nothing for the moment, my lady."

"Then you'll take the position?"

"Why, yes, I would be very happy to," said Honor, thinking this was one of the oddest conversations she had ever had, and grateful that she'd had a little warning as to how it might be.

"Thank goodness for that! What a dear you are, and I just know you are *kind*. Now," she said, rising, looking enormously relieved to have the interview over, "why don't I take you to meet the children? Don't expect too much; as I said, they're not very forthcoming, but I'm sure they will warm to you. It's Sir Henry we must worry about. He does so believe in strict governesses of . . . seasoned years. But perhaps I shall be able to bring him around. We do have a month before his return from London."

Honor followed. As she started up the stairs, she felt eyes on her back and turned. A man was conferring with Spencer just outside of the front door. His clothing was shabby, but he was of a muscular build, in a way that spoke of time spent outdoors. He looked up at her and smiled, and she stared in astonishment as she took in the familiar features. She had known that Jake Renard would be here, for Julian had told her how he had arranged it, but she had never expected such a transformation from the dapper, diplomatic captain to this. She smiled in return, and he went back to his conversation.

Honor went after Arabella.

The children were found in the day nursery, the older girl quietly reading to the younger in the window seat. The little girl was lovely; she looked like a china doll with flaxen hair and enormous blue eyes, but the elder couldn't have been more different. She had brown hair with no inclination to curl, her eyes were an indefinite shade of hazel, and her skin was sallow. Honor felt a rush of sympathy. She was at a difficult age and with time would grow into her features, but her sulky expression as she looked up from the book did nothing to improve her.

"Miss Winslow, these are my children, Lady Jocelyn and Lady Minerva Montague. My darlings, meet Miss Winslow, who has come to look after you. Make your curtsies now, my sweetings," said Arabella coaxingly. "Minerva, darling, take your thumb out of your mouth."

Minerva obliged, but only for a moment.

"Good afternoon, Jocelyn, Minerva," said Honor, going over to them and kneeling down to come to their height. "I am so pleased to meet you!"

"If you say so, Miss Winslow," muttered Jocelyn, looking at her with undisguised hostility. Minerva said nothing, only stared at her with those huge expressionless eyes. Honor looked over at their mother and smiled. "Why don't you leave me with the children to become acquainted? We have much to get to know of each other."

"You have no idea how very happy I am you have come, Miss Winslow," said Arabella with a great sigh, as if handing a burden over, and with one last backward look, she hurried out.

"Come now, girls; why don't you come and sit over here with me," said Honor, taking stock of the nursery. It was a large room, and full of light; the carpet was a rich, deep green and the damask draperies at the long windows were a burgundy red, with cushions on the window seat to match. A low table and chairs were placed in front of the softly glowing fireplace, and two comfortable armchairs with embroidered footstools sat next to the corner window with a small mahogany table between them. But the room had a strangely empty quality and Honor finally realized what it was. There were no toys scattered about. Shelves lined one wall, with neat rows of books and one of dolls, beautifully dressed, but they appeared to be untouched.

"Are these your dolls? How pretty they are!" said Honor cheerfully. She went over and took one down, dressed in old French court costume.

"No, Miss Winslow," said Jocelyn disdainfully. "Those belong to Phoebe Rutherford. We're not to touch her things."

"Oh . . ." said Honor, replacing the doll. "But haven't you any dolls of your own, then?"

"No. I am too old for dolls."

"Too old? Where in heaven's name did you get that idea?"

"Miss Torch said so. I am a young lady, Miss Winslow, concerned only with the higher things in life."

"I see . . ." said Honor, thinking that she had her work cut out for her. "Well, you may think you're too old for dolls, but Minerva most certainly isn't, and I'm sure Miss Rutherford wouldn't mind if Minerva played with hers."

"Yes, she would," said Jocelyn smugly, then took Minerva's free hand, effectively shutting Honor out. "Come, Minnie," she said. "I'll finish reading to you from Proverbs."

"How very exemplary," said Honor dryly. "Minerva must find it fascinating. Well, then," she continued as Jocelyn shot her a poisonous glare, "as it seems you have no need of me, I'll just find my room and unpack. No doubt you're both far too old for a governess as well."

She found her room with no trouble; it opened off the night nursery, where the girls had their bedrooms across the hall from her. She looked around her; the room was comfortable enough, with a four-poster tester bed, a heavy armoire in the corner, and a sofa and chairs grouped near the fireplace with a table off to one side, where she supposed she would be eating her meals alone. A stand holding a porcelain jug and basin stood next to a small dressing table with a mirror above it. Her portmanteau stood next to the bed. She took a deep breath and walked over to the washstand with a determined stride. One step at a time, she told herself, and poured out some water, actually hot, she noted with surprise, and washed the dirt of travel from her hands and face. As she used the towel that had been provided, her eye caught her reflection in the mirror.

Honor Winslow? The face looked back at her, a stranger's, as if she had never seen it before. Her life had not lent itself to mirror-gazing; there had been no need for beauty, certainly not for womanhood. Yet here was a woman looking back at her, as if she had sprung fully formed from nowhere. A woman with grave gray eyes and short fair curls in a drab, badly fitting brown dress. It would be obvious to anyone that she had just stepped out of half a lifetime in a convent, despite how false that impression was. In the last few years her hair had always been kept closely cut, partially because of the heat, partially for convenience while in the field of battle. There had been no time for grooming and, as revolting as it sounded, head lice were a serious problem. And of course, most important, was the fact that in dealing with the wounded day and night, there was no place for elaborate coils of hair that could come loose and fall down at the most inopportune moments. In truth, there had been no place for much other than skill and persistence in the face of pain and deprivation and often filth, and the constant effort of warding off fear—her own and that of the men she nursed. There had certainly never been any place for womanhood.

She sighed and leaned closer. Not pretty, for her nose was too long and her chin too set, and her hair was an indiscriminate color, neither truly blond nor brown, but there was character there, she supposed—which translated into the fact that she was stubborn, determined, and outspoken. Still, if nothing else, she knew the meaning of dedication, and of duty.

Duty. It had been pounded into her by her father, by all the people she had grown up with, a part of every waking moment of her life, never to be forgotten. And today she began a new life, in which both dedication and duty would play very much a part. Hold fast, she silently told herself. It was a challenge ahead. "Here you are, Honor Winslow," she whispered. "Now make the most of it."

A tap came at the door, and impatiently she ran her fingers through her curls, which hardly needed a brush, and turned from the mirror. "Come in," she called.

"Oh, miss," said the young girl, no more than fifteen, who entered the room. "I be Betsy and I come on Mrs.

Lipp's orders to ask if you be comfortable and if you please would you be so kind as to visit her in her rooms.''

Honor smiled. Betsy was a funny little thing, putting her in mind of a robin, with bright red cheeks and curious, darting eyes. "I'd be happy to, Betsy. Thank you for bringing me the message. Was it you who was so kind as to provide me with hot water on my arrival?"

"Yes, miss," said Betsy, bobbing an awkward curtsy and beaming with pleasure. "I reckoned you'd be dusty from your travels and in need of it."

"Thank you for your thoughtfulness. Would you see to the children while I am gone?"

"Yes, miss," said Betsy, looking doubtful. "I often saw to them for Miss Torch, not that it didn't give me a chill, and that's a fact. That Lady Jocelyn can stare you down like you was the devil himself. She be a strange one, that, what with her praying and preaching, and that poor little sister of hers just as queer, and has been since the day she crossed this threshold not six months ago with nary a word. If you ask me, they be downright unnatural, and that Miss Torch with her strange ideas weren't no help when she came. I think she only made them worse. The only time I ever saw them smile was when Lord Chesney came to visit, the one time only, and more's the pity, for he be very kind on the eyes, miss, and we was all in a flutter. But then there was some close goings-on with Sir Henry and her ladyship and we haven't seen him since. But here I be chattering away, and Mrs. Lipp waiting this whole time. Down the corridor, down the stairs, through the passage, and there it be, the first door you see."

"Thank you, Betsy," she said, amused at this protracted speech. "That would be very kind. I shan't be long."

She went down the corridor as she'd been instructed, past vague ancestral portraits of corpulent gentlemen and languorous women in various period dress. Red hair seemed to predominate, she noted with interest. She also noted that everything was slightly shabby and not very clean. Spencer, Betsy, now Mrs. Lipp. Where were all the other servants? she wondered as she reached the back stairs. Here the carpeting stopped, and the stairway twisted down, steep and narrow. The next floor opened onto the passage, and she found herself in a dark hallway. The promised door was there, and she tapped lightly. "Mrs. Lipp? It's Honor Winslow."

"Do come in," said a slightly peevish voice, and Honor opened the door and had to choke back a gasp of laughter at the spectacle that met her eyes.

Mrs. Lipp was an enormous woman, weighing a good sixteen stone. She possessed a number of chins, and her eyes were swallowed up in folds of cheek. She sat draped in shawls in a large armchair, her foot on a stool, and the offending foot was heavily swathed in bandages. A smell permeated the room, a peculiar medicinal odor mixed with something else that seemed familiar but which Honor couldn't place at that moment. But most astonishing of all was the mass of flaming red hair which crowned Mrs. Lipp's gigantic head, of a color so very red that not even nature could have managed to outshine it. A white lace cap sat perched upon this masterpiece, decorously tied under one of the many chins by satin ribbons which had been coaxed into a bow of admirable proportions.

"Don't just stand there, girl, come in, come in! I can't get up at the moment, as you can see; my rheumatics is kicking up. It's this cold and damp that does it every time. Come closer where I can see you." She fumbled for her spectacles, which hung by a ribbon somewhere in the region of her ample bosom, and perched them on her little nose, then proceeded to give Honor a thorough inspection, which made her feel very much like a prize cow at a fair.

"Humph," Mrs. Lipp finally said, nodding her head vigorously, and her chins trembled like jelly. "Well, Spencer said you were a young snip of a gel, and for once he was right about something, not that it counts for anything." She spoke in overly refined accents, torturing the vowels. "Too tall for fashion and too slim for my taste, but then, Spencer says you were raised in a nunnery, and I don't suppose they're overly generous with their food. I suppose they cut all your hair off to fit that headgear, and a shame I call it, not that there's any call for comeliness in a governess."

Honor's hand went involuntarily to her curls, but she quickly dropped it again, fixing her eyes on the ground.

"Now, sit down over there," carried on Mrs. Lipp, oblivious of Honor's embarrassment, "and we'll have a little chat while I put you in the way of things. I hope you know your business, my girl, for I have enough on my hands. We're very shorthanded around the place, and you can't be just another mouth to feed, not with the tight budget I'm expected to run this house on. Miss Torch thought she was too good for the rest of us and never lifted a finger to help out."

"I'll do what I can, Mrs. Lipp, as long as it doesn't take away from my duties with the children."

Mrs. Lipp nodded approvingly and settled herself more comfortably in her chair. "That's the attitude, my girl. We can't have you getting ideas above your station, can we? Now, supposedly you'll answer first to Lady Rutherford, but she has no idea what she's about, and I don't know what Sir Henry thought he was doing, up and marrying her like that when she has no more idea how to run a household than a peahen, but that's neither here nor there. So you'll be taking your orders from me. Now. The children visit their mother for an hour in the morning and again at tea, and when Sir Henry is at home they will be taken to the Blue Saloon for half an hour at five o'clock. He can't abide noise, so you're to see that they are kept quiet. As for the staff, there's Betsy, whom you've met. She's as simple as they come, but at least she knows how to work with no complaints. Mrs. Spencer is the cook and thinks she's God Almighty, no different from that husband of hers, but you just remember whom you take your orders from and we'll get along. She has two girls who come in to help, but they stay downstairs. There's the new groom, Jake; he's come just this week to replace that bounder who up and went without so much as a by-your-leave, just like that Miss Torch, not that anyone will be missing her. He keeps himself to the stables, so you shouldn't be having much to do with him—but handsome is as handsome does, as I've always said, so don't let me catch you making calf's eyes at him, or you'll find yourself with the door at your back. There'll be none of those goings-on in my household.

"I expect you to be my right hand when I'm indisposed. You'll learn soon enough. Now, bring me my medicine bottle from that bureau there and run along.'' She leaned back in her chair as if exhausted by the speech.

Honor obligingly fetched the dark brown bottle and departed, waiting until she was safely through the passage and halfway up the stairs before collapsing with laughter.

2

I am giddy, expectation whirls me round.
The imaginary relish is so sweet
That it enhances my senses.

 —William Shakespeare, *Troilus and Cressida*, III, ii

Honor quickly learned that despite all of Mrs. Lipp's pronouncements, the woman had little control over the house, which ran in a decidedly uneven fashion. Grasping the situation, Honor quietly began to override Mrs. Lipp's orders when they threatened to overthrow the already precarious household. Often enough Mrs. Lipp forgot she had ordered a particular menu for lunch or dinner and would countermand her own directions, throwing the cook into a frenzy. Arabella was unable to cope with either the confusion or Mrs. Spencer's tantrums, and Honor took to bringing the menus directly to Arabella herself, and gently prompting her in making decisions. As Mrs. Lipp rarely emerged from her room, issuing her commands from that place either to Honor or by way of Betsy, she was none the wiser. Honor began to wonder if Mrs. Lipp's long periods of indisposition were due less to rheumatism than to a fondness for her medicine bottle, which Honor suspected contained pure gin. Spencer was no problem at all, for despite his perpetually disapproving air, he was not often in evidence, and when he was, he was almost always in a somnambulant condition.

Honor thanked heaven for Jake Renard, who had arrived at Croftsfield with a strong Yorkshire accent replacing his own well-bred tones. He conspired to hold up his own end of the establishment, and although that was limited to the stables, as a groom he was often pressed into service running errands. He adopted an air of humble respect for his betters, which, given the people he was accustomed to fraternizing with, often had Honor biting her cheek against a sudden urge to laugh.

But where Mrs. Lipp and the household were quickly and relatively easily organized by a combination of meek appearance and gentle suggestion always credited to another source, the children were another matter. Minerva and Jocelyn were quiet but gave her not one inch. Minerva didn't speak a word, and spent hours sitting quite still, gazing out of the window. Jocelyn was never exactly insubordinate but never truly cooperative, and seemed to spend an inordinate amount of time reading the Bible, when she wasn't hard at work at her lessons, priggishly quoting it back at Honor whenever the occasion suited. When she couldn't find an appropriate passage from the Bible, she would quote Miss Torch instead, which made Honor grit her teeth.

Honor accompanied them on their visits to their mother. It was left to Honor to make inconsequential conversation. Jocie bordered on hostility, Minerva said nothing, and their mother was no match for the withdrawn silence. Honor began to despair that she was no match for them either; even when she took them on walks, they didn't play and shout as most children; they did as they were bidden without protest, but equally without enthusiasm.

But then one afternoon a week after her arrival, Honor found the opportunity she had been waiting for. It came when she opened the window in the nursery an inch or two to let in some fresh air.

Jocelyn looked up from her history lesson. "Miss Torch said cold air is harmful to the lungs."

"And stale air is harmful to the brain," replied Honor tartly, "and furthermore, Miss Torch is gone and has no more say in the matter."

Jocelyn shrugged and went back to her history. Honor shook her head and returned to the bookcases, which she had been sorting out. She pulled from the stack a beautifully illustrated book of fairy tales. Inscribed on the inside in a large childish scrawl was "Andrew Montague, Chesney, 1791."

She smiled, imagining the small boy who had written it so proudly. "Jocelyn, look what I've found. Do you like fairy tales?"

Jocelyn looked at her with scorn. "I don't read fairy stories. They don't improve the mind."

"No? But look; this book belonged to one of your relatives. Are you acquainted with him?"

"Uncle Andrew? Of course. He is the earl, now that our father is dead," said Jocelyn superiorly, as if amazed that Honor should not know such an important fact.

"Indeed," said Honor. "And tell me, how do you find his mind?"

"He is very clever," said Jocelyn, not seeing the trap. "He is a solicitor."

"Really? How do you suppose he came to be so clever?"

"He worked very hard, and went to university."

"And all this cleverness despite the fact that he obviously read fairy stories!"

"Yes," she said with a frown, then paused, seeing Honor's point too late. She changed tactics. "But Miss Torch said—"

"I don't give a fig for what Miss Torch said. She sounds a most unimaginative woman."

"Miss Torch said that imagination can only lead to ruin," said Jocelyn darkly.

This time Honor couldn't help herself. She burst into peals of laughter. "Did she! And tell me, Jocelyn, did she tell you what sort of ruin you were to fall into?"

"No, but she said that discipline of mind and body was the only course to salvation."

"I think I begin to understand," said Honor, still smiling. "I suppose she had you wear a hair shirt to bed at night?"

Jocelyn looked intrigued, as if this thought had not before occurred to her. "A hair shirt? The monks and nuns wore them for penance to purge evil thoughts from their souls, didn't they?"

"A century or two ago. I imagine such garments were extremely uncomfortable and did very little for the soul. You know, Jocelyn, I spent years in a convent and never saw a single hair shirt. Fancy that! I never even saw a single nun slide from grace, and some had wonderful imaginations."

Jocelyn regarded her with even greater interest. "*You* were in a convent, Miss Winslow? Did you not complete your vows? I have always wanted to be a nun, even though we are not Catholic. But I shall be devout and devote my life to God, and never marry. Marriage only leads to carnal sin."

"Oh, dear," said Honor, sitting down at the table and trying very hard to maintain her composure. "My dear Jocelyn, I can see that we have some talking to do. I didn't become a nun, because I had no vocation. I went to the convent because I had been orphaned and the sisters were kind enough to take me in and continue my education. I'm afraid I was a dreadful nuisance to them. It takes a very special sort of person to live that kind of life; most people would be terribly unhappy under those circumstances. I was in the end, and I think you would be too."

Jocelyn glared. "I am unhappy now. That proves that I was meant for a religious life."

"Absolute nonsense! Of course you're unhappy," said Honor succinctly.

Jocelyn was startled out of her truculence. "Why would you say that?"

"Because you still miss your papa. It has not been so long since he died, and it takes time for people to come to terms with grief."

"Yes . . ." said Jocelyn, her face twisting miserably. "I do miss Papa dreadfully. But Miss Torch said when she came that we shouldn't dwell on the past, that it was our Christian duty to be grateful to Sir Henry and to love him as our new papa."

"Oh, Jocelyn," said Honor, her heart going out to the girl. "It's been very difficult for you to be uprooted from your home and to have to make your life in a new place, hasn't it? But it wouldn't be natural for you not to grieve for your father. That doesn't make you ungrateful."

"But I'm *not* grateful, don't you see? I hate it here, and I hate Sir Henry, and that makes me wicked! Miss Torch said so. And it's much worse to know you're wicked and to keep on being wicked anyway. It's the sort of thing you burn in hell for."

Honor gently took her hand. "My dear, you are not wicked in the least. Your feelings are perfectly natural. It is terribly difficult losing a parent, and it would be very unfair to ask you to love someone instantly who has taken his place. Perhaps with time your feelings for your new stepfather will change, but it doesn't make you wicked that you don't love him."

"I'll *never* love him, no matter what anyone says. And I hate my mama too," she muttered.

"Why, Jocelyn? Your mama loves you so much!"

Jocelyn raised angry eyes. "She does not! How could she love us and do what she did? H-how could she have gone and married Sir Henry when she knew we would be so unhappy! She took us away from Chesney, and all that we knew and loved! If she had truly loved Papa, then she never would have thought to marry again. It was carnal lust, just as Miss Torch said—"

"My dear girl," Honor interrupted gently but with a gleam of laughter in her eyes, "goodness only knows what you think carnal lust is, but rest assured that it doesn't apply to your mother. Has it ever occurred to you that she might have been lonely and unhappy, and needed someone to care for her? It doesn't mean she doesn't care for you."

"But you don't understand! Nobody does. Sir Henry doesn't like us, and our new stepsister, Phoebe, hates us, and I can't bear that she's coming home, and Uncle Andrew, who is the only person who cared about us since Papa died, hasn't even been to visit, not in ages! Nobody cares anymore. If Mama had loved us she would never have married horrid Sir Henry!" Jocelyn burst into a flood of tears, burying her head on her arms.

"Oh, Jocie," said Honor quietly, reaching out a hand and stroking her hair. "How very dreadful it's been for you. Will you let me help?"

Jocelyn raised tear-filled eyes. "Help?" she said, sniffing, and ran a hand under her nose, for once forgetting her dignity. "How can *you* help?"

"Just let me try. I think we must concentrate on playing more, and not worrying about improving your mind all the time, for your mind seems perfectly good to me. I think part of the problem is that you take yourself far too seriously. You have a healthy streak of drama in you and, despite what you may think, a lively imagination, and we should put them to good use. And think of Minerva. She needs fun and laughter, and you can help me give all of that to her. Your mama needs your love too, very much. Can you not see how unhappy you have made her by keeping it from her?"

"Yes . . . but I was angry with her. I didn't think she was lonely. I thought she had Sir Henry and didn't care about us or Papa any longer. I have been very wicked," she said theatrically. "Even more wicked than I had thought!"

"No, Jocelyn. You have just been unhappy and confused, but things will get better, you'll see. And, Jocelyn—why don't you and Minerva call me Honor? It would make me feel so much more comfortable, more like a friend. I want to be your friend, you know."

"I'd like to be your friend too," said Jocelyn shyly, with the first real smile Honor had seen, and it transformed her face. "I think I am very glad you've come."

"Do you know, I think I am very glad I've come too," Honor said.

That same night, Honor went to sleep happily enough with the beautiful book of fairy tales, for she had always had a passion for those lovely stories, a passion that had not been left behind with childhood. But she came awake to the sound of Minerva's terrified cries. Quickly lighting her candle, she hurried across the hall.

"What is it, little one?" Honor asked gently, putting the candle down and drawing the small child into her arms. To her gratification, Minerva did not pull away. "Can you tell me?"

Minerva looked up at her with great blue eyes swimming with tears.

"It's all right, Minerva. You can trust me. Would you like to tell me? Perhaps it will make it better."

Minerva gulped. "It was dark. I saw the bad man."

"The bad man? Does he come often and frighten you, my sweet?" asked Honor with a quick breath of relief. She'd begun to think Minerva would never speak.

Minerva nodded soundlessly, sucking furiously on her thumb. "He looks at me. I hate him. I want him to go away. He is wicked."

"Then we shall have to chase him away. I shall tell you what we will do. I will leave my candle in here and the bad man won't come back. And I shall leave my bedroom door open as well and he will know we have the better of him. Do you think you can sleep now?"

Minerva drew her thumb out of her mouth for a moment and nodded with serious eyes.

"Good girl. Do you know, when I was a little girl and something frightened me, my mother would sit by my bed and sing to me, and then I could sleep. She never shut my door, saying that the angels could come in and watch me while I slept. Shall I sing you a lullaby and guide the angels in?"

Minerva nodded again. "Papa too?"

"Of course! He will stay with you all night long until you wake." Honor kissed her brow, then settled her down and softly began to sing a long-forgotten song, and before long Minerva's eyes closed and her breathing deepened into sleep. Honor went to bed, leaving her own door open as promised. But she spent some time mulling over what Minerva had said—and what she had not. The bad-man dream was interesting, and most likely Minerva's fearful interpretation of her new stepfather, which Jocelyn had already indicated. But there was something else that needed some careful thought, because she really didn't think that Minerva's problem was shyness at all.

She finally fell asleep that night with the book of fairy tales in her hand, after having turned back to it as a way to settle her mind. But it had set off a chain of association which did nothing for her sleep. For the first time in years she came suddenly awake, having had the familiar dream that had comforted her throughout her childhood and into adolescence. She had always been reluctant to wake up, for the dream was pure happiness, and when it vanished she felt empty and sad, as if she had suffered a loss.

It had always been the same: there was a boy, perhaps eleven or so, a beautiful boy with laughing eyes the color of sapphires and a lovely broad smile. He was so comfortable and real somehow, and she had loved him for as long as she could remember. She had always supposed that her dreams of an imaginary friend were brought on by a fevered longing for a brother. But no brother had come along. Her mother had died and the war began, and she and her father had moved to the Peninsula and there had been little enough time for sleep, let alone dreams. They had become fewer and fewer and eventually faded altogether, although never completely from her memory. For five or six years now she had been without them.

But that night, completely without warning or expectation, the dream returned in full force. But what had made it so alarming was the fact that the boy was no longer a boy; he had changed into a full-fledged man, still with the same laughing eyes and smile, and with the same sense of connection to her, but so different. He was no longer the easy companion she had dreamt of for so many years, despite the closeness she still sensed. He was a stranger to her, tall and dark, a god built of broad muscles and a terrifying but utterly attractive newness, and with one look from those piercing eyes he had struck her senseless. And then with a smile he had reached out a hand and touched her cheek, sending a jolt throughout her entire body. Just then the dream had rippled and faded, leaving her longing for him. It was quite mad, she told herself firmly. She was obviously feeling deprived of her true identity, and was hanging on to any past comfort, no matter how feeble.

She sat up in bed and rubbed her eyes, trying to restore sanity, what little there was of it, to her present circumstances. This had been the old world intruding, and she was Honor Winslow, and that was all there was to it. If her sleep betrayed her, there was nothing she could do about it, and it could hardly matter.

She rose to begin another day.

* * *

Time passed quickly, but the dreams returned again and again to dominate Honor's sleep. And yet somehow they lent her comfort even in this new and distressing form. It was easy enough to dismiss what she perceived to be the yearnings of a lonely heart. She had so much to concentrate on in her waking hours that there was no room for anything else. Jocelyn's newly discovered affection for her and her own easily given love soon caught Minerva up, and she began to participate in their activities with a degree of enthusiasm. During lessons, Honor fashioned simple letters and made up games to coax her into spelling her name with them. She tried hard and began to smile, a beautiful, heart-warming smile that lit up her whole face. But she rarely spoke, and when she did, it was in the simplest of sentences.

* * *

Honor introduced Jocie to Shakespeare, and they acted out scenes, Jocie reveling in the newly discovered pleasure, while Minerva listened and clapped her hands in delight at their antics. They went for long, brisk walks and thrashed in piles of leaves, and played at soldiers in the woods, which fast became a favorite game. One night, warmly bundled up, they attended a bonfire, and Minerva and Jocelyn squealed with pleasure and went home happy and tired, smelling deliciously of smoke and cold, crisp night air. And also as promised, Jocelyn's behavior toward her mother underwent a gradual change as she attempted to be more forthcoming. Arabella exclaimed time and again that Honor had wrought a miracle with them, and Honor only smiled and said it was probably because she was not much more than a child herself.

Arabella discovered during one of their conversations that Honor had enjoyed riding as a child, and quickly offered her the use of a riding habit and a mare in the stables, insisting that she should have some pleasure after all the help she had been to them. Honor accepted gladly and fell into the practice of rising very early so that she could have an hour to herself. That hour gave her more pleasure than she could express, although she struggled with the unfamiliarity of her perch, feeling precariously unbalanced on the sidesaddle.

comfortable, although she constantly swore at the feeling of being a sailor manning the deck in a high sea.

After a short period she became more confident of her riding skills, despite the fact that she longed to tear the sidesaddle from the horse's back and charge off unencumbered. But, persisting with it, she discovered an old path that led through the thick woods and out and across a series of fields. She ambled along, not particularly sure of where she was going, and not really caring, for although she would have loved a good gallop, a sedate trot was about all she was prepared to attempt. But after three miles or so, her attention was suddenly torn from general enjoyment of the countryside to a riveted focus as she reached the crest of a hill. There in the distance a beautiful house nestled in a valley. It was enormous, a vast expanse of sand-colored stone, but despite its size, it emanated a feeling of warmth.

Her breath caught in her throat and she stared, and then shook her head and stared again. It was not only the most beautiful house she had ever seen, but it was somehow so intimately familiar. She wracked her brains, trying to think whether she had seen it in a picture book, or perhaps a magazine. And then it fell into place with a great crash. She did know this house. But she knew it from her own memory, the same memory which had held the boy, and now held the man.

She felt a burst of terror, as if her carefully fabricated world had finally tipped out of control, that all of the fragile pieces she had so carefully tried to keep in place were coming unraveled faster that she could keep them together. She looked a minute longer, and then violently turned her horse's head for home.

It occurred to her on that disjointed ride back that either the stress of the last few months had driven her completely over the edge, or somehow she was still in her right mind, and somewhere she'd seen that house before. But then, that made no sense either. She'd lived away from England, virtually from the time of earliest memory. How could one have an instinct toward a house, let alone the fantasy inhabitant? Loneliness could do many things to a person, she knew. And perhaps her imagination, strong as it had always been, had overdone itself. With that, she put it to one side. Or so she thought.

Oddly enough, Jocie dragged out a book of drawings that same night, reproductions of paintings at Chesney that ranged from her great-great-grandfather all the way down to her own father. "These are the earls of Chesney," she said, turning the pages. "There hasn't been a break from father to son for six generations, you see, until now. It's a shame that Papa didn't manage to have a son, and so the title passed to Uncle Andrew. There's no picture of him yet. He's not married either—and without issue, as they say—so it makes it very difficult if he should die with DSP after his name. Chesney would go out of the immediate family for the first time ever. So everyone says that Uncle Andrew will have to marry soon and produce a son. Oh, never mind. It's stupid talk anyway," she said quickly at the expression on Honor's face, which she took for disapproval of the subject.

But Honor's thoughts were far from Uncle Andrew's lack of issue. She was mainly concerned with the backdrop with which three of the esteemed earls had been painted. It was the same place, without any doubt, that she had seen that very day.

"What a lovely house," she managed to say.

"Oh, Chesney? Yes, it is, and I'll always love it and I'll always hate being taken away. But I told you all of that, Honor. And you're right, of course, that we must get on with our lives and do as well as we can with what we've been given, not that it will ever be the same, or that I'll ever like it here. But I do wish Uncle Andrew would come home, for that might make it easier, and he's so nice. I suppose that's too much to ask for, though. People don't do what you expect of them. Perhaps that's the comfort in religion: it's always there, exactly the same, and you don't have to expect anything, so you can't be disappointed."

Honor burst into laughter. "Oh, Jocie, you are precious, and far beyond your years, and you're quite right. There's great comfort in religion, but it doesn't help us much when it comes to the inconsistencies in human nature, does it? Don't worry about your uncle, for I'm sure that he loves you very much. And he's bound to come home. After all, you've just told me that Chesney is his now, and who would neglect such a beautiful place? I saw it today, as it happens, and I couldn't have been more taken with it.''

Jocie gave her a keen and slightly unsettling look. "Everyone is taken with it, Honor, but most people don't see the real Chesney. All they see is the size and grandeur and all the money behind it. There's much, much more to Chesney than that. But then, it's not our home anymore, and no doubt Uncle Andrew will marry someone because he has to, and she will marry him because of Chesney and his title, and it will never be the same.'' She folded her mouth together as if there were nothing more to say on the subject.

"My dear child," said Honor with a smile, "don't for a minute imagine that all of the world is quite as jaded as you might believe just now. There are people who care for more than appearances, you know. And I'm sure that no matter whom your uncle might choose as a wife, you will always be welcome at Chesney, if that is what is worrying you.''

"We'll see," said Jocie blackly. "*I* have learned that appearances are not what they may seem.''

Honor put her to bed, reflecting that Jocie had seen a great deal too much and understood far too little of it. But she was quite right about one thing: appearances were most certainly not what they seemed.

The dream came that night, of course. As Honor had become accustomed to it, even to look forward to it, she had rediscovered the old feeling of friendship, the ease, the ready laughter in his company. They walked together on the rise, content with each other as people are who know each other beyond the need for words, but with the new undercurrent of excitement running beneath the surface. She loved him, she knew that as a certainty, but with a woman's love, not any longer the simple love of a child. He had laughed, the wind blowing through his dark hair, and made some remark. And then he had drawn her close to him, his arm around her waist, and they had stood on the hill, perfectly happy, and looked down at Chesney gleaming in the sunshine.

Honor sighed as she woke, the memory lingering, and she drew her arms around herself. It had been a lovely dream, and it was no wonder she had picked Chesney to set it in, for wherever she had seen it in the past, the house had obviously inspired her.

But dreams were dreams, and she had work to do. She shrugged herself into her robe and went to see to the children.

3

They are not ever jealous for the cause,
But jealous for they are jealous.

—William Shakespeare, *Othello*, III, iv

The day finally arrived for Sir Henry and his daughter's return. Honor sensed Arabella's growing apprehension, and her own was no small thing. Mrs. Lipp had roused herself and bustled about the household tossing frenzied directives right and left, thereby throwing the staff into more of a confused state than they'd already managed for themselves. Honor soothed them, sorting out injured feelings that were brought to her on an hourly basis, but it severely disturbed her efforts to calm and reassure the children that life would carry on as normal, and they had no reason to fear Sir Henry's return. Jocelyn had been in a thoroughly bad temper the entire day, arguing with everything Honor said, and finally Honor pulled her into her arms, where Jocelyn promptly had a good cry and felt much better. When Jocie heard the carriage pull up to the house shortly after four, she jumped up from the table and ran to peer out the window, kneeling on the window seat, but safely hidden behind the curtains.

"They've arrived—come and look, Honor!" she cried as Honor came into the room with Minerva.

"Certainly not," said Honor primly, longing to do just

that. "Come away from the window at once, Jocie, and finish your lesson."

"Oh, Honor, you're not going to become a real governess, are you? Not now!"

"I most certainly am," said Honor with a smile. "I shall show Sir Henry that I am the epitome of one, whose charges are perfectly behaved. I must confess, I'm as nervous as a cat, though."

"He will send you away?" whispered Minerva, clinging to her hand.

"Of course he won't," said Honor, frantically wondering the same thing herself. "Not if he sees that you are well and happy and behaving yourselves. But you must help me and be the best of children, and polite and kind to your stepfather. Will you do that, just for me?"

Minerva nodded and Jocelyn shrugged. "Oh, all right, but only because you ask. It doesn't mean I don't hate him, but I don't want him to dismiss you."

"Good, then. Let's get you ready, for I'm sure that your stepfather and stepsister shall want to see you directly."

It was another hour before the summons came via a frantic and flustered Betsy, and Honor made good use of the time, scrubbing the girls until their faces shone. She had dressed them in their best frocks, laughing and teasing, trying to lighten their gloom.

"You both look lovely," she said, inspecting them carefully. "Now, Minerva, do try to remember not to suck your thumb, as Jocie tells me that Sir Henry doesn't like it. No sulking, and for heaven's sake, smile! Remember, it's a new beginning for all of you, and you must give Sir Henry and Phoebe a chance to like you, which I know they will."

She smoothed her dress into place, a worn dark green wool. Her heart was pounding as she shepherded the children downstairs. This would be her big test; Arabella had accepted her easily enough, but Sir Henry was another matter.

"Oh, Honor, here you are!" said Arabella nervously, coming toward them and ushering the girls into the room. "Children, welcome your Uncle Henry home."

Honor, lingering by the door, took in a florid, corpulent man somewhere in his fifties. He was dressed in evening clothes, and his head was crowned by wiry red hair, which was matched by brows and lashes of the same color. He looked remarkably like the portraits of his dissipated ancestors. He was not in any way an attractive man, but had a commanding presence, and he turned it now on the children. She immediately understood why they held him in such dislike. She already harbored an acute hatred of him in her own heart.

"Jocelyn, Minerva? What do you have to say for yourselves?" His voice was stern, and Honor held her breath.

"Good evening, Sir Henry," said Jocie, pulling Minerva into a curtsy next to her, and Honor breathed again.

"Very prettily done," said Sir Henry with approval and surprise, clearly expecting their habitual recalcitrance. "I can see your new governess has finally taught you some manners." He looked over toward the door and his eyebrows shot up in surprise as he took Honor in. His gaze went from head to foot and back to her face again and he frowned. "*You* are the new governess?"

Her heart in her throat, Honor swept him a curtsy. "Good evening, Sir Henry," she said with lowered eyes.

"Arabella, what is this?" he said, turning to his wife. "I expected someone very different from your letters! This . . . this . . . person is hardly more than a child!"

"Well, yes, my dear, but I didn't see it fit to mention, as she has been so very good with the children." Arabella's voice was almost pleading. "Her age hardly seemed to matter in light of that, and Andrew did recommend her highly. She was brought up by the nuns, and is quite beyond reproach!"

"And she is so very good at lessons, Sir Henry," interjected Jocelyn sweetly, to his astonishment. Jocelyn had barely ever spoken to him before, and never civilly. "I am learning all about the Peninsular War, and Shakespeare, and Minerva can even write her name and some of her numbers."

"I can," whispered Minerva, and he stared at her.

"Why, my dear child! So you do speak, after all! It does seem that some improvement has been effected in my absence. The Peninsular War, is it? Quite out of the usual curriculum. Tell me, then, Jocelyn. What important event marked August of last year?''

"Wellington entered Madrid in triumph, sir. But some say that it was a mistake because . . ." She glanced over at Honor, who nodded encouragingly. " . . . because the French were advancing from all over Spain, and after the unsuccessful siege on Burgos, Wellington had to retreat to Ciudad Rodrigo.''

"More and more astonishing! A mistake, was it?'' he said, leveling a curious look on Honor. "A matter of opinion. Nevertheless, I can see that you've been teaching the children some substance. Welcome to Croftsfield, Miss Winslow," he said with a small, tight smile.

"Thank you, sir," Honor said with infinite relief.

"Tell me, how do you find life with us? The children are behaving themselves?''

"Very well, sir. I find them most enjoyable charges, and they have made an effort to make me comfortable," she said softly.

Sir Henry nodded. "So, you were raised by the nuns? I see that they instilled a sense of modesty in you along with an education.''

"Thank you, sir," said Honor. "I hope you find me suitable despite my age. I shall endeavor to do my best.''

"I am sure you shall." He looked over her shoulder and smiled indulgently. "Ah, here you are, Phoebe, dear. Come and make Miss Winslow's acquaintance. She is looking after your new sisters.''

Honor turned around and saw a striking girl enter the room, with the same red hair as her father, but darker; she had catlike green eyes which tilted up at the corners and a full mouth which could only be described as petulant. Her skin was milky white and her lashes and brows made a dark contrast against it. She was dressed in the height of fashion, wearing a pale blue gown of crepe with a high waist and clinging skirt. She took Honor in with an expression of disdain, but something else flickered in her eyes that Honor couldn't read.

"Miss Winslow. I see you are here too, Jocelyn and Minerva," she said, her expression turning to boredom. "Papa, although my stepmama has been very kind in assigning me my old rooms, I should much prefer to be closer to you, away from the noise of the children. After all, I am a young woman now. Can it be arranged?'' She took his arm and flashed him a devastating smile, showing small, even teeth.

"Of course, my dear. Arabella?'' he said in an expectant tone, and Honor saw her flush.

She came forward, twisting her handkerchief between her fingers in an agitated gesture Honor had come to know. "I'm so sorry that you find your apartment unsuitable, Phoebe. You must forgive me . . . Of course, you have lived here all your life, and I am so newly arrived. Please, you must make any arrangements you like. . . . Honor—perhaps you might fix it?'' she finished helplessly.

Honor's heart went out to her. "Certainly, my lady. If Miss Rutherford would tell me which rooms she would like, I shall see that they are prepared immediately.''

Sir Henry nodded approvingly and Phoebe inclined her head. "I think the green suite would do nicely. Please see to it at once, Miss . . . ah. . .''

"Winslow,'' said Honor.

"Yes, of course. Miss Winslow.'' She managed to attach a distaste to the words, as if they soured inside her mouth.

"As you say, Miss Rutherford. I'll return to fetch the children in half an hour, my lady.'' Honor turned to go, thinking that the peace of the last month had just been irrevocably shattered. She did not know why exactly, but for some reason she felt she had just made an enemy in Miss Phoebe Rutherford.

Honor was exactly right. Phoebe couldn't really explain it herself, but she had disliked the girl on sight. There was something about her that didn't belong in a governess, something in her eyes, her carriage, which was not meek enough for her position. She was not beautiful; Phoebe knew that she came close to outshining virtually every young woman she had ever met. But this girl had something else, a certain sense of command, despite the fact that she never seemed to raise her voice, a way of watching and listening that made Phoebe suspicious. Honor Winslow would not do. She had read stories about young governesses upsetting families with their devious ways, luring the gentlemen into their beds. Her father had obviously been swayed by Miss Winslow and could not see through her. It was up to her to find a way of getting rid of the girl before she caused trouble. She could watch and listen too.

Over the next few days, Phoebe did just that. She noticed from her window that Honor rode early in the mornings before the children woke. She always seemed to head in and return from the same direction—the south woods. The rest of her day was taken up with the mundane activities of managing the children and helping out around the house, and Phoebe noted that Honor seemed to be in charge. So she did everything she could to cause difficulties with the staff, hoping the blame would be attached to Honor's mismanagement. Even that seemed to have no effect. The girl somehow managed always to put things right.

And then one night after the stable clock had chimed midnight, Phoebe was sitting in her window gazing out across the moon-washed garden, inexpressibly bored with her life and planning a dazzling future in London society. She longed for romance in her life, and knew it was just around the corner, waiting for her like some shining star— she would be swept off her feet by a dashing lord, the likes of Lord Jadfrey in *The Marquess and the Maiden*. He would fall in love with her at first sight, naturally, and lay the world and his immense fortune at her feet. She would be the envy of all of London, and their wedding would be unequaled by anything society had seen before. Something caught her eye, a quick movement in the shadows, and she looked more closely. She saw the cloaked figure of a woman coming across the grass toward the house, keeping always to the dark of the shadows. Phoebe smiled slowly. Not two minutes later, she saw an even more intriguing sight. A man, unmistakably a man—Jake, the groom, if she was correct. He looked around him, then quickly moved on toward the stables, where he slept. How incredibly lucky. Miss Winslow and the groom? It was too good to be true! How deliciously low and lacking in dignity. And Miss Winslow thought she was so clever. . . . Phoebe would see about that.

Honor returned to her room breathless with excitement. It had finally begun. The letter she had found in Sir Henry's desk surely would convince Julian that Sir Henry was doing something suspicious: it had clearly stated, after all, that his services had been appreciated as always and that he would find a deposit of one thousand pounds in his account. Honor had carefully copied the contents and replaced the original, so Sir Henry would suspect nothing, and Jake would post the letter to Julian tomorrow. Sir Henry was not as careful as he ought to be, given the filthy business he was involved in, and that was her good fortune. She made herself ready for bed and slipped between the sheets with a great sigh. At least she had the comfort of knowing that while she slept she had a friend, for just like a fairy tale, her mysterious lover had appeared every night, only to be banished by the dawn. She smiled at her idiocy and closed her eyes. Still, no matter how idiotic, the nights helped to get her through the difficult days.

Honor had settled Jocie by the window the next afternoon with a book of French grammar and was tidying Minerva's block letters when Phoebe came sweeping into the nursery without bothering to knock. She looked straight off a fashion plate as usual, wearing a pomona-green silk gown, the hem embellished with a broad flounce, ribbons worked into the bodice.

"Oh, there you are, Miss Winslow," she said, looking around her with her usual expression of boredom.

"What can I do for you, Miss Rutherford?" said Honor, straightening, and wondering what devilry had brought her to the nursery, where she had never before set one of her precious feet.

"My novel has disappeared. I though perhaps Jocelyn might have taken it. I saw her leafing through it yesterday, and had to remove it from her as unsuitable." The implication was very clear.

Jocie colored hotly. "I wouldn't be found reading one of those Minerva Press romances if you paid me a hundred guineas. I was only looking to see if it was as stupid as I had imagined."

"Oh, you think you're very clever, Miss Jocelyn, don't

you? Well, you may be clever, but you're homely and you'll never catch a husband, being a blue stocking.''

"I'm *Lady* Jocelyn," Jocie said wickedly, somehow knowing it bothered Phoebe that her stepsisters outranked her. "And I won't need to catch a husband, unlike you. I have a fortune in my own right, and I shall be very content. And furthermore, I see nothing wrong with being plain.''

"You're not plain, Jocie," Honor said gently, hoping to remove the sting from Phoebe's words. "You have not grown into your looks yet, that is all. Everyone goes through an awkward stage of growth.''

"Spoken like a true governess, Miss Winslow. But then, you would know about awkwardness.''

"I do indeed," she said, smiling reassuringly at Jocie, who looked torn between mutiny and tears. "But something magical will happen, Jocie; you'll begin to fill out in all the right places and your skin will glow, and the next thing you know, you'll be a beautiful young woman surrounded by admiring beaus, most of whom will want to marry you, and you shall pick and choose and break a hundred hearts.''

"Oh, is that what happened to you, Miss Winslow? I hadn't noticed," said Phoebe snidely. "Tell me, how many hearts have you broken to date from the walls of your convent?''

"Had there been even one, it would be my business alone, Miss Rutherford," said Honor quietly, and saw Phoebe's eyes widen slightly in surprise at the rebuff.

"You're very high and mighty for a mere servant, Miss Winslow. It would be well of you to remember your place.''

"I shall never forget my place, Miss Rutherford. Indeed, it was carefully schooled into me. But I was also taught kindness and consideration for others' feelings.''

Two violent spots of red appeared in Phoebe's cheeks. "You are impertinent, Miss Winslow!''

"I beg your pardon. I was only speaking the truth.''

Minerva, sensing trouble but not really understanding the cause, slipped her hand into Honor's.

Phoebe's fists clenched by her side. "You have spoiled the children appallingly, giving in to their every whim. You think you run this house—oh, yes, I have seen how it is, how you overrule even our cousin, who has every right to be here, whereas you have not!''

"Your cousin . . .''

"Lipp, of course. My father took her in as housekeeper years ago when he discovered she was disgracing herself in a theater troupe.''

Honor overcame a treacherous desire to laugh, thinking that it explained the woman's alarming appearance and melodramatic airs. And no doubt Sir Henry had "rescued" her to give himself a free, if incompetent, housekeeper. No wonder Mrs. Lipp drowned her sorrows, stuck away in the country as she was. "I am sorry, I did not know.'' She stood, turning her back to Phoebe so that she might not see her expression.

"A poor relation, to be sure, but nevertheless, a connection. I don't know who you think you are, Miss Winslow, marching in here as if it is yours by right and taking over. And I know all about your secret assignations too.''

"My . . . my secret assignations?'' said Honor, turning around quickly. "Just what are you implying?''

"Oh, I saw you come in late last night, sneaking upstairs. Do you deny it? I also saw Jake go scurrying off across the gardens not two minutes later!''

"Miss Rutherford,'' Honor said as calmly as she could manage, "I often walk at night when I cannot sleep. There is no crime in that. Nor is there any harm in Jake's doing the same if he chooses. If you are insinuating that . . . that I have been meeting with the groom for some sordid reason, you are quite wrong. And I wish you wouldn't speak like this in front of the children.''

"I know what I saw, and I have half a mind to report you to my father! He'll have your bags packed and you out of the house in the snap of a finger.'' She had already told her father, and he had dismissed her with a laugh, saying that what the servants did with their time off was their affair, but Honor need not know that.

"No!'' said Minerva, staring at Phoebe with horror. "You are a liar. You are wicked!''

"And you are stupid,'' said Phoebe. Her hand flashed out and pinched Minerva's little arm hard, and Minerva immediately burst into floods of tears. Jocie sprang at Phoebe like a spitting cat, and Honor quickly stepped in front of her, restraining her by the shoulders as Jocie struggled.

"No, Jocie. It is not the way," she said quietly.

"I shall make you pay!" cried Jocie.

Phoebe smiled. "I doubt it," she said. "I am the daughter of the house, after all. You are merely stepchildren here."

She turned on her heel and marched out, leaving Honor to comfort both the girls.

After that incident, Minerva showed every inclination of completely withdrawing again, and had to be coaxed to go down to the Blue Saloon every evening with her sister to endure the half-hour's torture in the presence of Sir Henry and his spoiled daughter. On these occasions Honor sat quietly in a corner, sending reassuring glances to the girls and enduring Phoebe's spite.

"I am so looking forward to my Season, Papa," Phoebe said during one of these interminable sessions. "Have you begun to make arrangements for my ball?"

"That is up to your stepmama, Phoebe," said Sir Henry absently, engrossed in his newspaper. "I am going to be far too busy in Parliament for such things."

"But she won't have the faintest idea what to do, Papa! She can't even manage things in the country!"

A deep flush spread over Arabella's face. "I know I am so foolish when it comes to these things, Phoebe, dear," Arabella said, tears threatening at her eyes, "but I shall do my very best to see that you have a lovely Season. Honor can help me make arrangements—"

"Her!" said Phoebe in disgust, as if Honor were not present. "What does she know about society and balls and making the appropriate arrangements? She's nothing but a common orphan! And in any case, she'll be here at Croftsfield looking after the children."

Honor bit her tongue, longing to give Phoebe the setdown she deserved.

"No, Phoebe," said Sir Henry firmly. "I am closing Croftsfield for the Season. It is too expensive to keep two establishments open. The children will come to London."

Jocelyn, delighted, watched Phoebe for her reaction.

"I cannot credit it, Papa!" said Phoebe. "How am I to receive suitors with those two running about the house? Really, it's beyond all belief."

"I am sure Honor will keep them out of your way, my dear Phoebe," offered Arabella. "And you shall be far too busy even to notice that the children are there. But speaking of the Season, I have something I've been meaning to tell you. Lord Chesney has written to me, and has offered to introduce you when you go to London. Isn't that kind? So there really is nothing to worry about. He is removing to Chesney any day now and will be calling to make your acquaintance."

Sir Henry started. "Lord Chesney? Why didn't you tell me of this sooner, Arabella? You know what I have been planning!"

"Why, it slipped my mind until just this minute, Henry. I meant to tell you after breakfast when I opened my letters, but you went off before I had a chance."

Jocie squeezed her hands together in her lap and tried to look neutral, but Honor could see that she was about to burst with excitement. Even Minerva had looked up.

"Lord Chesney?" Phoebe shrugged, remembering the brother, who had been middle-aged, rotund, and as boring as anything. "Why the fuss, Papa?"

Sir Henry smiled indulgently. "Because I have been expecting this. I know exactly why he is returning to Chesney. It is no coincidence that he comes just after you have arrived yourself, my pet."

"What is that supposed to mean, Papa?" she said, frowning.

"It is quite simple. He is unmarried and without children, which was all well and fine when he was a younger son, but now that he is the new earl, he must look to the succession. Which means he will also be looking for a wife. It has been in my mind for some time that although your portion is not as large as I would like, our land does run with his, which he can only see as fortunate. You have breeding in your favor, and very presentable looks, and our family is already connected with his. It would be a most auspicious match. And if he has offered to introduce you, it is clear to me that he is thinking in the same direction. Do you find it an agreeable idea?''

Phoebe's mouth pulled down, thinking of her prince awaiting her in London. ''I want my Season, Papa, without being already spoken for. I should be very unhappy to be married off without having a chance to choose for myself. I don't want to be stuck away in the country with an old bore.''

''Phoebe!'' said her father sharply. ''This is not a question of what you want or what you don't. I have made up my mind, as has Lord Chesney, apparently. You will go along with my decision. But,'' he said more cajolingly, ''do you not want to be a countess?''

''I should be quite satisfied with being a countess, Papa, but—''

''Perhaps you are unaware that the Chesney fortune is one of the largest in Great Britain. And Lord Chesney is the most eligible man in the country as a result. You would live in great style for all your life, with far more excitement than one Season can bring you.''

Phoebe's eyes widened. She hadn't known that the Chesney fortune was so large . . . Oh, well. One had to be practical, after all. She would have money for all her life, and with luck her bore of a husband would follow in his brother's footsteps and die early. It might not be so bad, and she could always take a lover. In fact, that might be truly romantic. She had read a story in which Lady Vanessa Lockridge had . . .

''Phoebe! Will you pay attention!''

''Yes, Papa,'' she said demurely. ''You are quite right, as always. How old did you say he was?''

''I did not say, but he is thirty, not such a repulsive difference in your ages, is it, my dear?''

''Not at all, Papa,'' said Phoebe, thinking it sounded ancient. ''I have always held that it is much better for one's husband to be more mature, so that he can guide one.''

Honor, hardly able to believe the conversation, looked up, only to see Phoebe peeping a look at her father from beneath her dark eyelashes, an affectation Honor found repulsive. Poor Lord Chesney, she thought to herself.

''Do you really think, Papa, that Lord Chesney might be

considering me?'' asked Phoebe, warming to the idea. ''There are so many others to choose from.''

''Never you mind that, my girl.'' Sir Henry poured himself a glass of sherry as he spoke. ''He knows on which side his bread is buttered. He knows that your stepmama can have no more children, so Croftsfield goes to you, along with the lands that are already your dowry. He'd be a fool to pass up a chance to increase Chesney. And once he sees you, it will only add fuel to the fire, for what man would pass up a beauty in the bargain? Now, mind you, Phoebe,'' he added, ''this is an opportunity not to be missed, and I won't take it kindly if you scotch it. You keep your eyes down and speak only when you're spoken to, do you understand?''

''Yes, Papa,'' said Phoebe. ''I will do just as you say. Lord Chesney will find nothing to fault in me, I promise.''

''Very well, then,'' said her father approvingly. ''You just see that it stays that way, and I promise you a husband any girl would be happy to have.''

''Yes, Papa,'' agreed Phoebe, already practicing lowering her eyes and visualizing the jewels around her neck. But she could still hear the creaking of his corsets in the back of her mind.

''Really, Honor,'' said Jocelyn later, her voice muffled beneath her nightdress. ''Have you ever heard anything more disgusting? 'Oh, Papa, I should be quite satisfied with being a countess,' '' Jocie mimicked in identical tones. Her head popped out and she made a face. ''She is the most horrid creature! She may reckon herself a beauty, but she's rotten through and through. And I couldn't bear the thought of having her live at Chesney. I *told* you something like this would happen! I should warn Uncle Andrew.''

''It may all be quite true, Jocie, but I absolutely forbid you to say anything rude to your uncle about Phoebe. If he finds a disgust of her, it shall be without your help, do you understand? It would be most unworthy of you to interfere.''

Jocelyn scowled.

''Promise, Jocie,'' said Honor, turning from poking the fire and looking at her sternly.

"Oh, very well, then, Honor. But imagine planning Uncle Andrew's future for him as if he were nothing more than a title and a bag of money."

"Jocie, I know how it must seem to you, but often marriages are arranged this way, and they work out nicely. It's not our place to judge what others do. You've done very well up until now to keep the peace; for heaven's sake, don't ruin it now. Come now, put away your books and I'll listen to your prayers and tuck you into bed."

Jocelyn only shrugged, but when she said her prayers that night, a good amount of time was spent begging God to keep Uncle Andrew safe from Phoebe.

4

If this were played upon a stage now,
I could condemn it as an improbable fiction.

—William Shakespeare, *Twelfth Night*, III, iv

It snowed during the night and Andrew woke to a carpet of sparkling white stretching everywhere the eye could see. The storm over, the sun now beat down and caught in the minute crystals, leaping and shimmering like a thousand stars. He flung the window open and stuck his head out, breathing deeply of the cold, crisp air. He felt vital and alive, and infinitely happy to be back in the country.

Chesney was Andrew's favorite of all the Montague estates. Here was where he had spent most of the hours of his childhood, and it held very happy memories for him. The earls of Chesney had by tradition been devoted to their land, with the minor exceptions of Andrew's brother, George, who had allowed much of the fifteen thousand acres to fall fallow in favor of his hunting. Andrew determined to correct this situation as soon as possible, now that his other concerns had been seen to. Here he intended to make his permanent home, and, he thought with a stab of guilt as he looked out of the window over the extensive gardens, to raise his children.

He pulled his head back in and closed the window, frowning as his eye fell on the four-poster bed and heavy blue hangings. To raise children, he needed a wife, he thought for the thousandth time. But there was no way on earth or in heaven that he would be forced into a marriage of convenience. He'd already seen what that had done to a number of his friends, where the two people lived under the same roof, bore children, and shared precious little else. And he had also seen what a marriage of love could do, for Julian, whom he'd never thought to see happily married, had found his Bryonny and had not looked back. No, if he were ever to marry, it would be for love and nothing else. And that would be how his children came, not from some indifferent coupling in the night, during which the wife turned her head away and tolerated the act, but from mutual passion and caring.

He frowned again, thinking of poor Arabella, whom he considered very much his responsibility. How could she have married Henry Rutherford after having known the joy of a love match with his brother? And those poor children. It was so damnably unfair on them. But that lack of affection he would correct to the best of his ability. If Henry Rutherford found his constant attendance in his house an irritation, it would be deflected by the fact that he was helping his daughter into society. How could Henry possibly object to that? And he would indeed try to manage to see the daughter, Phoebe, married off this Season, which would be a burden off Arabella's shoulders, for she was not equipped to handle that sort of thing at all.

He wondered how easy it would be to see this Phoebe Rutherford married; as Julian had said, she was reported to be a beauty, which was all to the good. But only seventeen, and in the country for most of her life, she was bound to be shy and nervous, which would not help. He'd have to take advantage of the few months he had to give her some confidence, or she'd never take in her first Season, no matter how beautiful, given that her dowry was not much to speak of. From his discreet investigations just after Arabella's marriage, he had learned of Sir Henry's severe gambling debts. Just about all he had left were his lands and Arabella's once extensive but now severely diminished dowry that she had brought into her second marriage. No wonder he had set his eyes on Arabella so soon after George's death. Thank God the children's money was safely in trust, where Henry couldn't touch it.

On that encouraging thought he dismissed the entire subject from his mind and yanked his nightshirt off, pulled on a pair of buckskin breeches and a white cambric shirt, and shrugged himself into a coat of blue superfine. Last, he pulled on his Hessian boots and took himself downstairs.

He met Hobson coming up the stairs with a jug of hot water.

"Good morning, my lord!" Hobson said in surprised but vaguely offended tones. "You should have rung for me before rising! I had no idea you would be up quite so early—"

"Thank you, Hobson, but as you can see, I've managed very well on my own. Tell the bailiff that I'll see him in the library in an hour."

"Yes, my lord, but your breakfast—"

"I'll take my breakfast later."

"Yes, my lord," said Hobson, rooted to the spot with his jug, staring after the earl, who had gone down the stairs and out the door before he had a chance to offer him his cloak. He shook his head and went to confer with Nugent over the troublesome habits of their master, which would surely lead to galloping consumption.

Andrew headed to the west, his large gelding, Cabal, snorting and stretching his neck out in a fast canter. He finally pulled him up on the crest of the highest hill and looked down over Chesney, satisfaction filing him like a cool drink of water after a long thirst. The long ribbon of drive led up to the house, small now in the distance, smoke curling up from its many chimneys, looking warm and inhabited, as it was meant to be. From his vantage point he could see the tenant farms stretching out in a haphazard fashion on the other side of the hill, and behind them and lower down in the valley nestled the little village of Pickney, drowsily coming to life in the early-morning light.

Andrew smiled, his head full of plans for the future, but his smile faded as his eye caught a movement on the path to the north through the woods that led to Croftsfield. There was someone riding toward the woods, a woman, for she rode sidesaddle. Her seat was adequate, although slightly lopsided, he noted, and wondered whether it might be Phoebe Rutherford. He watched her until she disappeared into the cover of trees, then sighed. The launching of Phoebe Rutherford was not something he looked forward to. In fact, it was a downright nuisance. If there was one thing he could not bear, it was an ingenue. But it was high time to begin the process, and more than time to see his nieces again. He would go around that afternoon, he decided. First and most important came Chesney business. He turned Cabal's head around and nudged his sides with his heels, heading back toward the house at a slower pace, taking the long way through the fields over the layer of fine dry snow.

Honor shifted on the blanket, pulling her legs more comfortably up underneath her and drawing Minerva, who had fallen asleep, thumb safely planted in mouth, more closely into her lap. Her brown woolen cloak was loosely settled about her slender shoulders, the hood thrown back, and her curly head was bent to the pages before her. Jocie lay on her stomach, her chin in her hands as she listened intently to Honor read from the book of fairy tales.

They often retreated to the Croftsfield stables, which had become a favorite place on cold days, and a safe refuge from the house and Phoebe's constant complaints. Jake, explaining his find with the broad Yorkshire accent that still made Honor want to laugh when she heard it, had shown them the empty stall at the end of the building, which he'd laid with fresh hay, and the noises of horses pawing and nickering lent an air of coziness. Best of all, Jake had discovered a nest of seven kittens in the manger, whose tabby mother had no objection to sharing her shelter or her offspring. One of these, a tiny marmalade, snuggled in Minerva's arms and Jocelyn stroked a little tabby replica of her mother.

"And so the princess finally found her prince despite all

the efforts of her wicked stepmother to kill her," said Honor with a happy sigh, closing the book. "You see, love triumphs over all, Jocie, despite what you like to believe. And furthermore, they lived happily ever after. What do you think of that?"

"I think it a highly suitable ending, and one to which we might all aspire," said a deep voice filled with amusement, and Honor looked up with a start. A tall man was leaning over the door of the stall, dressed in a tasseled and corded Polish greatcoat. He was very dark, with brilliant, laughing blue eyes and a full, well-shaped mouth. Her heart nearly stopped in her chest. She blinked hard, as if to clear her vision, for it didn't seem possible, and for a moment she thought she had lost her mind. But she hadn't, for when she opened her eyes again, he was still there. This was no phantom from the realm of dreams. This was solid flesh. A rush of hot color flooded her cheeks.

"Uncle Andrew!" shrieked Jocelyn in the same moment, jumping up and flying across the stall. Minerva's eyes flew open. The little marmalade cascaded to the floor unnoticed as Minerva struggled out of Honor's arms and dashed across the hay. Andrew reached down and pulled her up into his arms, where Jocelyn was already ensconced, and she soundlessly buried her head in his broad shoulder.

Honor, thrown into even more of a state of confusion upon learning his identity, quickly bent to collect the marmalade kitten, who was mewling where he had softly landed among the straw. She spent more time than necessary comforting him and putting him and his sister back in the manger with their mother, who, sleeping soundly, had not noticed a thing amiss. She woke only long enough to give each progeny a quick lick and closed her eyes again.

"All safe and sound?" queried Andrew with a laugh.

"My lord . . ." Honor met his eyes and blushed even deeper, feeling completely at a loss. "I didn't . . . we didn't know you were there . . . I mean, that you had come . . ." She trailed off in a fit of embarrassment.

"Not at all. It was I who should have announced myself. But you were telling such a gripping tale that I couldn't help but listen. I've always loved that particular story, you see. Especially the part when the wicked stepmother is sent over a cliff to suffer eternal torment. I once knew someone exactly like that, who suffered the same fate.''

"Did you really, Uncle Andrew?" asked Jocelyn, her curiosity piqued.

"Naturally, my sweeting. A very wicked woman indeed, who had a penchant for killing people who crossed her.''

"My lord, I beg you!" said Honor quickly, forgetting her own chaotic thoughts for a moment, for she saw exactly where Jocelyn might take this. "You mustn't fill the children's heads with such things. Fairy stories are one thing, but from you they might think—''

"But it's quite true, I assure you," Andrew said with amusement. "And Jocie is such a bloodthirsty little girl that I thought she might be pleased to hear that such wicked people are truly punished. Were you, Jocie?''

"Oh, yes, Uncle Andrew. Do tell us more! How did the wicked woman fall over the cliff and—?''

"Jocie, enough!" said Honor, laughing despite herself. It was all just as she remembered, his smile, his easy bearing. "My lord, you will please refrain from indulging your own gruesome penchant. It is time I took the children back for their tea.''

"Most certainly," he said with a bow, and deposited the girls on the ground. "I must see to my horse, but I shall see you back at the house.''

"Oh, please, Uncle Andrew!" said Jocie. "You will stay, won't you? We haven't seen you for the longest time, and there's so much to tell you!''

"Of course, sweetheart. I wouldn't think of leaving before you had a chance to tell me all about everything. And you must make me a proper introduction to your stepsister, you know.''

Jocie shot him a black look, then grabbed Honor's hand and tugged her away before she had a chance to speak, with Minerva in their wake, leaving Andrew to stare after them in astonishment.

"His lordship has arrived, miss," announced Betsy breathlessly, having just raced up the stairs two at a time in an agony of excitement. "Ooh, he's just lovely, and so dignified, just like I told you. They be waiting for you in the

Blue Saloon, and Mr. Spencer says you're to come down quick-like.''

"Thank you, Betsy," said Honor with a faint smile, the most she could summon. "I'll bring the children down directly." Her own heart was pounding, and had been since the encounter in the stables. She couldn't understand it—it simply wasn't possible! How could a figment of her imagination suddenly appear in real life, and turn out to be Uncle Andrew of all people! The only thing that did make any sense at all was the fact that he belonged to Chesney. And how in heaven's name was she going to behave as if he were a complete stranger instead of the intimate friend she had come to know so well over the years, and all in her sleep no less! Worse, she wasn't even supposed to be his social equal—she was a governess, and he was an earl. They couldn't even become friends. Honor groaned. Now she was believing her own fairy tale. She didn't know him, not at all. It was all some insane coincidence. She shivered. For no matter what she told herself, she could not dismiss the eerie sensation that she knew him as well as she knew herself.

Andrew sat sipping his wine, chatting amiably with Arabella and Sir Henry, outwardly unconcerned. But his attention was focused on the door, waiting for Phoebe to come through. No one could have been more surprised than he when he had heard a low voice coming from an empty box as he was putting up his horse, and had found her sitting in the hay, her short fair curls framing as sweet a face as he had ever seen, reading to his nieces, completely engrossed in her story. Her reaction upon meeting him had delighted him, for after her initial confusion, which had amused him considerably, she had treated him with ease and assurance. Here was no spoiled child, a mass of simpering airs, but a warm, natural girl who enjoyed fairy tales. His book of fairy tales, that he had treasured so much as a child.

She was not the classic beauty he had expected, given the picture that had been presented to him, but there was a strength of character in her face that he had not expected. And her wide gray eyes with their finely sketched brows held worlds of expression and a clear intelligence. She reminded him vaguely of someone, but he could not place it.

He found that he looked forward to growing to know her better. It would be no problem at all to find her a husband, he felt quite sure. All the despondency he had originally felt at the prospect of launching Phoebe Rutherford had vanished.

He heard footsteps approaching and his face lit with pleasure as he saw Jocelyn and Minerva come through, and behind them, the girl who had been occupying his thoughts.

Surprisingly, she was wearing a day dress of gray wool, demurely cut, high in the neck, with long sleeves. No lace adorned it, and the dress was not in the latest mode. He wondered that Sir Henry did not see to dressing his daughter more fashionably, but perhaps things were worse than he had thought.

"Uncle Andrew!" chimed Jocie, and Minerva favored him with one of her brilliant smiles.

"How very lovely you look, both of you," he said, standing, his eyes going to the girl behind him. He smiled. "I see that you have managed to remove all traces of hay from yourselves."

"Hay?" said Sir Henry, frowning.

"Why, yes. I found my nieces in the stables, having a very enjoyable time indeed."

"The girls do so enjoy looking at the horses," said Arabella quickly, forestalling her husband's rebuke. "Miss Winslow is so clever at amusing them on cold afternoons."

"Miss . . . Winslow?" said Andrew, shooting a confused look at Arabella.

"Yes, Andrew. Do you not remember the governess you recommended to me? She has been such a help, you have no idea! Miss Winslow, allow me to present my dear brother-in-law, Lord Chesney."

Andrew felt his heart sink. The truth of the matter was that he had forgotten completely, and he had made the most dreadful mistake. And he should have remembered, for Julian had said she was young. He made a slight bow. "Of course. We had not been introduced. Are you enjoying the post, Miss Winslow?"

"I . . . I have been treated most kindly here, my lord. I

have you to thank for recommending me to the position."
She didn't know how she managed to get the words out.

"Not at all. I only followed my friend's suggestion. I am
delighted that you find yourself content. Come, Jocie, Minerva. Tell me all about how you have been amusing yourselves with Miss Winslow."

The children snuggled into his arms and Jocie began to
tell him all about their activities. Honor retreated thankfully
to her usual seat by the window. She looked up once to find
Lord Chesney's eyes on her, and quickly looked down again,
biting her lip against a warm rush of embarrassment. She
felt as if he had seen straight through her, had read her
thoughts, and she had a strong impulse to run from the room
where those too-perceptive eyes would not be able to follow.
Instead, she concentrated on her stitching and tried to empty
her mind of the alarming direction it insisted on taking.

"Papa, Aunt Arabella!" Phoebe stood in the doorway,
dressed in a white silk gown with a demitrain, the bodice
low but covered by an almost transparent gauze shawl. Her
hair fell enchantingly around her shoulders.

"Lord Chesney, allow me to present my daughter, Miss
Rutherford," said Sir Henry proudly. "She has been so
looking forward to making your acquaintance."

"How gratifying," murmured Andrew, bowing over her
hand, somehow feeling a twinge of disappointment. "It is
my pleasure, indeed." She was indeed beautiful, even more
beautiful than he had expected. Yet as he spoke to her, she
did not meet his eyes, looking down at the ground. How
unfortunate, he thought. It was just as he had anticipated—
a country mouse ill-at-ease with the male sex. He gave an
inward sigh.

"My lord. It is an honor." She made her curtsy, then
rose, her eyes still lowered.

"Indeed, the honor is mine. Why don't you come and sit
over here next to me, Miss Rutherford?" he said, trying to
make her feel comfortable. "My nieces have been amusing
me with their stories. Only now am I realizing how much I
have missed them."

"They are enchanting, aren't they?" said Phoebe. "I do
so love children. I hope to have many myself one day."

Jocie simply stared, but Honor's hand slipped and she

pricked herself with her needle, uttering a stifled cry. Andrew's surprised eyes met hers and fell to her finger, which was beading with a drop of blood. She covered it with her other hand. "It is time I took Minerva and Jocelyn upstairs," she said quickly, rising, and avoiding Andrew's keen look of interest. "Say good evening, children."

"Will you come back?" asked Minerva, regarding him solemnly with enormous blue eyes.

"Of course, my pet, and very soon. I shall think of something amusing for us to do. Now, run along with Miss Winslow," he said, kissing her cheek, and then Jocie's, but his eyes went to Honor.

"Good night, Uncle Andrew, Mama, Sir Henry," said Jocie, pointedly ignoring Phoebe, and took Minerva's hand, following Honor from the room.

"Good night, my darlings," said Arabella, calling after them. "Andrew, dearest, tell me how Chesney is looking these days. I have missed it so."

Phoebe picked up a piece of embroidery and began to take dainty little stitches, a task she despised but thought modestly becoming. Her mind and her pulse were both racing. Lord Chesney was far better-looking than she had hoped for, even in her wildest dreams! Here was no middle-aged man going to seed as she had feared. His eyes were a heavenly blue, thickly lashed, his mouth full and his teeth even and white. His hair was thick and dark with a hint of curl in it. She sighed deeply. This was a man she wouldn't mind marrying in the least. Mind! She would be ecstatic, for she had fallen in love at first sight, just as she had always dreamed she would. She slanted a look over at him. He was well-built and broad, needing no buckram padding for his chest or shoulders. His legs were long and the thighs beneath the breeches strongly muscled. He was in the height of his manhood. Phoebe suppressed a little giggle at the thought. She would find out about that soon enough. . . .

"Miss Rutherford? Have you been wool-gathering?"

Phoebe started and blushed. "I . . . beg your pardon, my lord. You were saying?" She raised her eyes to his and made them wide and interested.

"Nothing of any importance. I was talking about Chesney. I'm surprised I didn't put you fast asleep."

Phoebe smiled and made a pretty denial, and set herself to the task of making Lord Chesney fall in love with her.

Andrew rode over to Croftsfield two days later in response to Arabella's dinner invitation. He had spent the time very carefully considering how to approach the training of Miss Phoebe Rutherford. She was very young and naive, but perhaps it was good that she was not set in her ways. She was certainly dazzling, although somewhat lacking in humor. Still, if he could set her at ease, there might be hope for her. . . .

He was shaken out of his thoughts by shouts of laughter coming from the nearby copse in the woods. Curiously, he directed Cabal over in that direction. And then a freezing ball of snow hit his face with a great whack. "What the devil . . ." he cried, stunned.

Honor heard the exclamation and came out of the copse, the children on her heels, and her heart sank. "Oh! It's you! I . . . I mean, Lord Chesney!" She stopped dead in her tracks and swallowed hard against the sudden thumping of her heart, for she had spent the last two days trying to banish his image from her mind. "Please forgive me—I . . . I was teaching the girls how to aim at the tree, you see, and I had no idea you were lurking there behind it!" She stared at him in horror, and then, as she watched the snow sliding down his face, a little giggle escaped, and another, until she began to shake helplessly with laughter, the girls joining in.

"Just what is it you find so amusing, may I ask?" he said with a grin, wiping the snow from his face.

"Oh, forgive me, my lord, but you looked so funny—I do beg your pardon," she said, trying to sober, with no success. "Jocie's aim is still unreliable, you see." She burst into another fit, tears rolling down her cheeks.

Minerva pulled on his leg, her cheeks and nose rosy with the cold and exercise. "I'm a soldier, uncle."

"You made a very fine Napoleon, my lord," said Honor with a smile. "Had it been a bullet, Jocie might have won the war for us single-handedly."

"Oh, please do come down, Uncle Andrew," said Jocie.

"We've been having such a good time, even though I wish I had a real gun to aim with."

"God forbid!" said Andrew, swinging his leg over and dismounting. "Your snowballs are quite lethal enough. I think perhaps I'd better help you perfect your aim, my dear Jocie, before any worse accidents befall me." He strode into the copse, where he found a pile of snowballs heaped into a pile.

"Cannonballs," said Honor, picking up one and handing it to him. "Do your worst, my lord. Twenty paces, I think." He took it from her, the warmth of his hand transferring itself through her glove, and she flushed.

He took the twenty paces back, leveled his eye at the crook in the tree where Honor had set a bottle, drew his arm back, and threw. The bottle went flying.

"Well-aimed, my lord. You have a good eye," said Honor.

"Thank you, Miss Winslow," he said with amusement, and reset the bottle. "Your turn. Ten paces."

"Indeed?" she said indignantly. "Twenty paces, I think, or it would not be fair. Or perhaps you underestimate me."

"Perhaps I do," he said with a slow smile. "Would you care to make a wager?"

"Certainly. What shall it be?" Honor said, feeling quite weak at the knees and wishing he wouldn't look at her like that.

"Should you miss your target, your ear after dinner tonight."

"Her *ear*?" whispered Minerva, her eyes wide. "What shall he do with it?"

Andrew burst into laughter. "That is between Miss Winslow and myself," he said, and saw Honor smile. "Do you agree?"

"Very well, my lord," said Honor, her smile broadening. "And should I win?"

"You must choose my forfeit." He cocked an eyebrow.

"Then I choose that when we go to London you shall take us to a fair, for it is Minerva's greatest desire and we cannot go unescorted."

"Done," he said, and shook her slim hand. He watched her take her twenty paces in long, easy strides. Then she turned, impatiently pulled her cloak back off her shoulder, aimed carefully, and threw. To his surprise, the bottle toppled into the snow.

"Bravo!" cried Jocie, and Minerva clapped her little hands together in delight.

Andrew bowed. "A clean win. A fair it will be. But may I still have your ear?" He looked down at her and grinned.

"If you treat it with propriety, my lord, it is all yours."

"With none but the very greatest of respect, ma'am, you have my word."

He walked back through the copse and swung up onto his horse, a big bay gelding with a strong chest and well-proportioned back, and then he kicked the horse into a canter, his cloak flowing behind him. Honor admired the fluidity of the horse's paces. So many people had no idea how to buy a horse, she thought, going for showy looks and too often buying a like temperament. This horse had muscle and breeding, but sense, the sort of horse that would do well in battle.

"Come, girls, it grows cold and we should make our way home. Jocie, the bottle, please. Minerva, take my hand, there's a good girl." She led them back to the house, wondering nervously what Andrew wished to speak with her about in private. It was bad enough, being thrown together with him in the company of others, but alone? Once again she determined that she would put these foolish thoughts from her mind, for it was sheer idiocy to be affected by a specter from a dream. And in any case, she told herself firmly, she had made it all up.

5

He reads much;
He is a great observer, and he looks
Quite through the deeds of men.

—William Shakespeare, *Julius Caesar*, I, ii

Honor arrived home to chaos. Mrs. Lipp and Mrs. Spencer had practically come to fisticuffs over the ordering of that night's meal, and were in the process of confronting Arabella in the morning room, while Mrs. Spencer raged and Mrs. Lipp cried. Honor heard the noise as soon as she came into the house, and saw Betsy lurking in the hallway with her ear to the door.

"Oh, miss!" she said as soon as she saw Honor enter. "There be the most terrible goings-on! Her ladyship said to fetch you as soon as you was back!"

"Oh, dear," said Honor with a sigh. "Take the children upstairs for hot baths, will you, Betsy? Where is Sir Henry?"

"He left not two hours ago in a tearing hurry, he did, with Jake pushing the horses like there was no tomorrow, miss, and thank goodness he's not here right now is all I can say, for he'd be in a taking sure enough to come home and find everyone topsy-turvy. And Lord Chesney is to be here for dinner, if there is to be one." Betsy's face was pink with excitement.

"Thank you, Betsy," said Honor, absorbing all of this quickly. She made sure Betsy had safely taken the children up, then knocked on the door of the morning room and entered.

"My lady? Betsy said you'd summoned me."

Three faces turned to her. Arabella looked pale and flustered, Mrs. Lipp's alarming hair had come partially undone and her cap was askew, and Mrs. Spencer, a thin, tall woman with a sharp face like a weasel's, was shaking with fury. Mrs. Lipp and Mrs. Spencer began to speak at the same time. Arabella said nothing, simply looked at Honor imploringly.

"Mrs. Lipp, you must sit down," said Honor, seeing that the situation had obviously gone beyond Arabella's control. She led Mrs. Lipp over to the delicate sofa, which threatened to collapse beneath her weight. "You know it is not good for you to upset yourself. Mrs. Spencer, why don't you sit over here, for I know you are on your feet all day long and must be tired. Now, what has happened to put you both in such a state? Did I make another one of my mistakes? I must apologize, for I do get into such a muddle."

Arabella sank gratefully back in her own chair.

"*She*," said the cook imperiously, pointing a scrawny finger at Mrs. Lipp, "had the gall to enter my kitchen and inform me that there was not to be goose tonight for Sir Henry has no taste for it, when it was on the menu her ladyship approved. What I am to do for the main course when the shopping was done this morning is beyond me, unless the old sow expects me to produce herself on a platter with an apple in her mouth, and more than enough to go around, I'd say, not that anyone wouldn't keel over from the sight!"

"Why, you shriveled old bag!" started Mrs. Lipp. "If anyone were to—"

"Oh, it's just as I feared," interrupted Honor. "I'm afraid it's all my fault! Lady Rutherford went over the menu with me this morning, and I misunderstood completely. I had no idea that Sir Henry disliked goose, and I must have been thinking of the duck he enjoyed so much last week."

"He most certainly does not dislike goose," insisted Mrs. Spencer. "He's had it any number of times since I've been in service here, and never a word was said! If I can't cook as I like, I'll leave and take Mr. Spencer with me, and then see where you'll be! I'll tell you—you'll be the one out on your ear, mark my words, relation or no!"

"Mrs. Spencer," said Honor gently. "Please do not blame Mrs. Lipp, for I obviously made the mistake."

"But he does like goose," said Arabella helplessly. "I cannot understand why you think he doesn't, Mrs. Lipp. And I did approve the menu this morning, just as I told you."

"But Miss Phoebe said her father will not eat goose," insisted Mrs. Lipp. "She told me herself: 'Lipp,' she said, 'you know my papa cannot abide the stuff.' She said that she had seen the goose brought in from the stableyard and came straight in to tell me when she heard from Cook that Lady Rutherford had approved the menu and sent it back with you, Miss Winslow, for you know I was indisposed this morning and could not see to it myself. I hurried in to amend the error, only to have the old bag throw a dish at my head, and that's God's honest truth!''

''I might have known,'' said Honor under her breath. ''Oh, dear,'' she said more loudly. ''Well, then, that explains it. But perhaps, Mrs. Lipp, if it is true that Sir Henry does enjoy goose, then we might still have it for dinner? It does seem very late to make other arrangements, and her ladyship took so much trouble to plan the dinner. Mrs. Spencer, you really mustn't blame Mrs. Lipp for the error, for she was only looking out for Sir Henry's interests, and not trying to disturb your kitchen, and as for Miss Phoebe, she has been away from home for these few years and has most likely confused her father's likes and dislikes. Perhaps she was thinking of something else. I'm sure that it has been very upsetting for both of you. But, Mrs. Spencer, now that you've sorted out the trouble, I know you will want to return to your kitchen in order to prepare one of your remarkable dinners.''

Mrs. Spencer smiled slightly, nodded superiorly at Mrs. Lipp, and rustled out of the room.

''And, Mrs. Lipp,'' continued Honor, ''perhaps it would be best if you rested now. I do know how much excessive emotion upsets you, and we can't take any chances with your precarious health. Goodness only knows how Lady Rutherford would manage should you be required to take to your bed again!''

Mrs. Lipp shot a withering look at her rival's retreating back, hoping she had heard and taken warning, then rose precariously. ''Thank you for your assistance, Miss Winslow. You are improving admirably under my tutelage, if I do say so myself. But I would thank you to approve the menus with me after conferring with her ladyship. It is my impression that you take my periods of indisposition too much for granted, and we can't have you forgetting your place.''

"Indeed I won't," said Honor with a choke. "I only hoped that you might be spared some of the more tedious tasks, knowing how you . . . you suffer from your rheumatism. I beg your pardon for the mistake."

"I accept your apology," said Mrs. Lipp grandly. "Now then, I suggest you return to your place with the children. Good evening, your ladyship."

"Oh, Honor!" exclaimed Arabella when Mrs. Lipp had sailed off like a battleship in victory. "I don't know what I should do without you! Those two had me in such a state, I cannot tell you!"

"Not at all, my lady. It is unnerving to deal with such opposing temperaments when one is gently reared. Fortunately I was not bred for nerves, so such encounters do not upset me." Honor's eyes danced with laughter.

"And just what were you bred for, Miss Winslow?" asked Andrew, coming away from the door of the adjoining room, where he had been listening with great interest to the majority of the fray.

Honor spun around, her hand flying to her throat. "For service, my lord," she replied, steadying herself. "What else?"

"Indeed. Then your breeding was successful, it seems. What a treasure you have found in Miss Winslow, Arabella. She has won the loving obedience of not only your children, but also your staff."

"Oh, Andrew, it is true," said Arabella, rising and offering her cheek to him. "Honor—Miss Winslow—has extracted me from so many scrapes, you would not credit it!"

"I believe I would credit her with a great deal." Andrew looked at her thoughtfully.

"I must see to the children," Honor said abruptly, looking away from his searching gaze.

"But of course. You won't forget our agreement?"

"No, my lord. My lady." Honor sketched a curtsy and promptly fled from the room, which had become too warm by far.

As she entered the hall, she saw that Sir Henry had returned and was making his slightly unsteady way upstairs. She waited until he had disappeared and then crossed to the stairs herself, but Jake appeared, seemingly from nowhere,

and stopped her. Looking quickly around to see if his un-
authorized appearance in the house had been noticed, he
pressed a note into her hand. "His lordship said after midnight," he whispered, and without waiting for an answer,
melted away again.

Honor waited until she had reached the privacy of her
room before opening the note and scanning the contents.
She read it carefully, deciphering the code, and her pulse
quickened as she realized the implication of what Julian had
written. The gist of it was simple enough: he had discovered
who Sir Henry's contact was, a certain French colonel, and
Sir Henry had met with a mutual contact that very afternoon. He had agreed, within Jake's hearing, to pass along
some sort of secret government document for a very large
sum of money. The money was to be deposited as soon as
the document was received, and Sir Henry assured the gentleman that he would have it delivered the next day. Julian,
who had met Jake outside of the inn where Sir Henry had
been celebrating, wanted Honor to find the document if at
all possible. He would be waiting in the woods that night
for her to bring it to him. All haste was required, for he had
a good idea of the contents, and they could not be allowed
to pass into the hands of the French.

Honor smiled, then crossed the room to the fireplace, and
crumpling the note into a small ball, fed it to the flames.

Andrew was at his most charming at dinner that night,
politely conversing with Phoebe, trying hard to find a subject in common.

"Do you enjoy riding, Miss Rutherford?" he asked as a
compote of pigeon was being removed, to be replaced by
the infamous goose, and he had to bow his head to keep
from laughing aloud.

"Oh, no, Lord Chesney," said Phoebe, showing her little
white teeth in a self-deprecating smile. "I wish I could say
I did, but horses and I do not agree. I took a fall when I
was young, and since then I have not been able to stop
trembling whenever I am near one of the animals." She
couldn't stop trembling in his presence either, she happily
thought to herself.

"How very unfortunate for you," he said absently, wondering whom he had seen riding toward Croftsfield. But he dragged his attention back to the immediate conversation. "I hope you do not mind being driven? That would be even more unfortunate, for one must get about somehow. Thank you, Spencer," he said as that gentleman laid a large slice of goose on his plate. "It looks most . . . exemplary. Caught in full flight, no doubt."

Phoebe looked sidelong at his dancing eyes and wondered if he was poking fun at her. "I enjoy being driven very much indeed, my lord. My aversion does not extend that far. I imagine you must drive very well. Are you a member of the Four-in-Hand Club?"

"No, nothing as exalted as that. I wouldn't think of competing with the Corinthian set." This wasn't exactly true; Andrew was extremely skilled with the ribbons, but found most of the young bucks and their showing-off a bore. "In any case, brass buttons and violently striped waistcoats were never quite my taste."

"Oh," said Phoebe, nonplussed, for she thought that someone as dashing as he would surely have belonged to so prestigious a club. "Perhaps your tastes run more to White's or Brooks's?" she continued hopefully.

Andrew replied with gentle humor, "No, Miss Rutherford. It seems I am to become a farmer. Delicious goose, Arabella; don't you agree, Sir Henry?"

"Marvelous. There's nothing like a good goose to set one up. Compliments to Mrs. Spencer. Pour some more wine for his lordship, Spencer."

Phoebe looked down and for the first time noticed what was on her plate, unaware that Andrew was watching her carefully. She frowned. She had been quite sure that Lipp had countermanded Honor's order . . .

"Miss Rutherford? Have I lost your attention so easily?"

"A farmer, did you say? How droll, Lord Chesney. You are funning me, of course."

"Only in a manner of speaking. I intend to spend most of my time at Chesney, looking after its concerns. Do you enjoy the country, Miss Rutherford, or do you prefer the city life?"

"Why . . . I love the country. I have grown up here and known nothing else, except for the ladies' seminary in Bath.

But one can't call Bath a city, can one? I do look forward to going up to London for my Season, for I have been only once or twice as a child, which cannot be compared to being a part of all the exciting things. There's the opera, and the assemblies, and the routs and balls. But then, you know it so well, my lord. It is still an exciting mystery to me.''

"I am sure I found it just so myself, Phoebe dearest," said Arabella reassuringly. "I was raised in the country, although much further north, but found one Season in London was quite enough. I met my dear George that spring and married him that summer, and after that we hardly strayed from Chesney. I'm sure it will be just the same for you.''

Andrew caught the look of anger Sir Henry directed at his wife, and wondered at it. "Perhaps it was so for you, Arabella," he said quickly, covering for her. "But then, not all young girls are as suited to country life as you are. To many, the allure of London society is quite irresistible. Look at Lady Hemming, for example. Her poor husband is hard put to remove her to Sussex even when most of London has emptied out. I remember a time when she and Sally Jersey took it into their heads to start up a whole new fashion . . .'' He carried on telling an amusing anecdote until they were safely off dangerous ground. Dinner went on in this manner until the ladies had excused themselves from the table and he and Sir Henry were left with the port.

"What do you make of my little Phoebe, Chesney?" inquired Sir Henry jovially, his face flushed from an excess of drink, as it had been since he had arrived home before dinner. "Arabella has informed me you have offered to ease her way in London. Very kind of you, I'm sure.''

"I'm sure that she shall do very well," said Andrew coolly, wishing he had never conceived the idea of smoothing Phoebe's way, not even to rescue Arabella and provide easy access to his nieces. Henry Rutherford was a nightmare and he could well do without his company. But he had made an offer to help, and he honored his commitments. In any case, it was a way of keeping his eye on the man. "I know how much Arabella dreads social occasions," he continued. "As you know, I'm very fond of her, and her interests become my own. It's the least I can do for George.''

"Yes, yes, of course," said Sir Henry, feeling somehow chastised. "My dear wife has always spoken fondly of you. Well, then, what do you make of the progress of the war? I heard rumors that Wellington is pressing the invasion of France. At this rate, we should see a victory in the new year. What have you heard yourself?" He poured himself another glass of port and, to Andrew's dismay, prepared to settle in.

But finally it was over, the tea tray was shared with the ladies, who then departed, and Andrew, after enduring yet another glass of indifferent port with Sir Henry, and declining an offer of cards, asked him if he might borrow his study to have a brief interview with Miss Winslow about his nieces' progress. Sir Henry graciously complied, wending his drunken way to bed, and Andrew had Honor summoned. He stirred the fire as he waited, looking forward to the discussion more than he had realized. At least it was bound to be intelligent.

"My lord," Honor said calmly as she entered, "what did you wish to discuss with me?" She sat down in the chair he indicated.

"May I offer you sherry?"

She nodded and accepted the glass he poured from the decanter, waiting patiently, but her heart thumped painfully despite her calm demeanor.

"Miss Winslow, as you probably know, I have not been able to spend as much time with my nieces as I would have liked over this last difficult year. What I had seen during that time had concerned me. I find them much changed indeed since then, and happier than since my brother's unfortunate death. I must attribute this change to your exemplary care."

"Thank you, my lord," said Honor quickly, her hands clasped tightly in her lap. "It has taken them time to adjust to their new situation, but I believe that they have finally become accustomed to the change in their circumstances."

"Yes, it is true," said Andrew. "Jocelyn certainly seems to have lost her truculence—"

"Oh, not altogether, my lord," said Honor with a smile. "Truculence is as much a part of Jocelyn's nature as . . .

as service is to mine. She has merely learned to restrain her more inflammatory feelings. She is a highly spirited girl, and I don't believe in repressing spirit.''

"No, I can see why you wouldn't. You have enough of your own, despite what you say about your call to service. I suppose the nuns taught you that?''

Honor inclined her head. ''I was not the best of pupils.''

"No. From what I have seen, you do better leading than following.''

"My lord, I should hope I have not given you the impression—''

"You have given me the impression, Miss Winslow, that you rule with a steel fist inside a velvet glove, surprising in one so young. Your performance today in the morning room was remarkable. Tell me, did you run the convent in such a manner?''

Honor flushed under the intent gaze of his sapphire eyes. ''Certainly not, my lord. I confess that I am a trifle headstrong, but we digress. It is the children you wished to discuss, surely?''

Andrew smiled. ''Your point, Miss Winslow. It is the children, indeed, we were discussing. Jocie seems to have lost the religious fanaticism I found creeping up on her. I confess to surprise, given that I would have expected your own background a perfect breeding-ground for religious conviction. She has not yet thrown a single biblical quotation at me.''

"Jocie has had enough unnecessary influence from her previous governess to last her a lifetime. I do not intend to add to it. Morning and evening prayers suffice, and I would prefer her to seek a more secular life.''

"As you have done?'' He crossed one long muscular leg over the other and continued to regard her intently.

"As I have done. But again we stray from the point.''

"Ah, yes, the point. I come now to Minerva.'' He frowned. ''Tell me, Miss Winslow, what do you make of Minerva?''

Honor leaned forward earnestly in her chair. ''The truth, my lord?''

"Naturally the truth. I fear the truth has been suppressed for too long.''

"Yes . . ." Honor looked at him with a troubled face. "You, then, too, see what I see in Minerva?"

"I cannot in truth say, for I do not know what you see. I have wondered for some time if she is not . . . different."

"Yes, my lord. She *is* different. Minerva will never be like other children, or even other young women as she grows older. She will always be a child. A sweet, innocent child."

Andrew sighed and looked down at the glass in his hand. "It is as I feared. Her birth was not an easy one. But perhaps it is something I should not be discussing with you—"

"Not at all. I have had some experience with nursing, and I have seen cases where a long and difficult birth has resulted in a diminution of mental faculties. I had wondered what circumstances had caused Minerva to be the way she is. I did not like to ask her mother, who prefers to see Minerva as shy and retiring by nature, but the child has great difficulty with learning anything more than the simplest facts. And then, there is her speech, or lack of it. I believe her brain to have been injured in a way that cannot be repaired."

"Yes," said Andrew heavily. "I believe you are correct. For years I had hoped she would grow out of it. But in the last year I began to wonder if it were not a permanent condition. I thank you for being so candid with me. What can be done for her?"

"What Minerva needs is love and encouragement, and no pressure to push her beyond her limited capacities. She is very sensitive to her environment and the people around her, and is hurt deeply by criticism; she withdraws very easily from the world when it is harsh. Her father's death was inexplicable to her, and being removed from her home confusing. Jocelyn is the greatest stay on her stability, but then Jocie is possessed of such intelligence and sensitivity that I believe she understands Minerva's problem already. I don't think that Jocelyn's loyalty will ever sway from her sister, despite the problems that are bound to occur. She is very protective of her."

"Miss Winslow," said Andrew, taking all of this in carefully, and with a feeling of inexpressible relief that Minerva was finally in capable, understanding hands, "I cannot think what gift of God brought you to this doorstep, and I can only thank my dear friend Lord Hambledon for putting you in our way. I shall help you with Minerva as best I can, and Jocie, too, of course,'' he went on, ''but I do want to thank you for your devotion to them. It is more than I had ever expected.''

''My lord, I care for the children deeply, even though I have been with them only for these few short weeks. There is time yet to see what might be made of Minerva; Jocelyn will make her own way in the world, with or without our help. She is strong.''

''Yes. Yes, I can see that. But I will spend what time I can with them, for I know they miss their father badly. I will ride over early tomorrow morning, if it will not interfere with their lessons, for I have appointments all afternoon.''

''Your attention to the children is far more important than their lessons, my lord. Those can always be given at another time.''

''I thank you for your understanding. And I also thank you for giving me your honest opinion. We will talk again later.'' He rose, signaling the end of the interview.

''Yes, my lord.'' Honor carefully put down her glass, curtsied to him, and left the room.

Andrew watched her retreating back, then smiled to himself. There was a great deal more he wanted to know about the astonishing Miss Honor Winslow.

Phoebe, watching from the top of the stairs, saw Honor leave the study, and prepared to duck into the corridor, but Honor did not come upstairs. Looking over the railing, she saw Lord Chesney leave the room not two minutes later. She was overcome with an unreasonable rush of jealousy. She had half a mind to run down the stairs when she saw him, with a pretext of forgetting her book, but she decided against it. It was too soon, and it might appear unmaidenly. She couldn't afford to make any mistakes, not when he was watching her so closely and making up his mind to his future bride. She had to appear in the best possible light. She had to admit that she hadn't been her best at dinner; the incident of the goose had distracted her. How had Honor managed to straighten it out? And what had she been doing closeted in the library with Lord Chesney? Probably discussing those dreadful little girls. Her thoughts were stilled as Honor came back through the hall. She went into the study, and reappeared a few minutes later with a tray of glasses, disappearing in the direction of the kitchen.

Phoebe crept down the stairs and followed after her. But when she reached the kitchen, all that she found was the tray of glasses sitting next to the sink. There was a draft coming from the door, and Phoebe went quickly over and discovered it off the latch, and Honor's cloak missing. She thought of locking the door against Honor's return, but then reconsidered. It would be much more to her purpose to discover what the horrible Honor was up to. With any luck, she was meeting with the groom. Phoebe grabbed up a spare cloak from the peg, probably Betsy's, she thought with a shudder. She'd catch a disease for sure.

It was a foggy night, the cold coming after a fairly warm day, and the moon was only a tiny sliver in the sky, giving very little light to see by. Honor was more than halfway across the garden and Phoebe followed at a discreet distance. She saw Honor slip into the woods, and she hurried after her, but she caught her hem on a briar and lost a few minutes while she untangled it. Had it been just the cloak, she would have jerked it away without worrying about the consequences, but this was one of her new dresses and she did not want to ruin the flounce. Finally she freed herself, and continued across the grass. In five minutes' time, she had entered the wood on silent feet. The fog swirled about her feet, and she wished she had thought to change her slippers for sturdier boots; her feet were soaking from the melting snow, and very cold. But then she heard a low exchange of voices coming from the copse to her left, and she forgot the cold in the excitement of tracking down her prey. A horse's bit jangled, a sharp clank of steel and a soft snort in the silence of the night. Phoebe crept closer, drawing the rough woolen cloak more closely about her, her blood pounding in her veins in an agony of anticipation. She felt very daring, like a heroine in a book. She stumbled and scratched her face against the bark of an oak tree, and swore softly under her breath. And then in the swirling white mist she made out the outline of Honor's cloak, and a horse with a tall dark man mounted on its back. He bent over her hand and murmured something.

It was Lord Chesney! There was no doubt in her mind, despite the mist. Who else was so tall, so heroic a figure? And who else would be on horseback on the Chesney path meeting Honor Winslow? It was unspeakably vulgar: the governess consorting with Lord Chesney. She might have known.

A flood of anger poured through her, so overpowering that for a moment she could see nothing but red before her eyes. She leaned against the oak, clutching onto it, scraping at the trunk with her nails. But just as she was about to stumble forward, Honor melted back into the fog, and the horse reared once, then leapt off at a short command from its master. Phoebe heard nothing but the pounding of great hooves on the earth. And then there was silence.

6

My mind is troubled, like a fountain stirred;
And I myself see not the bottom of it.

—William Shakespeare, *Troilus and Cressida*, III, ii

Honor missed her ride that morning. She slept the sleep of exhaustion, and when she woke, it was abruptly, with a small cry. It took her a moment to orient herself. Something had happened, but what was it? Not the dream; that hadn't come since Andrew's appearance, and she thanked God for that. No, it was something else—but she couldn't think what. She rubbed her eyes and looked at the clock. Everything else was driven out of her mind, and she jumped out of bed in alarm. It was already past eight and the children would be stirring. Quickly she washed and changed into a warm blue woolen dress, grabbed up a shawl, and went next door to the nursery, where Betsy had laid a blazing fire and pulled the draperies back. Winter sunshine streamed into the room. The windowpanes were covered with frost and the sill was high with fresh snow. It all looked so normal, but Honor could not shake the feeling that there was something terribly wrong.

Minerva came padding silently into the room, shivering in only her nightdress and bare feet, and Honor scooped her up in her arms with a laugh.

"Funny girl, where are your slippers and robe? You should have waited for me to come and get you—you must be very cold indeed! Here, we'll go in front of the fire and it will warm you." She pulled up a chair and settled Minerva on her lap, wrapping the shawl around her.

The flames crackled and leapt, and Minerva gazed into them with wide, unseeing eyes.

"Are you warmer now, little one?" Honor asked after a few minutes. "Shall I go down for your cocoa?"

Minerva shook her head.

"What is it, then? Is something troubling you?"

Minerva nodded and took her eyes from the fire for a moment. "Uncle is cold."

"Is he, sweet? I should think that he has just come out of bed like you, and forgot to put on his slippers and robe. And he is old enough to know better! He'll be visiting later."

"No. He has gone to see Papa."

"All the way to heaven without his robe and slippers? Goodness, no wonder he is cold! We shall have to scold him when he comes. Have you seen the snow, Minerva? We have had a lovely snowfall during the night, and we shall go out later and play in it. That will give us something to look forward to, as well as your uncle's visit."

Minerva just shook her head adamantly and refused to say another word.

But when eleven came, Andrew still had not arrived. Honor could not sit still a moment longer, and put away the books. She still felt uneasy, but attributed her nervousness to Minerva, who had been silent and disturbed all morning.

Jocie could get nothing more out of her than Honor had. Minerva seldom had these moods anymore, and Honor decided that maybe the fresh air would shake them both out of it.

"Jocelyn, I think I've discovered what's troubling Minerva," Honor said in an undertone, coming out of Minerva's bedroom. "I can't find her scarf anywhere, and I think she might have forgotten it in the copse yesterday. She must be worried that she'll be punished for leaving it. Why don't I go out and see if I can't find it, and then she'll feel better. Will you look after her for me? I won't be too long."

Honor pulled on her boots and gloves and bundled into her cloak, pulling the hood over her head. It was a beautiful day again, but Minerva was quite right, it was cold. There was a bite in the air, and her feet crunched on the frozen snow, which came up well over her ankles. She hurried, wanting to get back to Minerva as quickly as possible.

The woods looked like one of the illustrations from Andrew's book of fairy tales, the trees and ground covered with a mantle of sparkling snow. Honor was about to turn left toward the copse when her eye caught a dark shape further ahead on the path, and beyond it, a horse, a bay gelding she had admired only the day before. Her heart jerked sickeningly, and she picked up her skirts and ran forward.

He lay facedown, and the snow had turned a deep pink around his head. With a horrible feeling of anticipation she gently rolled his motionless body over. His skin was terribly white, with a bluish tinge about his lips, and his dark hair was matted with blood, still seeping from a long, ugly gash in his scalp. His arm lay at an awkward angle.

"Dear God . . . Andrew!" Her hands shaking, she moved over his bones with experienced fingers, pulled his cloak around him, then removed her own cloak and covered him with that as well. She felt his neck for a pulse and found it, but it was faint, far too faint. Without wasting another second, she pulled her skirts up and removed her petticoat, tearing it into strips, and forming a pad. This she carefully placed against the gash, and, resting his head on her lap, tied the pad in place with the other strips. She couldn't move him on her own; she would have to fetch help, and quickly.

Her heart pounding in her throat, she approached the horse, speaking softly to it as she collected the trailing reins. He trembled, but he let her mount, and she hitched up her skirts and swung up astride his back, not bothering with the long stirrups. She kicked him forward. The wind howled through her hair and cut sharply through the wool of her dress as she galloped toward the stables, her body moving as one with the beast, her will urging him forward.

"Jake!" she cried as she saw him emerging from the stables, a large wooden bucket of water in one hand. "Jake!"

He stopped abruptly when he saw her. "What is it? What's happened?" He dropped the bucket and started toward her.

"It's Lord Chesney—he was thrown from his horse and has been badly injured!" She reined the horse up next to him, trying to catch her breath. "He's in the woods on the Chesney path. We'll need a litter, and the hay cart—and a roll of the liniment bandages. Get two of the stableboys to help you—I'm going back. And for God's sake, hurry!" She was shivering helplessly.

Jake nodded curtly, his mouth tight. "Go on. We'll be there as soon as possible. Wait—take my cloak. I'll borrow one." He pulled it off and handed it to her.

Honor took it gratefully, then wheeled the gelding around and took off again.

She tied the horse to a nearby tree and dismounted. He was lying just as she'd left him, and the bandage she'd fashioned was already stained through with blood. She sank down into the snow and pulled his heavy weight up into her arms, cradling him against her chest to share her warmth, her arms around him. It seemed an eternity before she heard the clatter of wheels, and then the cart appeared. Jake jumped down, calling orders to the boys, and he brought the bandages over to Honor, taking in the situation with a glance. "How bad is it?"

"Bad. I need the bandages for his collarbone; he's broken it and it will have to be set in some fashion before we can move him, although that's the least of his worries. Here, help me lift him.'' She pulled the cloaks away and laid his arm across his chest. ''Now, keep his arm like that so I can get the bandages around his chest.'' Quickly, efficiently, she strapped his arm in place and covered him again with the cloaks. ''There. Let's get him onto the cart.''

''I sent a message with one of the boys for the doctor. He should be here shortly.''

''Thank you. Take the cart slowly. I don't want him jostled and his head to start bleeding heavily again. He's lost far too much blood as it is. I'll ride back and meet you at the house.''

Jake nodded, and directed the boys with the litter. They carefully moved him onto it, then lowered him into the cart onto a springy cushion of hay, and the cart rolled off cumbersomely.

Honor went back to the horse and was about to untie the reins when her eye caught something shining across the path at shoulder height. She slowly straightened and put out her hand. It was a thin wire, tied to the oak on one side and stretched tightly across the path, where it was attached to a tree on the other side, almost invisible even now, and impossible to see if one were bearing down on it quickly. She had heard of the trick being used before to bring a man down. But to what use? And why Andrew of all people? Frowning heavily, Honor untied the wire and put it in the pocket of her skirt. There was no time to puzzle it out now while Andrew's life hung in the balance.

The stableboys carried the litter into the house and Honor followed.

''Oh, miss!'' cried Betsy, wringing her hands as Honor came through the door. ''What has befallen his lordship?''

''Never mind that now, Betsy dear,'' said Honor more calmly than she felt. ''When the doctor comes, direct him up to the front bedroom, the red one. Spencer, please find Sir Henry and tell him what has happened. Jake, follow me.'' She was almost at the top of the stairs when Phoebe appeared, still in her nightdress, having heard the commotion.

''Miss Winslow . . .'' she said with bewilderment, rubbing at her eyes. And then she caught sight of the litter bearing Andrew, alarmingly pale, and she uttered a stifled scream. "Lord Chesney—no! Oh, no! What has happened? Is he dead?" She shook Honor. "*Tell* me, is he dead?" Her voice had risen to a screech.

"Please collect yourself, Miss Rutherford," said Honor, removing her hands from her shoulders and firmly setting her to one side. "Lord Chesney has been injured, and this is no time for hysterics." She moved past her, leaving Phoebe staring at the litter as it went past, her hand pressed against her mouth in horror.

Honor saw Andrew gently settled onto the large bed. "I thank you all for responding so quickly. You may go now, and rest assured that Lord Chesney is very much in your debt. Jake, will you stay for a moment?"

He nodded and the stableboys filed out of the room.

"Will you start a fire and then help me with Lord Chesney's clothes? He's soaked through and we must get him warm and dry."

"It won't take a moment," he said, going to the fireplace, and, true to his word, in a minute he had a warm blaze going in the hearth. He then obligingly helped Honor to strip Andrew. "He's far too pale, if you ask me. It looked as if he left half his blood out there in the snow."

"I know—it worries me." They pulled off his boots and breeches and gently toweled him dry, and Honor carefully inspected his body for any other injuries. Then she set the collarbone with sensitive fingers, and wrapped the bandages securely around his chest to hold his arm firmly in position. She sighed heavily, her brow furrowed with worry as she covered him with heavy blankets. "It's the best we can do now, Jake, until the doctor comes, and even then I think prayers are all we have left to us."

"Don't worry yourself too much. He's strong and fit, and that's all to the best," said Jake reassuringly. "You've seen worse than this come through. But we'll have to act quickly as to the other matter. It looks very suspicious to me, considering the events of last night."

"Yes, it's a nasty business, and I'm afraid that somehow Lord Chesney has been put in the middle of it," she said, sinking down onto the foot of the bed. "Please, will you see that word is sent to Lady Rutherford? I dare not leave

his lordship for a moment, but I shall speak to Lady Rutherford as soon as possible if she will come up. And a message will have to be sent to Chesney immediately. Can you
take care of it?''

"Right away."

"And Lord Hambledon? Do you know where he can be
reached? He'll want to know."

"I'll see to all of it, directed through the proper chan-
nels, naturally."

"Thank you, Jake. I don't know what I'd have done without you."

"Not at all. Only doing my job." He smiled at her, then
gave her shoulder a light squeeze. "And you know your job
as well as anyone. His lordship will be grateful."

"Let's just hope he has cause to be grateful, Jake."

"All will be well, you'll see." He rolled down his
sleeves, replaced his jacket and cloak, and with a worried
backward look hurried out.

Honor slipped her hand into her pocket and brought out
the thin, coiled wire. She stared at it intently for a few
moments, then slipped it into the back of the bottom bureau
drawer under a pile of linen and went back to watch Andrew.

"Ah, Miss Winslow, is it?" The doctor came into the
room, a relatively young man who Honor knew had trained
at the University of Edinburgh and had very modern ideas
according to Mrs. Lipp, who refused to let herself be treated
by him. That alone was enough to give Honor confidence.
He had thinning blond hair and brown eyes, and a profes-
sional air about him, unlike some of the doctors of Honor's
acquaintance, whose lack of regard for cleanliness and a
fondness for bleeding their patients did nothing to recommend them to her. She was relieved to see him, knowing
Andrew would be in the best of hands.

"Mr. Langley," she said, rising. "Lord Chesney has sustained a head injury that has left him concussed, and he
has broken his clavicle, but what I fear far worse is the
extensive loss of blood and exposure to the cold. I believe
he must have been lying in the snow for at least two hours,
possibly three, before I found him." She thought of Mi-

nerva, and shook her head, wondering. And wondered at her own uneasy feelings since she had awakened with a jerk.

"Ah, yes," said the doctor, examining Andrew carefully, prodding at his body. "Did you set this yourself, Miss Winslow?" He spoke with a faint Scottish burr.

"Yes, sir."

"And applied the head dressing?"

"Yes, sir."

"Very well done, I must say. Where did you learn such things?" he asked, opening Andrew's eyelids and peering into his unseeing eyes.

"I was trained in the . . . at a convent. The sisters nursed the community."

"They taught you well. Let's remove this dressing then, and we'll see what we have." He carefully unraveled Honor's strips of petticoat, throwing her a curious glance as he did so, and gently pulled away the pad, exposing a laceration a good four inches long and gaping. "Hmm," he said, looking closely at it. "It shall have to be stitched. Have you had experience with stitching, Miss Winslow?"

"Yes, I have," she said, taking the soiled dressings from him. "Shall I clean the area while you prepare?"

"Good girl," he said approvingly, turning to his bag. "It's not often that I find a young woman who doesn't fly into the boughs at the first sight of blood."

Honor smiled. "That would be very out of character. It might be unfeminine, but I'm afraid that I've never been very squeamish." She took the scissors he offered and carefully cut away a healthy strip of Andrew's hair, dabbing at the edges of the wound with a wet cloth.

"It's just as well he's unconscious," said the doctor, threading his needle. "They generally don't hold very still for this. But I'm sure you know. Now, Miss Winslow. If you'll just keep the area free from blood, we'll have this over in no time."

He sewed quickly and efficiently, and a quarter of an hour later Andrew's head had a neat line of thick black stitches. "There we are. Now for the rest of it. You're quite right about the clavicle. It has been broken, but I see no need to shift the position in which you've set the arm. I couldn't have done it better myself. There are no other injuries to his person that I can detect. However, I agree with you concerning his lordship's loss of blood. It has made him weaker than I would have liked, and the question of exposure is a serious one. Now we must combat the effect of chill. I warn you, Miss Winslow, it will be an uphill battle. He must be watched at all times. The concussion is severe, and fever will indubitably ensue. But no doubt you know how to deal with it. I'll be back tomorrow," he said, packing away his bag.

"Yes, doctor. Thank you for coming so quickly."

"It is I who thank you, Miss Winslow, for being so level-headed. Lord Chesney is fortunate to be in your care. He *is* in your care?"

"I shall stay with him for as long as he needs me."

"Good, then, very good." He gave Honor another curious look. "Good day, Miss Winslow."

"Good day, Mr. Langley." A mere pleasantry, but Honor couldn't help but think it was horribly inappropriate under the circumstances.

Honor stayed with Andrew as promised. She had assigned Betsy to the children, and had spoken with Arabella and successfully warded off Mrs. Lipp, who had tried to barge her way into the room to assess the situation, as was her duty, but had immediately retreated upon catching a glimpse of Andrew, her face suddenly as white as the patient himself. Phoebe also attempted to visit Andrew, but Honor refused her admittance, to Phoebe's fury.

"Once again, Miss Winslow, you are putting yourself forward!" she had cried, her face flushed with anger. "I know exactly what you are trying to do—"

But her father had come along just at that moment and had dissuaded Phoebe from persisting in her attack.

"Phoebe, dear, I know how distraught you are, and how much you might want to help, but you have had no nursing experience, you know, and Mr. Langley tells me Miss Winslow has been trained. We must think of Lord Chesney's health first and foremost. And in any case, this coarse work in beneath you. You must remember your more tender sensibilities. Think how shocked Lord Chesney would be if he thought you had been exposed to . . . to his condition . . ."

This last statement seemed to mollify her. "Very well, then, Papa," she said, slanting a superior look at Honor. "We shall leave it to those who were born to the baser things in life." She turned on her heel and swished off to spend the remainder of the day brooding in her room.

Sir Henry had then drawn Honor to one side and queried her closely about Andrew's condition, his concern seemingly genuine, although Honor questioned the cause.

And then there had been Hobson's arrival from Chesney. He had insisted—more than insisted—on seeing his master, and Honor had seen not only the valet's devotion but also his potential usefulness. She would need help, and nobody in Sir Henry's house was competent enough to help her, now that Jake was gone. Reluctantly she let him in.

"Oh, dear!" he cried distressfully, approaching the bed where Andrew lay still and pale. "It is as we all feared, just like his brother he is, with not a care to his health! Look at him, just lying there, waiting to meet his Maker, and the succession not ensured! Not that we don't love him in his own right, for a finer lord there couldn't be, but we did try to warn him!"

"It was not his fault, Hobson," said Honor impatiently. "If you truly care for your master, then he can use you now in this difficult time. Why don't we have a bed made up for you next door and you can be there to relieve me. I would be most grateful."

"Why, yes, miss. It's why I'm here, of course, to look after his lordship. I'll just fetch some clothes for him—"

"He won't be needing clothes for some time, Hobson. A nightshirt would only be irritating and painful to change. We must see him through this crisis first, and then I'm sure he would be happy for some things from home."

Hobson looked at her with shock, wondering at this strange, controlled girl who had no concern that his lordship be properly attired, at least given the dignity of a nightshirt, but what could he do? "Very well, miss," he sniffed. "As you say."

"Thank you, Hobson. If you don't mind sitting with his lordship for a few minutes, I should like to see the children and change my clothes."

Hobson nodded encouragingly. He had not missed his

lordship's blood all over the girl's dress, and it had struck him as very unsuitable indeed. In fact, the girl herself struck him as extremely unsuitable, and he couldn't think what Sir Henry was about, allowing a child governess to nurse his lordship. But he'd soon have the situation straightened out, he thought, settling himself into the armchair next to the bed, and the girl would learn her place and what was what in no time flat.

Honor quickly washed and changed, so as not to alarm the girls, and found them in the nursery with Betsy.

"Oh, miss, how be his poor lordship?" she exclaimed, jumping to her feet.

Honor ignored Betsy. She knelt and held out her hands to the girls, who were staring at her, Minerva blankly and Jocie with fear. She knew this scene was far too familiar to them. They slipped off the window seat and came to her slowly. Then Minerva let go of Jocie's hand and threw herself at Honor, clinging to her waist and burying her head in Honor's shoulder with a shudder.

Jocie glared, her body stiff. "Is he dead?"

"No, my darling. But he is going to need some very special looking after if he is to get well again."

"May we see him?"

"Not for some time, Jocie. He has hurt his head and is unconscious. Then he must regain his strength, and it is best if he has no excitement, even the happy sort that would come from seeing both of you. I shall tell you what we will do. I am going to be very busy looking after your uncle, and Betsy will be looking after you. But I will keep Betsy up-to-date on Uncle Andrew's condition, and she shall relay that information to you, so that you will be the first to know, just like dispatches. And I promise, I shall tell you the truth."

Jocie relaxed slightly. "When Papa was dying, nobody told us anything."

"That won't be the case now. And I'm going to do my best to see to it that your Uncle Andrew recovers. Minerva," she said gently, detaching the child and looking into her face. "Was this what made you feel so upset this morning?"

Minerva nodded solemnly. "I thought Uncle went to see Papa."

"And you were right, for he very nearly did, and if you hadn't left your scarf yesterday, I might never have gone to look for it and found your uncle. So we have you to thank that he is safe and sound in a warm bed, and you're a very clever girl to have known."

Minvera's face lit up with her glorious smile, and she tugged on Jocie's hand with pleasure. "I am clever!"

"You are, my sweet, very. Jocie, tell me quickly, for I must go," Honor said, drawing her away. "Has Minerva ever had one of these feelings before?"

Jocie thought for a minute. "I hadn't really remembered until just now, but the last day Papa went hunting, Minnie was very upset and made a terrible fuss about his leaving. Then he came home sick, and . . . and died. Nobody thought anything of it at the time because Minnie . . . well, you know, Honor." She shrugged.

"Yes, Jocie, I do know. But sometimes when God takes away from one place, he gives in another. Now, you're not to worry, and for goodness' sake, help Betsy and be kind to her. I shall visit you when I can." She kissed Jocie's cheek and then Minerva's, and gave them both a big hug, then hurried back to keep her vigil.

7

Love sought is good, but giv'n unsought is better.

—William Shakespeare, *Twelfth Night*, III, i

Honor drowsed in the armchair next to the bed, her head resting against her arm. A single candle burned steadily on the bedstand, and the room was quiet of all but the sound of Andrew's breathing. She dreamt lightly, of her father, of mud and rain, and of sisters in black habits, all jumbled together with bloodied bandages and men crying out in pain. "Honor," a voice whispered. And then again. "Honor . . ."

She came awake with a start and sat bolt upright, her eyes going immediately to the bed. Andrew was watching her with a steady gaze, his head turned slightly on the pillow, and his eyes were bright—too bright, she thought as she went immediately to his side and took his wrist. The skin was hot and dry and his pulse fast and light.

"My lord, I am glad you have returned to us," she said softly, her heart sinking. The fever had already set in.

"I'm afraid I did a very stupid thing. I parted company with my horse, did I not?" His voice was hoarse.

"You did indeed, although your horse fared far better than you, so you needn't worry yourself on that score. He is back at Chesney eating oats. How are you feeling?"

"My head aches abominably, and my shoulder feels as if Cabal must have lain on it for hours. I suppose he did, as I cannot move my arm for the bandage." He licked at his dry lips.

Honor poured a glass of water and helped him into a position where he could drink it. "You have broken your collarbone, my lord, and you have a line of stitching in your head that would make any seamstress proud."

"How very gratifying to know." He sipped the water. "Thank you," he said, sinking back on the pillows with a grimace. "I feel most incredibly thickheaded, although I imagine my friends would say it's a common state." He attempted a smile. "And now it seems you are saddled with another nursling. Poor Miss Winslow."

"Not at all, my lord. It makes a pleasant change from little girls and lessons."

"You are too kind," he said, shivering convulsively. "I am most dreadfully cold. Silly, isn't it?"

Honor pulled another blanket from the end of the bed and tucked it around him. "Not silly, when you consider that you made your bed in the snow for some three hours. You must try to sleep now, my lord. You need as much rest as

possible. Don't talk any more now. I shall sit here with
you.''

He nodded faintly and closed his eyes. "Bred for service,'' he murmured with a crooked smile, and slept.

He grew worse during the night, shaking with fever, and
Honor bathed his body with lukewarm water from a jug kept
off to one side of the fire. As morning broke faintly through
the windows, he began to cough tightly. Hobson sat with
his master while Honor slept for a few hours, knowing the
crisis was yet to come and she would need to be alert.

The doctor came that afternoon and expressed his concern. "It's as I thought, Miss Winslow,'' he said after listening to Andrew's chest. "His lungs have become inflamed.
There is nothing we can do for him except to keep him
warm and comfortable and wait for the fever to break. It
could be days yet for it to run its course. Will you be able
to manage?''

"Yes.''

"Good, then. I shall leave you with an infusion to help
break up the congestion if you can persuade him to take it.
I shall return this evening.''

"Thank you, doctor.'' Honor sank back into the chair to
continue her watch.

"Henry, how can you leave at a time like this!'' said
Arabella tearfully, pacing up and down the drawing room.
"Poor Andrew—it is so like when George took ill! He took
the fever in just the same way, and it was all over in a matter
of days. It is too unfeeling of you!'' She burst into a fresh
flood of tears.

"Arabella, will you control yourself!'' Sir Henry said
harshly. "My presence in the house will have no effect on
Chesney's survival. I want his recovery every bit as much
as you do, for Phoebe's sake, if for none other. Look at
how the girl has paled, and keeps to her room, refusing to
eat. I had no idea how much her affections had already become engaged. But that's neither here nor there at the moment. Valuable government papers have disappeared from
my desk, and the last person in my study was Chesney himself. And, by God, if he stole them, he is better off dead

than if I get my hands around his neck, Phoebe and the Chesney fortune or no!''

''Henry, don't be ridiculous,'' said Arabella sniffing. ''You must have misplaced them, as I told you yesterday morning when you were making such a fuss at that outrageous hour. Andrew has no interest in your papers. You were foxed when you came home and you probably forgot where you put them. I'm sure they will turn up safe and sound.''

Sir Henry scowled at her. ''It is not your place to tell me when I am foxed or when I am not! I had every right to my libations after negotiating a delicate piece of business. But perhaps you are right. I might have mislaid them, although I have turned the house upside down . . . Nevertheless, I must travel to London and make certain that nothing comes in the way of concluding my agreement. Stop your sniveling, woman. I shall return in a few days, by which time Chesney will be either alive or dead. And if I am successful, it will matter little either way.''

''I don't understand, Henry . . .''

''No, you understand very little, Arabella, as has become exceedingly clear to me. It is no surprise that Minerva takes after you!''

''Oh! You are cruel!'' cried Arabella, with a rare show of spirit. ''You have no care for anyone but yourself! Look at how you have thrown Phoebe at Andrew's head with no concern for anything but the Chesney money and what it might do for you. And Phoebe takes after you when it comes to that, for I am convinced that she cries and keeps to her room not because of tender feelings for Andrew's welfare, but because she is as concerned as you are that the Chesney title and fortune are going to slip between her fingers!''

''You are impertinent, ma'am!'' Sir Henry roared, and his hand lashed out and slapped her hard. ''I have warned you before not to cross me! Even the money you brought to this godforsaken marriage has not served to make it worth the trouble! You have no spirit and even less brains, and I will not have you interfering in my concerns. Take heed, or I shall make it very much worse for you, and you know I will! You will keep a civil tongue in your head and stay out of my way, and out of my daughter's. Continue on this course of action and you shall regret it. And remember, if your dear Andrew dies, you have no one to turn to but me! Spencer! I leave!'' He stalked out of the room, leaving Arabella staring after him with an expression of hatred, her hand clutched to her face. She could only be thankful it had not been worse this time, for she could not hide her bruises in her room while Andrew was so ill. And no one could know of her disgrace. She had made her miserable bed and she must lie in it. But how could life be so very cruel? She burst into tears.

Phoebe, in fact, had kept to her room because she had caught a cold from her nighttime foray into the wood, as her red eyes and nose attested. But her swollen appearance was due not only to her cold but also to her great emotional distress. Her beloved Lord Chesney lay on his deathbed because of her own folly. The idea had been brilliant, taken straight from *The Captive Countess*. But how was she to have known that Honor would not take her usual morning ride? Of course, she belatedly realized that her assumption about her beloved and the governess was quite foolish, for who would ever look at lowly little Honor twice, save for the groom? Certainly not the glorious Earl of Chesney. She must have been mistaken in what she'd seen, for Honor had indubitably chased him down herself, hoping for goodness knows what.

"Oh, well," she muttered nasally, putting aside her book. "Some things can't be helped. But if there is one thing I simply cannot bear, it is that that horrible girl is at his side, when it should be me who is standing vigil. He would see my love for him, and I know that it would restore him to health."

Sniffing into her handkerchief at this sad thought, she picked up her book and immersed herself once again in the terrible adventures of Lady Harriet Covensley, who had just been abducted by the dreadful Lord March.

"Hobson, do sit still!" said Honor impatiently, driven to distraction by the man's fretful pacing. "You won't improve his lordship any by wearing a hole in the carpet." Once again she wrung a cool cloth out in the basin and applied it to Andrew's hot forehead.

"Sorry, miss," said Hobson apologetically. His respect for Honor had grown by leaps and bounds as he had watched her skill and her devotion to his master, and he had relinquished his possessiveness for the most part, in favor of Honor's superior experience in matters of precarious health.

"I beg your pardon," said Honor, dark circles of exhaustion ringing her eyes. "I didn't mean to snap at you."

"Never you mind that, miss," said Hobson kindly. "You just look after his lordship and I'll see to everything else."

Honor bowed her head. "Thank you, Hobson. His lordship is lucky to have someone as loyal as you in his service."

"We are all loyal to his lordship, miss, as we were to his brother and father before him. Such a pity that a weakness of the lungs runs in the family," he said sadly.

Honor's tired eyes quickened with a spark of humor. "I don't think a family predisposition is Lord Chesney's problem, Hobson. And it would be very kind if you could fetch me another jug of water. This one is nearly empty."

"Certainly, miss. But perhaps another blanket might be the thing?"

"Hobson! Do you want his lordship to suffocate? Perhaps that also runs in the family?"

"Oh, no, miss. There hasn't been one case of suffocation since I've been in service to the earls of Chesney. The cook's sister, now, that was another matter. It was a cherry stone that did her in—"

Honor sighed. "I am profoundly sorry to hear it, Hobson. The water please?"

"I'm sure his lordship would be forever in your debt, Hobson," intoned a wry voice from the door. "Go, now, and let me speak to Miss Winslow."

Honor jumped to her feet. "Lord Hambledon!"

"The very same. How is my friend, Miss Winslow?" Julian entered the room, and with three long strides was beside the bed, looking down at Andrew with concern, taking in his labored breathing and flushed face.

"He struggles, my lord. But he is a fighter, and with luck will come out as well as ever."

"I thank you for summoning me." Julian's eyes raked over her slim form, assessing the circles under her eyes. "You look tired, Miss Winslow."

"Tired, perhaps, but not so much as to impair my faculties. I am used to it."

"Yes. So you are. Hobson, the water," he said to the man still hovering by the bed.

"My lord." Hobson bowed and hurried out, and Julian quietly shut the door on his back. "So, my dear. Just how serious is it?"

"It is serious." Honor wrung out another cloth.

Julian watched her for a moment as she stripped the sheets down and sponged his friend's naked form, then covered him up warmly again.

"I see that convent life has not made you shy, Miss Winslow."

Honor smiled tightly. "You know it has not, and it is no time for you to be making light of me. Let us be plain with each other. There is no one to hear."

"For the moment, but we cannot be too careful." He sighed and ran a hand through his hair. "My conscience bothers me. I placed you in this house for my own convenience despite your own eagerness—do not protest. I warned you how it might be. And now Andrew's life hangs in the balance when he is innocent in all this. I left you in the woods that night, and all was well. How did such a thing happen to him?"

Honor turned and looked at him with grave, pain-stricken eyes. "I fear he stumbled across a trap. I found this." She went to the bureau and pulled the wire out, handing it to Julian, who took it and pulled it taut in his hands, his face darkening.

"I see. Do you think we have Sir Henry to thank for this piece of mischief?"

"In truth, I cannot be sure. You know yourself how the situation might have been misconstrued. I blame myself for that—"

"Nonsense." Julian walked to the window, his hands behind his back, and looked out over the gray afternoon. "I arrived just now to find Sir Henry gone to London on an urgent piece of business, according to Arabella. It seems a peculiar time to leave his house, considering.''

''I was not aware he had left.'' Honor frowned. ''But if he has, it means only one thing. He discovered his papers missing and laid the snare for Lord Chesney, for I know he has not suspected me, and Lord Chesney and I were both in the study the other evening. I had not thought he would find anything amiss so quickly.''

''No, for he has been remarkably lax in protecting his correspondence since he's been home. If anyone is at fault, it must be me, for you took the papers at my request. I should have had you copy them as in the past.''

''There was no time, my lord, not with the length of the document and the seriousness of the matter. And Sir Henry was in his cups. It was the perfect opportunity.''

''Yes. And I shall see that the document is returned in a manner Sir Henry will not suspect. As of this morning, the contents are no longer of import, and all the appropriate people have been warned. But we paid far too dear a price.'' He looked over at Andrew again, and rubbed his brow. ''He is burning with fever. Is there nothing more you can do? You have had such experience with these cases.''

''There is only time on our side, and Lord Chesney's strong constitution. The crisis must come soon. It has been three days.''

''And then?''

''And then either his fever will break or he will die. I am sorry, Julian. I know you are as brothers to one another. I will do my best to see him through.''

''Yes, I know you will. He couldn't have a better person at his side. Where is Hobson with that water? The man moves like a snail!'' Julian went straight to the door and pulled it open. ''Hobson!'' he bellowed. ''Shift yourself!''

He came back and pulled off his jacket, waistcoat, and neckcloth and rolled up the sleeves of his fine linen shirt. ''I intend to stay through this crisis you spoke of. I think you're going to be needing better help than Hobson, and Jake has gone off to London with Sir Henry. He'll keep an eye on him while I'm engaged here. Ah, here you are at last, Hobson,'' he said to the man shuffling in with the jug.

"Pour the water into the basin here. Miss Winslow doesn't have all day. Now, then. Where do I start?"

Honor smiled with pure relief. "With the bed, my lord. We need to change the sheets."

Day turned into night, the doctor came and went again, looking even more concerned, and Andrew's fever continued to rise. He became delirious, crying out and muttering nonsense. Julian restrained him as best he could while Honor continuously sponged him down. He fought even against this. She left him only with a light sheet over his hips, hoping the cool air would circulate around his body, and Hobson did not bother to express his shock. He sat in a corner, with tears quietly rolling down his cheeks, fetching water whenever it was needed, and trays of food and drink, relieved to have the responsibility of Lord Chesney off his hands, for the situation was now beyond anything he could deal with.

Andrew's body was racked with coughing, his chest heaving for air, and Honor piled pillows behind his back and head to try to ease his breathing. The hours went by with no change, but Andrew was weakening. He ceased to struggle and now lay still and quiet, his body afire.

"It has to break soon—it has to. He cannot go on like this," Honor whispered to Julian, her eyes fierce.

Julian nodded and rose from the bed, going to the window. "It will soon be morning, my dear," he said very softly. "How long can such a crisis last?" His face was ravaged by private grief. The end was near, and he could not bear to watch it. Not even the brave girl by the bed could save his friend now.

"Come, Andrew, fight! You must fight! I won't let you die!" She could feel him slipping away from her, and she took his hand, long and slim, in both of hers and pressed it against her forehead, willing her life into him. Her heart felt as if it would break; great tears slid unnoticed down her cheeks. She held on to him as if she were holding on to his life.

She did not know how long she sat like that. The room had lightened, and she realized that Andrew's hand had gone limp and cool in her own. She sat up, her vision blinded by hot tears, a cry of anguish on her lips. To find Andrew's clear blue eyes looking into hers.

"Honor," he murmured, his face covered with cold sweat. "Honor? Why in heaven's name are you crying?"

"Andrew . . . Oh, Andrew! You have come through it! You are alive!" She was laughing and crying at the same time, and Julian was at the bed in a flash, and Hobson too, and their eyes were also wet.

"Naturally I am alive. You here, Julian? And Hobson—I might have known. Not a moment's peace. May I ask why you are all making fools of yourselves?" he said weakly, with a glimmer of a smile.

"You have been most inconsiderate, my friend, keeping us up at all hours of the night. What you see are the faces of exasperation and exhaustion," said Julian, grinning. "Your flesh has been weak, my dear Andrew, most weak, but it seems your spirit has some semblance of strength. Either that or you are not yet ready for immortality."

"I beg your most humble pardon, but I can't say I am overly distressed to find myself still chained to my body." He looked down at the sheet which barely covered him and frowned. "Ah . . . Miss Winslow. Do you think you might be kind enough to cover my so weak flesh in a more . . . modest fashion?" he said, reaching for the sheet.

Julian laughed. "A full recovery if I ever saw one. Wrested from the jaws of death, and you're worrying about your modesty."

Honor smiled, and pulled the sheet up around him, then covered him with a blanket. "Would you like your hat and cane as well, my lord?"

"Not for the moment, thank you," he murmured. "I feel extraordinarily tired. I think I might rest." He smiled and closed his eyes, and his breathing slowed into a deep, natural sleep.

Honor woke a few hours later and came through the connecting door, feeling infinitely refreshed and her heart a hundred times lighter. She found Julian wide-awake in the chair by the bed. He smiled as he saw her enter.

"You look much better, my dear. I've sent Hobson for hot water. Andrew has slept through the morning like a babe." He stood and stretched. "I think I'll just borrow that bed next door if there's nothing more I can do."

"Nothing that I can think of. But I thank you for all your help." She looked down at Andrew and lightly touched her hand to his cool brow.

"I think it is rather the other way around," he said, taking her hand in his. "I owe you a very great deal."

She smiled. "I only did what I was trained to do."

"So you did. Although I never expected you to have to use that training when I sent you here. Ah, well, you asked me for work and I gave it to you, although not quite in the way you had expected. Do you know, I believe I actually saw my friend blush when he realized the state of his dishabille. Consider his alarm, dear Miss Winslow, being nursed by a girl fresh from a convent."

Honor laughed and ran her hands through her short curls. "It is growing, my lord. There are times when I forget my old life."

"And I, looking at you now." He laughed and shook his head. "You have dealt remarkably well with your change of circumstances. I am pleased you did not find the transition too difficult."

"At first, perhaps. It was like stepping into a completely new world after so many years of the other. But I am grateful that you gave me this opportunity."

"It is I who am grateful." He smiled warmly at her. "Honor. It is a fitting sobriquet. I can see why you earned your other, 'the little soldier.' I had heard of you long before meeting you, you know. There must be many who owe their lives to you, Andrew not the least."

"I am glad to be of help. And we are achieving what we set out to do, although I will not rest until I can prove that Sir Henry was responsible for my father's murder." She glanced over at Andrew, who had shifted on the bed. "Do not worry about your friend. He will be fully recovered in a few short weeks. I will take good care of him."

Julian looked at her thoughtfully. "I cannot think you would let anything happen to him now. It seems he has need of you."

Honor blushed crimson, wondering if he had seen straight

through her. "He has been through the worst," she said neutrally.

"What are you two whispering about?" asked Andrew, opening his eyes and gingerly turning his head toward them.

"I think I'll let Miss Winslow tell you," Julian said laughing, and left her.

"So, Miss Winslow," Andrew said, attempting to pull himself up in bed as Honor leaned down to help him, "what has so amused my friend?"

"Nothing of import," she said, returning to her businesslike attitude. "Lord Hambledon must be easily amused."

"Hambledon? I would not say that in the least. Well, if you will not let me in on your joke, perhaps you might tell me how long I have been lying here."

"Four days and nights, my lord," she said, plumping up the pillows behind him.

"Four. I see. It seems only a few hours ago that I found myself flying through the air. Have you been with me all this time, then?"

"Yes, my lord. But you did not bother me with sensible conversation, so the time went by quickly."

"Sensible conversation? Insensible perhaps, but far more amusing, I should think." He laughed, but it turned into a cough, and Honor quickly handed him a glass of water, which he drank gratefully.

"Most insensible conversation, but I feel I know you far better for it. It is astonishing the things one can learn about a person from his wanderings, far more than what one may discover in drawing-room conversation. 'And how are you, my lady?' 'Quite well, my lord. Lovely weather we're having, is it not?' I don't believe it varies much."

Andrew smiled, and the creases deepened at the sides of his eyes. "You have an art for it, I think."

"I think not. I should not be very good at blushing and stammering and murmuring the commonplaces expected. No doubt I would say something truly shocking, and all conversation would stop dead. All eyes would swivel toward me, and I would find myself shrinking toward the door—"

"I can't imagine you shrinking toward the door, Miss Winslow, under any circumstances."

"No? Just roll to this side, my lord, and let me pull the sheets out." Honor was doing her very best to maintain her composure. She had never been rattled by a patient; nor had she ever been so acutely aware of the male body, now that he was conscious and watching her. She knew every muscle, every sinew of it from constant administrations, but suddenly the flesh, the muscle beneath, took on a whole new meaning.

"The hot water, miss," said Hobson, coming in. "My lord, what a joy it is seeing you on the mend! We were all in such a taking when you were about to take your leave of this world—"

"That's enough, Hobson," said Honor firmly. "I'm sure his lordship doesn't want to hear chapter and verse of his illness. Thank you for the water, and now I would be much obliged if you would have Mrs. Spencer make up some thin gruel while I give his lordship his bath."

"No!" said Andrew. "No gruel, and most certainly no bath, at least not by you, Miss Winslow. Hobson, order me up some kippers and bacon and eggs—you of all people know how I like them done—and a mug of ale. I have a fearful hunger and thirst—"

"Hobson, thin gruel. And, my lord, you will eat it. I haven't lost four nights' sleep to have you behave like a recalcitrant child. And furthermore, you'll have your bath whether you like it or not."

"Yes, miss. Gruel it is." Hobson threw her a rare smile and hurried out again.

Honor dipped the washcloth in the basin of water she poured, and advanced on Andrew.

"Spoken like a true governess," Andrew said, but submitted to her administrations, drawing the line at his waist, and only letting her resume at his knees, clutching the sheet with his one good hand.

"You're a prude, my lord," said Honor, sponging his legs, and secretly grateful for it.

"And you're a harridan, Miss Winslow, with no sense of decorum."

"If I had been worried about decorum, my lord, then you

would be lying in state in the parlor about now, with weeping women passing your casket.''

"Weeping women?'' asked Andrew with interest. "How
many weeping women, exactly?''

"I have no idea, my lord, not being privy to your personal life, but I assure you, they would all be weeping crocodile tears.''

She smiled as Andrew burst into laughter.

Andrew slept most of that day. Sir Henry returned home
that same afternoon, and Julian wasted no time in speaking
with him privately. "I wish you could have been there,'' he
later told Honor. "Sir Henry was filled with the most astonishing regret over Andrew's misfortune, and effusive in his
overwhelming relief that he might recover. It was all I could
do not to knock him down then and there, but I held my
tongue, and we settled down to discussing matters of political interest. By the way, I replaced those missing papers.
He'll feel the drunken fool when he finds them hidden in
his handkerchiefs.''

"But what are you going to do to stop him?'' asked Honor
quickly. "Surely you have all the proof you need?''

"Indeed, thanks to you. But the game does not stop here,
my dear. You see, I will now use Sir Henry to further my
own ends. He will believe himself to be cultivating me—
imagine his good fortune that I, who have never been more
than the slightest of disinterested acquaintances, should land
on his doorstep, full of gratitude for his kind treatment of
my friend. I will continue to seek out his company, have
long and intimate discussions with him, and allow him to
subtly pull confidential information from me, information
that he will be taking from the very top, from far more
secret chambers than he has access to. Naturally, the delicate information that I provide will be mostly lies, with
enough harmless truth to support it. I predict great victories
for England in the months ahead. By the by, Wellington
spoke most fondly of you in a private letter to me. He sent
his regards, and his thanks.'' Julian smiled. "It seems that
you have quite a few of us in your debt, and I more than
most.''

Honor met his eyes solemnly. "No, it is I who must thank

you. Without your help, my father would have died for nothing. And there are so many more who would have continued to die for their country, betrayed by one of their own.''

"There is that," he agreed. "I would ask you to leave, now that we have all that we need to bring the informer down. Not, of course, until Andrew is back to health, for I would see no other care for him. But I wonder if it would not be an insult to you, for there is no solid proof yet of Sir Henry's involvement in your father's murder. Would you go if I asked it of you?''

"If you asked it of me, Julian, I would go. But I would rather you did not, for I should prefer to stay. There is so much more for me to do here—I would like to find proof of my father's murder, for one—but there are the children. I could not leave them now. Not yet.''

Julian took her hand. "Be careful of your attachments, my dear. You cannot stay like this forever, you know."

"I know all too well," she said heavily.

He nodded. "Then I shall take my leave. I must go to London. But I plan to bring my family back to Chesney in January. Do you think he shall be home by then?''

"With luck. I shall keep you informed.''

"I know you will. Until next month, then.''

He went through the door to have one last look at Andrew, who was sleeping deeply, and then quickly departed.

8

Words, words, mere words, no matter from the heart.

—William Shakespeare, *Troilus and Cressida*, V, iii

The rest of the day and night went slowly for Honor. Andrew's condition was still so unstable that she dared not leave him, and she slept in a chair next to his bed, alert for the smallest sounds. He was so weak that it was easy to nurse him; his demands were few and basic, and Hobson helped much in dealing with those. He slept most of the time, which was all to the good. However, on the second day after his fever had broken, Honor wasn't at all surprised when Andrew woke in the late afternoon with a groan, his eyes wincing against the light, although it was faint.

"My lord?" she asked very softly, standing quickly and bending over him.

"It's my head. Filthy ache," he managed to say, but it was obvious that even that effort was painful.

"It's the concussion, my lord," she whispered. "Hold fast. I'll make you something to help it."

She drew the curtains, darkening the room, and laid a cold cloth on his forehead. With the water kept hot on the fire, she made an infusion of honey and angelica, which she'd had on hand for just such an eventuality. She helped Andrew to lift his head and sip.

"Here, do the best you can. It will help to ease it."

He opened his eyes for a moment and silently met hers, the thanks evident in them, and slowly, with her gentle prompting, finished the drink and sank back on the pillows.

That the pain was agonizing was clear to her, and it was also clear that he was trying with all of his might to keep it to himself. She pulled her chair close and took his hand, and his fingers tightened around hers, his face drawn and very pale.

"Shh," she said, "go along with it. There's little point in fighting against it, for you'll only make it worse. The herbs will take over soon enough, but for God's sake, don't try to be brave for my sake. It doesn't trouble me."

His hand tightened even more around hers, crushing her bones beneath the grip, but she bore it without flinching. Instead she watched his face; the clenched jaw, the eyelids frail and blue, the skin stretched tight against the bones of his skull, the intense, throbbing beat of the pulse in the temple giving testimony to the horrendous agony he was feeling.

For three hours she changed the cloth on his brow when it warmed, and she gave him another infusion. She sat as still and peacefully as she could while involuntary moans issued from his throat.

"Andrew," she thought silently to him in words she could never speak aloud, "this pain is more than worth your life, no matter how much you might wish yourself dead just now. Bear with it, and with me, and I shall see you well again."

Not very much later his grip relaxed on her hand and his breathing slowed into sleep. Honor did not know whether it had been her private entreaty or whether his headache had run its course, and she didn't much care. He was over the worst of it. But she knew from experience that there was probably more of the same to come before he was recovered.

She sat and thought of Andrew as she knew him now, and the unnamed man she had known in her dreams; she had ceased to try to deny that Andrew was one and the same. Too much had happened since then, and the fact that she understood none of it made little difference. The only thing that did make any difference was that Andrew was clearly unaware of the strange relationship they seemed to share, and she was in no position to enlighten him. Indeed, even if she had been, she could think of no way of broaching the subject: "By the by, my lord, did you know that I have dreamt of you all my life?" "In truth, my lady? It has been said to me before by a score of women. How entertaining. . . ."

Honor finally dozed and, against her will, fell into a profoundly deep sleep.

She did not dream of Andrew, for those dreams seemed to be over, perhaps because he was here in the flesh. But at some point she felt an awareness of him through the mists of sleep, a warm sense of his presence and something else running under it.

Her eyes opened sleepily, her lids still heavy, but all thought of sleep vanished as her hazy gaze met Andrew's deep blue eyes. He was steadily watching her and his eyes did not waver when he saw that she was awake. For a moment she felt as if all the breath had been drawn from her body, so intense was the impact. Andrew merely smiled, then closed his eyes again. But Honor was left trembling. She busied herself with the fire and with other simple tasks, and finally settled herself down to watch over him for the rest of the night. Sleep did not come again.

The next morning, Andrew seemed much better. Honor took advantage of the time that Hobson used to bathe his master to go and bathe herself and change her clothes. She spent a little time with the children, giving them a progress report on their uncle and explaining that it would be some time before she could be with them as usual. It was no more than an hour before she was back in Andrew's room, pleased to see that he was clean-shaven and in good color.

"Ah. Miss Winslow," he said as she entered. "Just the person I wished to speak with."

"Who else, my lord," asked Honor with a little smile, "given that other than the good doctor and Hobson, I am the only person allowed in your room?"

"Hobson bore that very fact in upon me this morning. I cannot help but wonder how this extraordinary state of affairs has come about. Forgive me, Miss Winslow, but I believe you to be twenty-two years of age?"

"I am, my lord," Honor said with a little smile, knowing exactly where the line of questioning was leading. It would not be the first time that she had been so questioned.

"I confess, Miss Winslow, that I find it extraordinary you should have the skill you seem to possess. My very existence testifies to that. You must have lived in a community of extremely—and consistently—ill people to have learned what you have learned so young in life."

Honor laughed. "Ah, but I did, my lord. You are very astute, it seems. Mine was a community struck by calamity time and time again."

"And you apparently learned to deal with all sorts of illness and injury in this tragic place."

Honor's eyes darkened. "I did, my lord."

"So I should think that over a period of time you have become hardened to misfortune, pain, and death."

"I suppose in a way, I have, my lord." Honor wondered what he was getting at, and he let her know exactly in the next sentence.

"I wonder, then, why you wasted your tears over me, whom you know not at all. It did not take too much deciphering to work out that you thought I was dead the other morning. Do you suffer so over all of your patients? If so, it is a wonder you can survive their misfortunes.''

Honor colored deeply. "It is not the same in every case, my lord. There are those who cannot be helped, and sometimes those who just will not be helped. And then there are those who need help desperately.''

"I see," he said quietly. "And which was I?''

She bit her lip. "I cannot say so simply. You are a strong and determined man, and that counted for much.''

"And the rest?''

"And the rest was luck and careful attention to what any person in the same situation would need.''

"I see. And for that I am very grateful. I understand that it was you who discovered me in the woods.''

"A lucky coincidence, my lord. Minnie had left her scarf in the copse.''

"I seem to have been very lucky all around. I owe you a great deal, Miss Winslow.''

"You owe me nothing, my lord," said Honor, looking away. "Rest now. It's best if you do not talk too much.''

Andrew frowned slightly, then sighed and closed his eyes. They most definitely had not been crocodile tears, he thought. He wished he could fathom her better. There was something about her he could not put his finger on. . . .

Andrew lay brooding in his bed in a state of complete frustration. It had been nearly ten days since the accident, and he had not yet been allowed to get out of bed. The pain in his shoulder he could bear easily enough, but the skull-splitting headaches he'd found more difficult, although mercifully they'd mostly subsided. Now that he was feeling better, he chafed against his helplessness and cursed the stupidity that had landed him in this situation in the first place. He still couldn't understand how it had happened, for he remembered nothing but Cabal suddenly stumbling, and trying to pull his head up, and then flying over Cabal's head, an explosion of pain and then nothing at all.

Now he had to tolerate his complete dependency on Honor Winslow. Only the plainest of food passed his lips—boiled eggs for supper again, he scowled to himself, and God only knew how long that would go on, for Honor had somehow managed to win Hobson over completely, and Hobson had point-blank refused to smuggle anything to him. It seemed that the only thing he was allowed was his modesty, for Honor had allowed Hobson to take over the bathing, and he could, at least, attend to his own other physical needs. Amazing, he considered, that she didn't insist on overseeing even those! He couldn't imagine the sort of convent to raise a young girl without a blush in such matters. But then, she had not exhibited a whit of feminine behavior that he had seen.

It annoyed him that he could not work her out, for he was generally good at judging people. But there was something about her that didn't fit. She gave him nothing, no clues, evading any personal questions, although she was more than willing to discuss anything and everything else, and had proved to be a well-educated and entertaining companion. He wondered why she had left the convent; had she decided she wasn't suited to being a nun? By the look of her hair, she had certainly been a novice. Honor as a nun. What a complete waste that would have been.

But it irritated him that she was so close-chested, for having been constantly in her presence, he had grown fond of her, and would have liked to know her better. And it was equally irritating that he had absolutely no right to ask any questions of her at all. Damnation, he felt that he did know her, but she wouldn't let him in beyond a certain point. All her talk of service and position and the rest of that nonsense was at complete odds with her behavior, for she acted in a decidedly relaxed and offhand manner, with no regard for their different ranks at all. In fact, she treated him with tolerant amusement, as an older sister might treat an out-of-sorts younger brother. She most certainly did not treat him as a man eight years her senior. What right had she to be so relaxed and easy with him, and retreat the moment he came at all close to her? And yet nothing seemed to shake her. She was so . . . so controlled. With the exception of the time he had seen her in tears—probably because she thought she had lost the battle—she had exhibited no real emotion other than sympathy toward him when he was in pain. And that was another thing; here he was, completely at her mercy, as vulnerable as a human could be, having been stripped naked, both figuratively and literally, and she was completely impersonal.

"My lord, are you attempting to glare a hole through me?" Honor asked, looking up from her sewing.

"My dear Miss Winslow, if I thought it would release me from this prison, I would glare ten holes through you."

"How kind, my lord. Glare away, but I'm afraid nothing will help you survive your incarceration but patience."

"I should like at least to get up from this bed and stretch my legs," he persisted.

"The only thing that would be stretched is your length along the floor. I have explained this to you, my lord. You are too weak from loss of blood, and your headaches are easily enough brought on. You don't realize it while you are lying warm and rested in your bed, but I do assure you that you would find it exhausting to leave it. A few more days, and you may sit in the window and watch the carolers come around on Christmas Eve. Will that do?"

"No, Miss Winslow, that will not do!" he roared, losing all patience. "You speak to me as if I am still in leading strings! I am a man of thirty years and I am accustomed to being treated as such!"

"You are accustomed to having your own way. No doubt you are also accustomed to being bowed and scraped to. I am most sorry, Lord Chesney, but privileges of rank and age are temporarily suspended until you have recovered." Honor looked down at her sewing, her eyes dancing with laughter. Teasing Andrew gave her great pleasure. If this disgruntled and very human man was not the romantic creature of her dreams, he was far more real and approachable, and she much preferred having him in the flesh.

"Why, you impudent little chit! It is no wonder the convent walls were too small to hold you. You are completely lacking in modesty and respect, and you are insubordinate on top of it all. Bred for service, indeed—I think you have fooled everyone in this house but me. You have *not* fooled me, Miss Winslow."

Honor looked up again with amusement, not the least bit perturbed. "What would you like me to tell you? That I was expelled from the convent for insubordination? You are only

annoyed with me because you are bored and impatient, and
I am the person who crosses your will for your own good.
As for my lack of modesty, perhaps you are angry that I
have gazed upon your precious body. It may come as a shock
to you, my lord, but it is very much the same as others.
And I beg your pardon if I have not dropped over in a dead
faint from the sight of it, but really, Lord Chesney, it isn't
that spectacular.'' She put her sewing down and stood. ''I
will get your broth; it might help you regain your senses.
It's such a pity that all the blood you lost went from your
head.''

She left the room still grinning, leaving Andrew feeling
even more irritated than before, and annoyed that on top of
everything else, she had an uncanny ability to read his mind.

It was the opportunity Phoebe had been waiting for. She
had been biding her time until she could find a rare moment
that her beloved was left alone. Honor guarded him jeal-
ously like a lioness at the door, and would never allow her
entrance, citing Lord Chesney's weakness as an excuse, but
Phoebe knew that she was keeping him to herself. He
needed to be reminded that it was she he had come court-
ing, and she set her mind to the task.

She watched Honor disappear down the hall. Hobson was
safely off at Chesney gathering some of Lord Chesney's be-
longings, so she knew the earl to be alone.

She tapped lightly at the door.

''Yes?'' he called impatiently, expecting Hobson.

Phoebe pushed open the door, slightly flushed and
breathless. Her eyes opened slightly at the sight that greeted
her in the bed. It had not occurred to her that Lord Chesney's appearance would be in any way altered from the
strong, virile man she had fallen passionately in love with.
He had lost weight, and it showed in the new hollows in his
face and his pale complexion. He looked utterly helpless.
''Oh!'' she said uncertainly.

''Why, Miss Rutherford,'' he said with surprise, struggling to sit up, and wincing with pain from the effort. ''How
kind of you to visit me.'' He wasn't at all sure that he meant
it, for he did not particularly feel up to small talk.

''I know you are not yet to have visitors,'' Phoebe said

shyly, "but I could not help myself, now that the dragon is away from the door." She peeped him a look from under her long lashes. "I shouldn't have imposed myself, but I have been so worried." She pulled a handkerchief from her sleeve and sniffed into it.

"My dear, how kind of you to have concerned yourself. But I am recovering as well as can be expected, so there is no need for you to be in the least upset. But do you really think you ought to be in here?" he added delicately.

"Oh, but, my lord, I could not stay away any longer! We have all been in such a state—but then, I should not be telling you about that. I have come to cheer you up, after all. Shall I tell you of the beautiful snow outside, and of the holly and ivy that bedeck the halls, heralding Christmas? Or perhaps you would rather hear of your dear nieces and their exploits? They amuse me so; why, just the other day Minerva—"

"No, no," said Andrew, wishing she would go. She really was the most tiresome child. "I hear all about the children from Miss Winslow."

"Oh, well, then," she said, settling herself prettily in the chair next to the bed, "I shall tell you about myself. I have been weaving a wreath from pine boughs, which I gathered from the woods. And I have fashioned it with berries and little ornaments for the tree. I know it was bad of me, but I could not help myself. The wooden angels looked so pretty among the green and the red of the berries. And Mrs. Spencer has been baking—there is to be Christmas pudding with a silver sixpence in it, and Mrs. Lipp is planning to make a wassail, even though she has been feeling so tired with Miss Winslow looking after you, and no one else to help out. Poor Betsy has been run off her feet trying to manage. My dear stepmama cannot keep up, you see, as much as she tries—but I should not bring you the household's problems either. I am sure that you need Miss Winslow here to look after you. We'll manage somehow." She took his hand and leaned a little closer. "It is *you* we worry about. Nothing else could possibly be a consideration next to that."

Andrew was about to pull his hand away, thinking that Phoebe really would have to be instructed more carefully before her Season or she would find herself compromised in no time, when Honor came through the door with a tray.

"My lord, I've brought you bread and butter, and even some jam to . . . Miss Rutherford! *What* are you doing in here?" She stopped abruptly halfway into the room and stared at them in astonishment.

"Miss Winslow—goodness, don't look so cross!" Phoebe jumped to her feet, schooling her face into an expression of distress. "I was only cheering Lord Chesney up! I'll go if you wish it. My lord, I hope to see you soon on your feet. Good evening, Miss Winslow," she said, giving Honor no time to reply as she hurried out of the room, throwing Andrew an apologetic look.

Andrew rested his head against the pillows, thoroughly entertained by the expression on Honor's face, and delighted to see her rattled for once. "You really are a dragon, aren't you, Miss Winslow?"

"And worse when it comes to preserving your health, my lord. You've lost what little color you had. You know you are to have no visitors until you are better: Mr. Langley told you so himself. My duty is to keep you as calm as possible, and that does not include social calls!"

Andrew looked at her with complete exasperation. "Oh, for pity's sake, Miss Winslow, will you forget about your blasted duty for one moment! God save us from convent girls! There are other things in life than service and duty—but no doubt you would perceive them as weaknesses of the human spirit, not to mention the flesh. And not the sort to which my poor—and apparently unremarkable—flesh should succumb."

"I see," said Honor, repressing a strong desire to slap him. "And which were you indulging in just now?"

Andrew grinned, unable to resist the retort. "Alas, the only weakness at my disposal, my spirit. Come now, Miss Winslow. Miss Rutherford was only trying to lift it up and remind me of the festive season, not trying to kill me. You will persist in making me feel as if I am to be a permanent fixture in this bed, eating bread, broth, and gruel for the rest of my days!"

Honor, deeply hurt, was finally stretched beyond her limit. "You, my lord, should be happy you're alive to see another Christmas, let alone celebrate it! Hobson has just returned. He can listen to your abuse. No doubt he is accustomed to it!'' She slammed the tray down and stalked out of the room, seething with indignation.

Andrew burst into laughter, but then he sobered, his conscience pricking at him. He had upset Honor, and that she had not deserved. She had done her best for him, unstintingly and without complaint, and he knew he had not been an easy patient. But from her reaction, which was so unlike her, it was obvious that she was overtired, and because of him. That he would remedy straightaway. He thought for a moment of calling her back, but his eyes closed in exhaustion and he slept.

Phoebe left a hastily fashioned wreath at Andrew's door the next morning with a sweet note apologizing for tiring him and for upsetting Miss Winslow, but saying that she wanted him to have a taste of the joyous season upon them, for she was sure that he must feel very alone at such a time. She knew Honor would be forced to deliver it, and took great satisfaction from the thought. For the first time, she realized that there might be unforeseen benefits as a result of Honor's nursing. After all, Honor had seen Lord Chesney at his very worst, which must have been terrible, given what he looked like now, and what man would tolerate that? Phoebe herself had to struggle to remember how handsome he really was, but it was a consolation to know that he would not look ill and weak forever.

Honor's step slowed when she saw the wreath with its note addressed to Andrew in Phoebe's handwriting lying on the door sill. Reluctantly she picked it up. How very clever, she thought to herself. Dear Phoebe, so attentive to her future husband. The thought made Honor's head ache anew. She had gone around and around in circles all night long trying to deny the obvious to herself, but it was no use. Jocie had been right. Andrew was to marry Phoebe Rutherford and connect the two estates. She, in turn, would provide him with his much-needed issue. Her heart felt like a heavy cold thing in her chest, as it had from the moment she had walked in upon the touching scene.

How could Andrew, with his quick intelligence and keen

perception, not have seen through Phoebe? How could he even consider such a marriage? Did he fancy himself in love with her, dazzled by her beauty and her innocent air? God help him when he woke up to the truth and saw her for what she was, too late to do anything about it. Not that it was any of her business; Andrew thought no more of her than of the man in the moon, and whatever her private feelings on the subject might be, they would get her nowhere.

Honor sighed and summoned up an impartial face. "Good morning, my lord," she said tightly, entering the room. "I trust you spent a restful night."

Andrew gave her a cautious look, trying to read her mood. "Restful enough, thank you. But I—"

"Look what Miss Rutherford has left for you, my lord," Honor said, interrupting him. "A wreath. How festive, and wasn't it thoughtful?"

"Very thoughtful, Miss Winslow. Much more thoughtful than I—"

"I'll hang it up in the window, shall I?" Honor said through the aching knot in her throat. "No doubt you'll find that the constant reminder will lift your spirits immeasurably."

"Do you think?" said Andrew, overcome by a sudden urge to laugh but repressing it at the look on Honor's face. "In truth, what would lift my spirits far more," he continued, "is if you would listen to me for just a moment. I'm fully aware, Miss Winslow, that nursing me has not been an easy or pleasant task, and for that I am profoundly sorry. So to make your life easier and to allow you to indulge in the festive season yourself, I am hereby releasing you from your duties with my most humble thanks. I am sure that you have more important things to attend to than my small complaints. I do feel very much better, and Hobson will be able to attend to any of my more mundane needs."

Honor froze in the act of hanging up the wreath, feeling as if she had just been slapped. Deliberately she finished the task with fingers that felt like ice, and slowly turned around.

"As you will have it, my lord," she said, curtsying. "I wouldn't think of forcing myself on you a moment longer than necessary. I wish you well for the remainder of your recovery.''

She swept out the door without giving Andrew a chance to reply, her self-control in shreds.

''What the devil . . . ?'' said Andrew in astonishment, staring at the slammed door. He ran a hand over his forehead and swore that he would never understand women in general and Honor Winslow in particular.

Christmas Eve came, and the snow swirled down from the sky in great soft flakes, but Honor's temper had not improved in the five days since Andrew had summarily dismissed her. She had spent a good deal of the little private time she had cursing him and his arrogance and complete want of feeling. He had asked for her through Hobson, but Honor's pride smarted too badly, and she had cited pressing household tasks in order to avoid him. He had Phoebe to keep him company, and no doubt that was the very reason he had dismissed her in the first place.

Sir Henry handed out presents to the staff before dinner that evening, obviously in a generous mood. No doubt due, thought Honor, as she received her own, to the recent fat deposit in his bank account. She saw the girls off to their beds, and was on her way to the kitchen quarters when Hobson came chasing after her.

''Miss Winslow! Please wait, Miss Winslow,'' he called, scurrying breathlessly down the hall after her. ''Lord Chesney has asked to have you visit him in his room. Please, won't you see him this time?''

''No, Hobson. His lordship has no more need for me. I am on my way to the servants' hall for the wassail.''

''Yes, miss, but his lordship specifically requested—''

''What, exactly, did his lordship specifically request?'' asked Honor tightly.

''For you to bring him and yourself a cup of the wassail,'' said Hobson apologetically. ''It would ease his mind considerably, miss, and he did so want to wish you the joys of the season personally, seeing as what you did for him.'' Hobson looked so nervous that Honor could not help but smile.

''His lordship has obviously threatened you within an inch

of your life if I do not appear with his wassail. Very well, Hobson," said Honor, vacillating between stubbornness and a longing to see him, and capitulating to the latter. "I cannot refuse a direct order. I shall bring it, and mine. Come then, we shall see them poured out together."

"Miss Winslow," Andrew said with pleasure as Honor entered with a tray of steaming drinks, "could it be that you have forgiven me? I confess myself profoundly relieved, although you have every right to wish me to hell and back again if it pleases you. I fear you took my last speech to you the wrong way, which was entirely your prerogative, but there was no insult intended. Please allow me to apologize for my boorish behavior. It was never meant personally, and I'm surprised you tolerated me for as long as you did. It has distressed me that you have kept away."

"I cannot think why, my lord. I am only a servant here to do your bidding." Honor put down the tray abruptly, her heart beating far too fast. Just the sight of him had caused her to thaw, and his infuriating charm went straight through her like an arrow to her heart. She was determined not to let him shake her. In any case, she could not even like a man with such a lack of moral fiber. "Your wassail, my lord." She handed him the hot cup with no care that it might burn his fingers.

"Ouch!" He gingerly put the cup down and shook his hand. "I suppose I deserved that. But really, Miss Winslow, I cannot believe you still hold a grudge. After all, it's almost a week since you had to deal with my ill temper. I would have thought that you are accustomed to disgruntled patients frustrated with their lack of freedom and, by association, with their keeper."

"Oh, I am, my lord. I don't know that I have ever had such a disgruntled patient as you, but then, you seem to be an exception to most every rule."

"I expect I am," he said with a little smile. "My meals have improved considerably since you left me." He did not know that it was Honor who had approved them.

"And your company as well, I expect, my lord?"

He chuckled. The subject of little Miss Phoebe seemed a surefire way to put up Honor's back, and indeed, he could well understand it, for the girl irritated him no end as well. But he wasn't about to let Honor know that. "Miss Rutherford has been gracious enough to sit with me on occasion, if that is what you are referring to. But I find I have missed your own, ah . . . companionship."

"I find that difficult to believe. Who would miss the companionship of an overbearing, insubordinate harridan?"

"Just that. Who else is daring enough to fly in my face?" He sipped his wassail, his eyes meeting hers over the cup. "Come," he said more gently, "let us put aside our argument. Toast the season with me, Miss Winslow, and tell me of what is happening outside these four walls. How are the children getting on?"

"They are well, my lord," said Honor, unbending slightly, taking a taste of her drink. "Minerva has a new doll which she will not let be removed from her arms for an instant, and I left Jocie in bed poring over her new Bible in ecstasy. Sir Henry was very generous. Mrs. Lipp has a fine violent-red petticoat." She smiled as Andrew choked on his drink. "And I have been given a new shawl. It is merely blue."

"How very nice," he managed to say. Although he had never had the privilege of meeting Mrs. Lipp, he had overheard her that once, and Honor had described her in such clear detail that he had a passionate desire to make her acquaintance. But he pushed aside the image of Mrs. Lipp and her new violent-red petticoat in favor of something far more important.

"I have something for you also, Miss Winslow. It is not much, I know, to thank you for saving my life, but I had Hobson fetch it from Chesney. It belonged to my mother." He drew a small package from the table next to him. "Here, please open it."

Honor took it from him, unwrapping it. It was a cameo cut in ivory, laid about in gold, and very beautiful. "My lord, I cannot accept this," she said with a gasp. "It is very kind of you, I'm sure, but it is far too much—"

"No arguments," he said firmly. "I am happy you like it. It is the least I can give you for all you have done."

Tears pricked at Honor's eyes. "Thank you," she said

simply. "I shall treasure it. I . . . I'm afraid I have nothing
to give you in return."

"Miss Winslow, I would not have expected anything more
from you. You have already given me a great deal, including
the one thing I can never repay you for." He took her hand
in his.

Honor flushed and pulled it away as if she had been burnt.
All of the feelings she had been resolutely denying came
flooding back at his touch. "The carolers come, my lord,"
she said quickly. "Can you hear them?"

"Ah. And here I was thinking forgiveness was mine,"
he said dryly. "You made me a promise, you know."

"Did I?"

"Yes. You promised that I might leave my bed to hear
the singing. Will you help me?"

"Yes! Oh, yes, of course!" She slipped her arm behind
his back and helped him to sit up. He put his good arm
around her neck and swung his long legs over the side of
the bed, checking first to see that his nightshirt was pulled
down over his knees, which Honor noticed with a little
smile.

"Lean on me, my lord," she said, helping him to his
feet, and together they slowly crossed the room to the window, Andrew's weight heavy against her side, his nearness
causing her blood to pound.

"Here, sit down in the window seat before you drag us
both down," she said breathlessly.

"It . . . it was a bit more difficult than I had thought,"
allowed Andrew, sinking gratefully onto the cushions.
"Look, you can see the candles lighting their faces."

"So you can," said Honor, kneeling next to him on the
cushions and peering out. The voices came up to the window, clear and piercingly sweet. "It is beautiful, isn't it,"
she said with a sigh. "It's the first real Christmas I can
remember in years."

"Did they not celebrate Christmas in the convent?" Andrew asked with surprise.

"Oh . . . oh, not like this," she said quickly. "There
was the Mass, of course, but no carolers." Other vivid im-
ages tumbled through her mind: of her father reading from
the Nativity, of rain and mud and nuns in black habits, of

the unceasing work and cries of pain. She pushed them away, unable to think of any of it without crying, and missing her father with a great rush of grief. Her eyes welled with tears despite herself.

"Honor? What is it that troubles you?" Andrew's eyes studied her face, the carolers forgotten.

"N-nothing, truly." She wiped at her eyes hurriedly. "It is the snow, and the music, and . . . and the wassail. I must be feeling sentimental."

"Sentimental? You look miserable. Come, what has happened to upset you so? Was the convent that terrible?" She sat up abruptly, rubbing her hand endearingly under her nose, and Andrew smiled, for she looked so like a lost child. "You can tell me, you know. You needn't feel you are all alone."

She lifted her eyes to his, her heart aching, wishing she could only tell him the truth, the truth about herself, who she really was and what she was doing at Croftsfield—and about him, and the dreams, and how she was falling in love with him. Alone? She was more alone than he could ever imagine.

"Honor?" he asked, wondering at the expression in her eyes.

She dropped her eyes quickly. "It is impossible, my lord," she said thickly. "We should not even be talking like this. You are the Earl of Chesney and I am Honor Winslow, the governess, and that is how it is."

"And we are both human, Honor, and we hurt and bleed and love in the same manner, regardless of social rank. Please, if only for tonight while we are here alone, forget 'my lord' and call me Andrew. You did once before, you know."

She shook her head. "I cannot." She watched with great concentration the pulse beating steadily in the hollow above his collarbone. But that was no good either, for she felt a strong desire to press her lips to that vital spot.

"You cannot tell me, or you cannot call me by my name?" he persisted.

Her eyes flew to his. "Can't you understand?" she cried in anguish. "I cannot do either! I can never. . ." She turned her face away, having said too much already.

"You can never what?" he asked gently, cupping her chin in his hand and turning her face back to his. "Honor, for the love of God, what is it? Is it something I've done, or said?"

She shook her head soundlessly, her tears falling freely.

He could not bear it, to see her in such pain. Without thinking about the right or wrong of it, he did what seemed perfectly natural. He bent his head and softly kissed her lips. And forgot everything else in the shock of the contact. His hand fell from her chin and his arm went fast around her back, pulling her against him as he deepened his kiss, knowing only that he wanted more in a way he had never wanted before.

Honor felt as if she were drowning, as if she had been coming to this moment for all of her life. At the first touch of his lips, her senses had caught on fire and her blood had begun to pound. She opened her mouth against his insistent lips, and then dimly realized what she was doing. This was no dream; this was reality.

She pulled away abruptly, her pulse racing wildly. "No, Lord Chesney!" she cried, horrified by her own impulses. "You have no right," she said more feebly.

"Honor, my dear girl, I apologize." He ran his hand through his hair, breathing hard and acutely shaken. "Please forgive me. I should not have taken advantage—"

"No, you should not have!" she said, seizing on this convenient excuse, for she could not let him know the truth. "I am not a serving-girl for you to take your pleasures with, without a care!"

"No, for that is not how it was meant, I swear it. I only thought to comfort you." And got a great deal more than he had bargained for, he thought with amazement.

"If you wished to comfort me, my lord, then you might have done it with more consideration for my feelings and . . . and my dignity. And you should think about your position. No doubt you'll soon be married."

This was too much for him, and he burst into laughter. "By God, Honor, are you looking after my virtue as well as my health? I didn't know you had the power of divination along with everything else!"

She blushed deeply, thinking he didn't know the half of

it. "It doesn't excuse the fact that you shouldn't be kissing the governess," she said, for lack of anything better to say.

"Hmm," said Andrew, looking at her thoughtfully. "I begin to wonder if you are not the snob. I have never before come across someone who thinks so continuously about position and duty. And as for all this humility, you are surprisingly able to manage everything and everyone who comes your way."

"With the exception of yourself, it seems," said Honor, striking out. "And as for that, it seems to me that it is you who are forever thinking about your precious position."

"Honor, that's unfair, and well you know it. When have I ever stood upon my position with you? But it is there, and there is nothing I can do about it other than dispatching myself. I have a tremendous responsibility now, to Arabella, the children, not to mention the lands that are in my care and must be passed down intact. There are certain disadvantages to a title, you know. I was perfectly happy without one."

Honor regarded him caustically. "Tell me, my lord. If I had been of noble birth, would you have kissed me just now?"

Andrew opened his mouth to answer, then closed it again. "I cannot say," he finally replied. "Most likely not, for I doubt we would have found ourselves in the same circumstances. Young women are generally not left alone in the same room with unmarried gentlemen late at night, for fear of compromising their reputations."

"But I have no reputation, and therefore whether I am compromised or not is of little interest to anyone but myself," she countered. "Is that what you are saying?"

Andrew grinned, beginning to enjoy himself thoroughly. "Miss Winslow, despite your somewhat unconventional care of me for someone of your tender and unmarried years, I cannot think that you have been compromised in any way. And I am quite sure the nuns saw to it that you left them in the same state of innocence in which you arrived. But tell me—and I know you will be truthful—have you ever been kissed before?"

Honor colored. "No I haven't. How could I have been? But I cannot see what that has to do with anything!"

"It has a great deal to do with all of it. You are quite correct: I should not have kissed you in principle—not that I regret it for a moment. But you reacted as if I had been on the verge of seduction. Look at me. Do I look like a man in any state to carry out a seduction?"

"I would not know, my lord, not knowing exactly what a seduction consists of," Honor said, smiling in spite of herself.

Andrew gave a shout of laughter. "Don't try pulling that one on me, for it won't fly, nearly nun or no; you know far too much about matters of a physical nature as it is. But generally speaking, a seduction begins with the ability to walk across the room unaided."

"Does it, my lord? I can't see that has very much to do with the matter."

"You, Miss Winslow, always have an answer for everything, and don't think you're going to put me on the spot. I begin to feel sorry for the poor sisters, for I imagine you must have kept them in a constant state of nervous anticipation."

"And you, my lord?" she asked with a grin.

He looked down at her, his smile fading. "I admit that you baffle me. You do not have the bearing of a convent-raised girl, and there are times when you seem far older than your years, as if a mantle of responsibility had been placed on you from an early age. But there is something else, something which I cannot define, and it puzzles me: a sadness, a distance perhaps, as if, underneath, you are someone quite different, but do not want me to know who that person is."

Honor frowned. "What do you mean?"

"I don't know exactly," he said, considering. "I sometimes feel that I know you very well, in the way one might know an old friend, and then in the next moment I know you not at all."

Honor stared at him.

"Yes. I thought you might understand what I was talking about. I'm glad you do not insult me by denying it."

"I would not deny it," she said, wondering if it were possible that she wasn't completely insane after all. "But

. . . but I had not realized that you had any thoughts on the matter.''

"I have had a great many thoughts on the matter, Honor. But you have been so busy scampering away from me that I have not been able to express them. If I asked you now, would you tell me what I want to know?"

Honor hesitated. How she longed to tell him who she was, but it was far too dangerous. It was already too dangerous that he had read her this well. She couldn't risk it, not when she was so close to getting the evidence she needed on Sir Henry.

She finally looked up and met his eyes clearly. "No, my lord. As I told you before, we should not even be having this conversation.''

"Oh, Honor, are we back to this old saw again, the earl and the governess? Because if we are, I must confess I am finding it very tedious.''

"Believe me, no one finds it more tedious than I,'' said Honor sharply. "If you would be my friend, then you will leave it alone.''

Andrew was silent for a long moment, but then he nodded and took her hand in his. "I would be your friend, Honor. If that is how you wish it, then that is how it will be.''

"Thank you,'' she whispered, looking down at where her hand lay in his. She felt as if her heart would break. But then, frightened at how close he was coming, she pushed away all thought, all feeling. "It is time you returned to your bed, my lord,'' she said briskly.

"The dragon returneth,'' said Andrew sorrowfully. "Must you always be so dictatorial? It is exactly what I meant. One moment you are there with me, so close, and the next as far away as the moon and just as unreachable. I feel as if I have just had a door slammed in my face.''

Honor colored hotly. "You need your rest, my lord.''

"And now you treat me as if I were five and had stayed up well past my bedtime. It offends my deepest sensibilities, Miss Winslow.''

"Instead of worrying about your sensibilities, my lord, you might thank me for my trouble, and do your best not to sabotage my efforts to see you well again. After that you may go your own way and do precisely as you please with nary a word from me.'' She helped him to his feet and assisted him to his bed, settling him under the covers.

"You, Miss Winslow, are a bitter pill to swallow,'' he said, turning his head on the pillows. ''I recant my words. The nuns instilled in you a distinctly withering quality.''

"I am sorry you think so,'' she said, blowing out the candle. ''But I cannot help thinking it is your pride which causes you to interpret things that way. Good night, my lord. And . . . and thank you for the cameo.''

"Honor,'' he said softly. ''Do you not kiss your charges good night?''

She sighed. ''You are incorrigible. But if you insist, I shall do what I do with all my five-year-olds.'' She bent down and brushed his cool forehead with her lips.

"No,'' said Andrew, taking her arm and pulling her closer. ''Not like that—not with this charge.'' He lightly kissed her mouth, then released her, looking up into her startled eyes. ''And to answer your earlier question, it would have made no difference if you'd been the Queen of England: if I'd found myself in these circumstances, I would have kissed you exactly as I did. I shan't do it again, Honor, and you have my word on that. But tonight . . . tonight, while you and I were just ourselves, with nothing else between us, I wanted to thank you. I owe you my life, and I am well aware of it. Tomorrow we shall return to being the governess and the earl, as you insist. Good night, Honor. Sweet dreams.''

"Sweet dreams,'' Honor whispered.

He heard the door shut softly after her, and smiled into the darkness.

Honor went to sleep that night with the cameo cradled in her hand, and tears running down her cheeks.

9

I am sure care's an enemy to life.

—William Shakespeare, *The Winter's Tale*, III, ii

Honor struggled through the next week as she had never struggled in her life. It had been difficult enough when her mother died, fading away until she simply didn't have the strength to take another breath, and more difficult still when she had lost her beloved father in the brutal manner she had. It had not been easy in the Peninsula, battling against disease and death, but it simply was, and she did what needed to be done. And later, at the convent, she had battled with herself, trying to make some sense out of her life.

But this situation was beyond anything she had ever had to deal with; there were no rules, no boundaries, no fixed points of departure or even return; indeed the lack of rules was so extreme as to be absurd. She was a governess but not a governess, in love with a man she had dreamt but who was more real than any dream, and he was attached to a young girl who was playing even more of a game than she was, and who would bring him deep unhappiness while Honor looked on—and said nothing at all. And yet there was nothing she could do about any of it. To have been able to tell Andrew the truth, if only just the beginnings of it, would have brought her some measure of relief. But she could not even have that small comfort. She was condemned to carry on the charade, to tolerate his company with no show of feeling, to watch Phoebe lay out her snare. If only the other night had not happened, she might have been able to bear it. But having had her heart laid bare by his gentle persistence, to discover that he, too, somehow knew her, to learn that he thought of her as a friend—that had been her final undoing. The only thing she could do was to keep the door, as Andrew had so aptly put it, firmly shut between them and pray that he would not see any further. She really didn't know how much more she could tolerate, and prayed for the day he would be well enough to leave Croftsfield.

* * *

Andrew slowly regained his strength, and by the time the new year had arrived, he was well enough to be taken by carriage back to Chesney. He took his leave of Sir Henry, Arabella, and Phoebe. His nieces also saw him on his way with hugs and kisses. They had been delightful in the last week of his stay, brought to visit him every day by Honor. She seemed untroubled, and had apparently dismissed the brief intimacy which had passed between them, treating him with a polite but friendly manner. Beneath the surface he sensed that she had distanced herself from him, and that disturbed him. She had not been there to say good-bye as he left, and that disturbed him even more.

When Chesney finally came into sight, Andrew was exceptionally glad to see it. "It's a fine sight, Hobson, is it not?"

"A fine sight indeed, my lord. There was a time I never thought you would lay eyes on it again in this lifetime."

"Now, Hobson. There's something I've been meaning to address to you." He regarded the sharp-faced little man almost with affection. "You have been very loyal, and served me far beyond the call of duty during my illness, but you have now seen that I am not an easy man to kill. You will please refrain from fussing over me in the future, for I really cannot bear it, and you will persuade the others to do the same. In return, I promise you that I shall do my very best to retain my good health. Do we have an agreement?"

"We are agreed, my lord." Hobson actually smiled, an extraordinary twisted expression, thought Andrew with fascination, as if his long, mournful face had not been designed for it.

The carriage pulled up in front of the house, the steps were let down, and Andrew was carefully assisted out by a footman. He adjusted his arm in its sling, and walked as steadily as possible toward the house. The massive front door swung open, and there was Nugent, bowing so low that his nose very nearly scraped the ground. "My lord, we are so very gratified—"

"As am I, Nugent, as am I." He saw with dismay that behind Nugent in the hallway was what had to be the entire Chesney staff, from the gardener to the boy who blacked the boots. "Good afternoon. How very kind of you all to welcome me home," he said with a sigh.

There was a flurry of bows and curtsies and forelock-pulling, and then Hobson said grandly, "Thank you all. Now, off about your chores and let his lordship have some peace." The crowd immediately dispersed.

"Why, Hobson, I do believe we might have a partnership!" said Andrew with delight.

"An agreement, my lord. A partnership would be most unfitting," he said, putting Andrew firmly back in his place.

All went well for the next few days. Julian, Bryonny, and their little son came to visit, brightening Andrew's spirits considerably. Andrew spent more and more time on his feet, and he passed long hours with Julian, discussing how Chesney might be improved, for Julian had implemented many modern ideas on his own estates. They discussed drainage and crop rotation and various other farming concerns, and Andrew was content.

Bryonny and Julian concentrated on attending to Andrew, and on visits paid back and forth between Chesney and Croftsfield. Julian's cultivation of Sir Henry was paying off in spades, and he wished for Bryonny to continue the illusion of friendship by spending time with Arabella and Phoebe. An honest and direct woman, Bryonny found Phoebe extremely difficult to swallow, given her painstakingly modest manner and averted eyes. Julian and Bryonny were both concerned about Arabella, however, who was obviously unhappy. But Bryonny was far more concerned about Honor, of whom she had grown very fond during her stay at the Abbey. She could tell there was something seriously wrong, and after a week of observation and careful thought, she pressed her husband to put an end to Honor's obligation, for she felt that the pressure had become too much.

Julian merely replied that the decision would have to be Honor's and refused to discuss it further.

Andrew woke early to a glorious day. For the first time he felt his old self and badly in need of exercise, and decided that a long walk would do him good. Not willing to have to deal with a confrontation with Hobson, for this rash act most certainly would not be allowed to slide by, he struggled into his clothes on his own, swearing a good deal during the process. But he finally had himself in order and crept down the stairs, feeling like a naughty schoolboy.

The day was cold but refreshing, and Andrew was happy simply to be alive. He walked quickly, breathing deeply, his mind occupied with the winter planting. Reaching the crest of the hill, he stopped to rest, for as much as he hated to admit it, he was tired. He sat down upon his cloak, his arm resting on his knee, and contemplated his favorite vista, that of Chesney basking in the sun. But a few moments later he was distracted by the sound of hooves and turned in surprise. A horse was coming up the other side of the hill, its rider slightly lopsided on her sidesaddle. He grinned, realizing now who the mysterious rider had been, for it was Honor. He stood.

"Hail and well-met, stranger," he called, and walked toward her, his dark hair blowing in the light breeze.

"My . . . my lord," said Honor, thoroughly disconcerted, for she had dreamt something very like this, Andrew smiling at her on this very hill, the wind in his hair . . .

"Honor? Why do you look at me like that? You'd think I'd grown another head."

She shook her head as if to clear it. Then, in her surprise, she said, "What in *heaven's* name are you doing all the way up here?"

"Don't you dare tell me I should be languishing in my bed, Honor, or I shall become enraged," said Andrew with a laugh. "Come, dismount that mangy beast and sit down here with me. It seems an age since I've talked with you properly."

Honor hesitated, then obliged, for she couldn't think of a polite way to refuse him. But she did decline his offer to remove his cloak for her, and settled on the skirt of her own. "How have you been feeling, my lord?"

"Very well, thank you. And yourself?"

"Very well." She colored, feeling inane, and Andrew laughed again.

"You're right. You don't do it very well."

"Do what?" she asked in confusion.

"Drawing-room conversation. I much prefer the other

kind myself, which you are so apt at producing. But seriously, Honor, how are you? At the risk of sounding rude, you look tired.''

''Do I?'' she said, stung, for she knew it to be true. ''Well, if I do, it's not from worrying over you.'' She could have bitten her tongue.

''So I gather,'' Andrew said dryly. ''Honor . . . tell me something. Why did you not say good-bye to me when I left Croftsfield?''

''I was busy. And you had plenty of others to wave you a weepy farewell.''

''Ah . . . But as you once pointed out to me, it is unlikely that any real emotion was stimulated in their breasts.''

''I would hardly know.''

''That I doubt. As a matter of fact, it seems to me that you know a very great deal. Did you know, for example, that my feelings were very hurt?''

Honor looked away, on the verge of tears. It was more than she could bear. ''Your feelings are no concern of mine, my lord.''

Andrew frowned. ''Honor . . . This is not like you. What is it? Please, if something is bothering you, I would rather you told me about it instead of shutting me out.''

''Why do you assume there is something bothering me, my lord? And if there were, why should I be obliged to tell you about it?''

''Honor,'' he said with a sigh, ''we have been through this before. I consider you a friend. I like to believe that I take a concern in my friends' interests. Besides, you helped me once. Can I not now help you?''

She turned back to him, her eyes bleak with what she was forced to do. She used the only weapon she had against him. ''You owe me no obligation, my lord. I nursed you back to health. It is what I was trained to do, and what I was instructed to do by my employer. As for anything else, my life, what little I have of it to myself, is private. I would not think of intruding in your own, my lord. Is it your *droit du seigneur* to intrude into mine?''

Andrew colored hotly and gritted his teeth against his anger. ''I beg your pardon, ma'am,'' he said coldly, rising to his feet and offering his good hand to help her up. ''I did not mean to offend your delicate pride. Please accept my apologies for my apparent intrusion; in the future I shall try to keep to the conventions you put such stock in. It seems that once again I have forgotten my place."

"That," said Honor, facing him, "I would very much doubt. The place you have forgotten is mine."

"Yes, and I don't know why, when you remind me of it repeatedly. Forgive me for having interrupted your morning, but you were on Chesney land, so I can hardly be held blameworthy. Perhaps if you will let me know when you care to ride up here, I shall be sure to absent myself."

All the color drained from Honor's face. "I beg your pardon, my lord," she said stiffly. "I did not mean to trespass." She cut herself off at the welcome sight of Bryonny coming up the hill.

"Oh, Andrew, there you are!" said Bryonny breathlessly, coming toward them. "Good morning, Miss Winslow! Andrew, Hobson was about to put the entire household into a panic and report you missing and no doubt dead, but thank heaven he had the good sense to come to me first, and I thought I'd come and see if you weren't meditating in your favorite spot . . ." Her voice slowed and stopped as she took in the two faces, one ashen and the other scarlet. "I hope I haven't intruded," she said in a carefully casual tone.

"Not at all," said Andrew. "It was a chance meeting. Miss Winslow and I were just admiring the fine morning. She was leaving, in any case. May I assist you onto your horse, Miss Winslow?"

"Thank you, my lord," said Honor, grimly suffering his hand beneath her boot. "Good day. Forgive me for interrupting your musings. Good day, Lady Hambledon."

"Good day, Miss Winslow," said Bryonny lightly, and took Andrew's arm. "Come now, darling boy, let's see if we can't get you back to the house without incident. Hobson would never forgive me if anything should befall you." She led him away, chatting about nothing in particular, but her mind was preoccupied.

Later that afternoon, upon Bryonny's return from another deadly boring visit to Croftsfield, where Phoebe had simpered and Arabella had hardly spoken, she took advantage of finding Andrew alone in the library.

"Hello, Andrew," she said, discarding her gloves and dropping an affectionate kiss on his cheek. "Goodness, they're exhausting, those relatives of yours." She heaved a great sigh and dropped into a chair. "Shall I go away? Were you working? I am so bad when it comes to interrupting."

"Nonsense, Bryonny," Andrew said, putting away his papers and rubbing his eyes. "It's always a delight to see you; you know that. It's very good of you to make such an effort with Arabella. I know she's a goose, even though an endearing one, but she's been so changed since her marriage to Henry. It does her good to have a female friend she can converse with. She and George were such a close couple, and it's abundantly clear that she doesn't share the same companionship with Henry."

"I think her relationship with Sir Henry is of a very different nature, Andrew." Bryonny frowned. She had not missed the faint bruise on Arabella's cheek, carefully covered with rice powder, and had darkly suspected the worst.

"He is not a warm man, to be sure. Arabella is the sort of person who blossoms under affection."

"Well, it seems she is receiving little enough of that. Phoebe treats her appallingly, although she thinks no one notices."

"Oh, Phoebe," said Andrew with a grimace. "She's a dreadful child, isn't she? But I'm determined to see her married this Season, if it means I have to drag her to every party and rout, just to get her off Arabella's hands."

"You, Andrew?" said Bryonny with a grin. "That is martyrdom indeed."

"I know," he said with a sigh. "But I have all the *entrées* that Henry lacks. And can you imagine what would happen if I left it to Arabella to manage? Poor woman. She made a bad mistake all around, I fear, but it is done."

"It cannot be easy leaving the life she loved so well."

"I tried to convince her to stay here after George died, rather than removing to the dower house, but she would have none of it. Said it wouldn't be fitting! And now look at those two little girls and the mess she's landed them in, not to mention herself."

"At least they have Miss Winslow," said Bryonny.

"Ah, yes, Miss Winslow." Andrew shook his head and rubbed at his eyes again. "The embodiment of a saint."

"Why, Andrew! You sound as if you've taken a dislike to her."

"A dislike? Whatever gave you that idea? But as far as I'm concerned, she can bloody well go back to the convent from whence she came. I can't think why she left it in the first place. Still, the girls do need her, and she's done them a world of good. I find myself incredibly grateful to her on a number of counts. But then, it seems that gratitude is inappropriate. Miss Winslow is of a most independent mind."

"Oh, yes," said Bryonny. "I noticed it straightaway, and you know how much I admire that quality in a woman. She is so calm and sensible, but not without humor. I don't think it's Miss Winslow's destiny to return to the convent, Andrew, nor to remain a governess forever."

"Oh?" said Andrew with a tired smile. "And just what do you see Miss Winslow's destiny as being, Bryonny?"

"I should think she will make some man very happy. I do hope she marries well, for she is far too bright to be content with the farmer's son, or even the vicar's, when it comes to that."

The idea of Honor marrying the vicar's son, much less the farmer's, had never occurred to Andrew, and the picture it painted made him frown. "I had not considered the matter, to tell you the truth. But perhaps you had better ask Miss Winslow if she desires to marry. Somehow I doubt it."

"I cannot think why she wouldn't. She is bright and attractive and wonderful with children, and she has a generous and caring nature. Look what she did for you, for heaven's sake! I think she deserves some pleasure in her life, for it cannot give her much happiness to be shut away with the children all the time. And I must say, I cannot think how she is ever to meet anyone to marry in that situation. Perhaps you know a local squire or two, Andrew? You owe her a favor, after all, and an invitation from Arabella to a small dinner would not go amiss."

Andrew, who was more than aware of what Honor had

done for him, and who felt guilty enough as it was that he had apparently offended her, shrugged. "Miss Winslow's marital plans or lack of them are a matter of indifference to me, but I shall see if I cannot arrange for her to attend a dinner. I must say it seems quite enough to have Phoebe on my hands without worrying about a squire for Miss Winslow." He closed his eyes and leaned his head back against his chair.

"Oh . . . I beg your pardon, Andrew," Bryonny said, seeing belatedly how drawn he had become. "You know what a terrible nuisance I can be. I shouldn't have gone on so."

"No, it is not that," Andrew said, drawing a hand over his eyes. "It is only this confounded headache that has come upon me. They have plagued me since my accident. I had thought I was free of them, but I suppose I am not."

"Oh, Andrew, I am so sorry! But you should lie down at once. I'll call Hobson and he will make you comfortable." She hurried off in deep concern.

Andrew's headache only increased in severity throughout the early evening, and Hobson took it upon himself to intrude in the library before dinner.

"Please excuse me, your lordship, my lady, but I am most concerned with the pain Lord Chesney is suffering. I can find nothing to alleviate it, and he is quite ill!" Hobson's gray face attested to this fact. It had not been so bad for a long time, and he was at his wits' end. "Shall I summon the doctor?"

Julian rose to his feet. "No. Have a message sent immediately to Croftsfield. Miss Winslow must come at once."

"Yes, my lord," said Hobson with relief. He had not dared to offer the suggestion himself, but he ought to have remembered that Lord Hambledon had been present when Miss Winslow had been able to do what the doctor could not. "I'll send one of the men immediately."

"And have him take the path, not the road. It will save time."

"Yes, my lord," said Hobson with a bow, and immediately removed himself.

* * *

Honor arrived at Chesney not half an hour after receiving the message. Her step slowed as she entered the house. She knew just how the large marbled hall would look, with its black and white checkered squares, how the door to the library would be paneled in oak, and it was most unsettling. But she dismissed her thoughts from her mind, for she had an immediate problem to deal with. She stayed talking with Julian and Bryonny for only a brief moment, to discover how long Andrew had been suffering and, having her answer, she went immediately with Hobson to Andrew's room. She found it swathed in darkness, with not even a candle flickering to break up the night.

"Hobson," she whispered. "Bring me boiling water and honey." She went softly to the bed.

"My lord, it is Miss Winslow."

He partially opened his eyes, barely able to focus through the waves of pain. "Honor?" he murmured. "What the devil are you doing here?"

She pressed out a cool cloth and laid it against his forehead. "I am here to see to your headache. What else?"

"What else, indeed?" Andrew said bitterly.

His expression cut deeply, but she spoke calmly, with no trace of emotion. "Quiet now, my lord. I will make your drink and you will be better soon."

Hobson came in shortly after with the requested articles, and Honor made the infusion of angelica, then strained it and sweetened it. "My lord?"

He opened his eyes.

"Here is your medicine."

With an effort, Andrew managed to drink the potion. "I am sorry to be such a continuous bother. It must vex you greatly."

"It does not, my lord. I am glad to be of service. Now, sleep, and when you wake, you shall feel yourself again."

"Honor and service," he muttered. "The two go together like a dog and his master."

Honor glared at him. "I serve no master but my conscience," she whispered fiercely, but Andrew's eyes had closed and he appeared not to have heard her.

Honor settled herself down, watching him carefully as he struggled silently with the pain, until he finally fell into a peaceful sleep. She quietly left, but her heart was heavy and her throat ached with unshed tears.

The next day, the last of the Hambledons' visit, Bryonny sent a note to Croftsfield requesting Honor to bring the children around so that they might meet her son, young Andrew. It was a beautiful day, warm and bright with sunshine, and all the snow had melted away. Honor, Bryonny, and the children went out into the fields, Andrew warmly bundled in Bryonny's arms. He was a delightful little boy, with his father's dark looks and his mother's irrepressible spirits.

"Look, Minnie," cried Jocie with delight, watching Andrew charge across the brown grass. "See how his fat legs roll when he walks, as if he were aboard a ship?"

Andrew, as if he understood, squealed with merriment, rolled forward one more time, and promptly fell over onto his bottom. Minerva beamed, and carefully helped him to his feet, and Andrew screeched with laughter again and ran on, his arms waving wildly.

"He's a dear child," said Honor with a smile. "I swear he has grown inches since the autumn."

"He has indeed. Do you know, I never thought it would be such a joy to be a mother. I'm sure one day you will be as lucky as I."

Honor's smile faded. "I would like it very much, but I think it is not in my destiny."

Bryonny's steps slowed. "I once thought such a thing myself, and not so long ago. Let me tell you a story, for I think you will understand, and I know I can trust you with it."

Honor looked over at her and nodded. "Whatever you choose to tell me will be held in confidence."

Bryonny smiled. "I came to England from Jamaica when I was sixteen. I was orphaned shortly after arriving, and Julian's father became my guardian, and eventually Julian, after his father died. It was an uneasy relationship, for I was accustomed to independence, and I constantly made Julian quite furious. But despite all of that, I fell in love with him, and he with me. And then, through a series of terrible misunderstandings, I married someone else. I was deeply unhappy, but I did not think it was my destiny to be with

Julian, you see. It was the most terrible mistake I could have made, not to trust my feelings.''

Honor halted in her steps entirely. ''What happened?''

''I was with child, Julian's child, although Julian had no idea of it. Naturally, he thought it was my . . . my husband's.''

Honor stared. ''I . . . I beg your pardon?''

Bryonny smiled. ''These things happen. It all worked out in the end, but the moral is that if I had believed from the beginning that my destiny lay with Julian, and had never doubted my love for him, none of the confusion would have happened, and we would have been spared a great deal of pain.''

''Why do you tell me this story?'' Honor asked directly.

''I have sensed that you are deeply unhappy. It reminds me of myself at that time in my life. I wanted to speak with you alone, for I know that you have no one to confide in, and perhaps it might help to talk about it. Our lives have been very different, but I think our hearts are not so far apart, nor our understanding. You spoke of destiny. I only want you to realize what it ultimately means. The truth of things is so easily covered, and often lost as a result.''

''Yes,'' said Honor slowly. ''But sometimes that is the way things have to be.''

''It is never the way anything *has* to be. I have learned that there is always a way to where we belong if we are willing to work at it hard enough. And to believe in our dreams.''

''Tell me something,'' Honor said quietly. ''Have you ever had a dream, a dream that was so true that you could almost touch it more solidly than if it were real?''

Bryonny looked at her intently as she thought. ''No, I cannot say that I have, although I have heard of such things. Do you mean foresight, knowing the future before it happens?''

Honor struggled to find the right words. ''No . . . not exactly. I have seen that in Minerva; she foretold her father's death and Andrew's accident. No, I mean something quite different, more of a complete meeting of the mind before one encounters that person in the flesh.''

''I have heard it spoken of in theology and sometimes

philosophy, but I have never encountered anyone who has experienced it personally. Have you?"

"Yes. But no matter how I look at it, the reality is so very different that it makes no sense at all."

"I see. . . . I cannot say I understand it any better than you, but it obviously disturbs you. Does it go against your religious beliefs, this dreaming?"

"No." Honor bent down and scooped up a handful of the deep rich earth, squeezing it tightly between her fingers. "I believe in God and his guidance, and I know there are many different ways that it comes. But this other thing—it is different, and I cannot understand it. Ah, well." She shrugged. "The dreams have stopped, so I suppose there is nothing more to be said."

"It is Andrew, isn't it?"

Honor looked over at her, her eyes brimming with tears.

"You can trust me as much as I have you," said Bryonny gently.

Honor swallowed hard against the ache in her throat. "Yes, it is Andrew. I knew him before any of this, in my dreams, as far back as I can remember. He was a boy, older than I, but he was my friend, and I loved him. I always thought that it was only my imagination, a pleasant story I had made up, and the dreams stopped a number of years ago. And then they started again when I came to Croftsfield, and the boy was a man, and it had all changed, and the feelings were different. Again, I thought that it was because I was lonely, and it was familiar. But then I saw Chesney and recognized it, and I started to wonder. And then Andrew came to Croftsfield, and when I saw him for the first time, I knew him immediately as my . . . as my friend."

"How incredible!" said Bryonny, fascinated. "And Andrew? What did he do when he saw you?"

"Nothing. I don't know that he has experienced the same thing in the same way, although he has said some things which have led me to believe it is possible. But if he has dreamt me, he does not remember."

"Yes, but many people do not remember their dreams. It doesn't mean they don't have them," said Bryonny sensibly.

Honor nodded. "I hadn't thought of that, and it is possible. But regardless, I think he senses something, Bryonny, and that worries me. If he discovers the truth about me, he'll eventually learn about Sir Henry and everything else. My father was killed because of Sir Henry's treachery; I could not bear for anything to happen to Andrew, and he has already been hurt once because Sir Henry suspected him. He cannot be involved. In any case, he would think me quite mad if I said anything about my dreams. I sometimes think it myself.''

To Honor's surprise, Bryonny laughed. ''I do not think you mad at all. You are far too sensible. As I said, such things are not unheard-of, although you should be very careful to whom you mention it.''

''I have never spoken of this to anyone. I am glad you understand, for I don't myself.''

''That,'' said Bryonny pragmatically, ''is the way it generally seems to happen. We never know how these things enter our lives, or even why, but I am certain that if something such as this has been given to you, it is for a reason. Perhaps your destiny is somehow tied to Andrew's. But I do wish you could somehow make peace with him, for it's making you so miserable. Can't he know about the dreams without knowing about the rest of it?''

''If I open up to him at all, he'd certainly know how I feel, and sense that I am hiding something. Knowing Andrew, he'd find out everything. And I can't let that happen. Not until it's all over with.''

''And then?''

''I don't know,'' Honor said heavily. ''But Andrew has other plans for his life. Believe me, I am not part of them.'' She let the clump of earth fall from her fingers. ''I don't think destiny comes into it, Bryonny; I think it is just a freak thing between us with no rhyme or reason. It's best to forget it. And when this is finished with, I'll be gone.''

Bryonny glanced at her for a moment, her eyes keen. ''As you say. . . . Andrew, darling,'' she called to her child. ''Must you eat the mud? Jocelyn, do distract him to something else. Look, there's an old nest in the hedge. I'm certain that would be more appetizing.'' She turned the subject back to children.

10

Wherefore are these things hid?

—William Shakespeare, *Twelfth Night*, I, iii

To Honor's vast relief, Andrew appeared only twice more at Croftsfield, and both times his visits with the children were brief. He was impeccably polite to her, and she to him. And then in early February he was unexpectedly called away to Scotland, or so she understood from Arabella. The brief note he had sent to Jocie and Minerva had said only that he must absent himself on a matter of pressing business and would see them in London in late March. His departure brought her a degree of peace, for she no longer had to worry about meeting him around every corner. She refused to think about March at all.

But March drew inexorably nearer, and all of Croftsfield flew into a state of bustling excitement as the trunks were packed and the house prepared to be closed for the removal to London. Phoebe, who had done nothing but mope since Andrew had left, cheered up tremendously and left her room, much to Honor's dismay. She did nothing but talk about Lord Chesney when she wasn't talking about herself, and along with the constant references to Lord Chesney and her forthcoming engagement, she contrived to find a number of ways to make Honor's life miserable.

Mrs. Lipp, having recovered from the cold and damp, now came into her most magnificent own, even forsaking the comfort of her medicine bottle for the pleasure of directing the proceedings. It had been many a year since life had held such excitement, and she looked forward to renewing some of her old friendships. London was on every tongue, and Betsy made tearful farewells to her family in the village, while at the same time planning for a greater future in the metropolis.

Jocie was greatly excited, for there were museums to be seen and libraries to be visited. Minerva could only think about the joy of visiting a fair, which her Uncle Andrew had promised to take them to. She talked of nothing else, and Honor was hard-pressed to keep both the girls from bursting at the seams. Her own mind was preoccupied with how she was to deal with Andrew.

She had thought long and hard about what Bryonny had said. It had helped to unburden herself to another human being, and cleared her mind. It was her own fault that she had left her heart like an open door for Andrew to go walking through as he pleased. All she had to do was to keep herself completely closed off from him and all would be well.

That should not be too difficult, she told herself crossly, folding another of Minerva's nightdresses, for Andrew would be so busy squiring Phoebe around that she would scarcely see him. And how she could have any feeling at all for a man foolish enough to be pursuing Phoebe Rutherford was beyond her. He deserved everything coming to him. She had more important things to do than worry about his future, including proving that Sir Henry was a murderer. On that thought, she banged down the lid of the trunk she was packing and went to seek out Mrs. Lipp, who was in a turmoil about the linens.

At last the great day arrived, and the procession of two traveling carriages, three chaises with servants and baggage, and Sir Henry's sporting curricle, recently acquired in a card game, according to Jake, made its way to London. It was a full day's trip with the entire retinue, whereas it might have taken only three hours otherwise, and Honor was greatly relieved when they finally pulled up in front of the town house Sir Henry had hired in Berkeley Square. Minerva was about to pass out with fatigue brought on by too much excitement, and Jocie had merely become tired and quarrelsome. Honor could only be grateful that Phoebe had gone in the other carriage with Arabella, so as not to plague them, although she doubted that Arabella was any better for the company.

Phoebe immediately swept upstairs, where her own personal maid, newly hired for the Season, was awaiting her. Sir Henry went out, only pausing to change into evening clothes, and Arabella went to bed in a state of nervous exhaustion while Honor saw to the children and the settling-in of the staff.

* * *

It was two days before Andrew presented himself at the door to pay his respects. Phoebe had once again been taken off by Arabella for various fittings to complete her wardrobe, and Sir Henry was away at the House. Honor knew London not at all, and was wondering how to go about taking the children out for an airing when Andrew was announced. He looked even more dashing in his town clothes, wearing dove-colored pantaloons, a dark blue coat of Bath superfine, modest shirt-points, a simply tied cravat, and a silk waistcoat from which hung one gold fob.

"Miss Winslow! How delightful to see you again," he said, entering the hall and handing his hat and cane to Spencer, who regarded them with disfavor.

"It is kind of you to say so, my lord," she said carefully. Infuriatingly, at the sight of him her heart had begun to pound as if with a mind of its own. She summoned up her resolve. "I am afraid there is no one at home but myself and the children."

"Ah. But as I have come to take you and the children driving, it is no crushing blow. Where are they?"

"Upstairs, my lord, but I really don't know—"

"Then if it is not too much trouble, perhaps you'll fetch them, Miss Winslow?" said Andrew with a little laugh. "My God, you can look chilly when you want to. What have I done now?"

"Nothing!" she said, coloring.

"Nothing. . . . Then will you explain why you're looking at me as if you cannot wait to see my back at the door?"

"I beg your pardon, my lord," said Honor, recovering her dignity. "I do not know if it is suitable for you to go driving with the governess."

Andrew sighed. "My dear girl, perhaps for once you'll allow me to decide what is fitting. Now be a good little governess and fetch the girls and I shall point out the other governesses and their charges to you, and the walks they frequent in the park. Maybe that way you will feel you are on duty, despite the fact that it is a fine spring day, and you should not miss a moment more of it."

Honor went reluctantly to do his bidding, telling herself that despite her own feelings, the girls would be thrilled, and so they were. Minerva's eyes shone as she was helped up into Andrew's handsome curricle, and Jocie talked non-stop as she clambered up next to her sister, asking a thousand questions, and giving Andrew no time to answer. He laughed, and helped Honor up last, then took his place next to her on the seat, far too close for Honor's comfort.

It was indeed a beautiful day, and London was dressed up in cherry blossoms and flowering pears and new green leaves, and everywhere there were flowers. The streets were busy, thick with carriages and curricles and high-perch phaetons, but Andrew confidently handled his pair of matched grays, talking all the while, pointing out sights of interest. He took them on a tour around the town, down to the river Thames, past the Houses of Parliament, and finally through the gates into Hyde Park.

There, parading on horseback and in carriages, was the cream of London society, out to see and be seen. Honor was sorely tempted to burst into fits of laughter, for this promenading seemed to be a deadly serious business.

Andrew gave a running commentary on various members of the *ton,* and seemed to have an amusing story about each. Jocie drank it all in, forgetting that she had ever had aspirations to spinsterhood, let alone a nunnery.

"I can scarcely wait, Uncle Andrew, until I might have my come-out! Why, look at that beautiful woman over there on the horse, all bedecked in lovely plumes, and surrounded by swarms of gentleman. She is having the most glorious time!"

"That, my dear Jocelyn," said Andrew, aiming a wicked grin at Honor, "is Mrs. Simington, and she may be having a glorious time, for which she is well-noted, but I assure you, she is very wicked."

"Then I want to be as dreadfully wicked as Mrs. Simington, for it seems that her life must be filled with the most wonderful adventures!" She regarded the woman in question with delight.

"Her life, my sweet, is certainly filled with adventure, but of the most unsavory sort, and she is never seen in the better drawing rooms. I would beg you never to aspire to a career such as hers."

"What is her career?" asked Jocie breathlessly.

"She . . . she is an actress," said Andrew unsteadily, as Honor was suddenly taken by a fit of sneezing. "Now, over here on our left," he continued quickly, "are Mrs. Pomescue and her daughters Ferdinanda and Georgette." He nodded at an enormous woman regally marching along, balancing a hat that appeared to be constructed from tropical fruit, with two hefty, downtrodden girls at her heels. "She considers herself to be a great matron of society, and not many care to argue with her. She has been the bane of every titled gentleman's existence for years; she gave birth to five daughters, each more unfortunate than the one before, and it has been her mission in life to see them all well-married. Heretofore I have escaped her immediate attention when she has placed a daughter on the marriage mart, but now, sadly, she will no doubt change her tune."

"You are very eligible now, are you not, uncle?" asked Jocelyn, assuming an innocent face. "Surely you will have many mamas and their daughters after you."

Honor looked over at him with a little smile, wondering how he would field this question.

Andrew shook his head. "You, Jocie, are far too perspicacious for my comfort. I may be eligible, but I am also very cautious. I have no intention of being corralled into marriage by a scheming miss or her mother."

"Won't you marry Phoebe?" piped Minerva, who had appeared oblivious of the conversation.

Andrew shot her a startled look. "Where did you conceive that idea, my pet?"

"I don't know," said Minerva, and popped her thumb into her mouth.

"Do try not to suck your thumb, Minnie, my sweet," said Honor in a strangled voice.

Andrew opened his mouth to say something, but apparently thought better of it. "Now, here, Miss Winslow," he said, turning to her, "is where the governesses have their own parade, showing off their charges. The higher the rank, the more privileged the governess and the bench she presides upon, those nearest the water being considered the *crème de la crème.*"

"I suppose I will be sitting out in the middle of the field," said Honor dryly.

"No, no, Miss Winslow," said Andrew with a little smile, for he knew she had taken his meaning perfectly well. "It was the rank of the child I was referring to. You have two daughters of an earl, so you would be outranked only by children of a marquess or a duke, and, naturally, royal children, but you would hardly be likely to see them in Hyde Park."

"I see," said Honor. "So if I aspire to rise in the world, I should do it through the ranks of my charges. Do you know of any dukes seeking a governess, my lord?"

"You, Miss Winslow, are utterly impossible," said Andrew. "You never miss an opportunity to—"

Jocie interjected before he could go on. "Look!" she said in an amazed whisper, twisting around in her seat. "Look, it's Miss Torch!"

Honor followed her gaze, and saw a tall, thin woman dressed in black, with a sharp face and stiff carriage, leading three beautifully dressed charges down the path toward the pond.

"By God, so it is!" exclaimed Andrew. "And speak of the very devil! Those are the Duke of Bedford's children, if I'm not mistaken. How very interesting—no wonder she dropped everything and left Croftsfield for such an exalted position! You see, it proves my point exactly, Miss Winslow."

Jocie scowled furiously. "She lied! She said she was going to look after her sick sister. And she said it was a sin to lie, and God would punish you. I hate her! She pretended to be so holy and she's not at all!"

"I reckon she hung holiness over your head to keep you in line the way some might use a switch," said Andrew wryly. "But never mind, Jocie, for you are far better off having Miss Winslow as your governess, don't you think? Now you don't have to worry about being holy at all, despite Miss Winslow's own proclivity in that direction. Or so I have observed."

"No," said Jocie, considering. "Honor said that martyrdom does not suit me, and that it's quite all right to hate S—" She stopped herself just in time as Honor quickly squeezed her arm. "To hate saying prayers all day long," she finished lamely. "I don't want to be a nun anymore. I want to be a fashionable lady **and** wear plumes, and go riding in the park like Mrs. Simington.''

Andrew grinned at Honor. ''Most commendable instruction, Miss Winslow.''

''I think it a very fine ambition, Jocie,'' said Honor, giving Andrew a black look. ''I'm sure you will make a lovely lady one day.''

''You would too, Honor,'' said Jocie. ''I think it's much too bad that you must be a governess all your life. If it were a fairy tale, then you would be Cinderella, and the prince would find you and sweep you off to live happily ever after.''

Honor colored hotly, thoroughly sick of the whole issue. ''This is not a fairy tale, and I am not anything like Cinderella.''

Andrew laughed. ''I would have to agree; you're not the least bit like Cinderella. God help the prince who tried to pick up your slipper. You'd probably hit him over the head with it and call him an interfering scoundrel.''

''As you say, my lord,'' said Honor quietly, stung to the quick. ''It's a lucky thing for you, then, that I'm not Cinderella and you're not a prince, isn't it? I think it's time we took the children back.''

Andrew's jaw tightened, but he refrained from responding. He silently cursed her for her pride and truculence, when he had only been trying to give her some pleasure in the outing, a relief from her usual duties. The least she could do would be to exhibit some graciousness.

The rest of the drive passed in silence.

''Thank you so very much, Uncle Andrew,'' Jocie said when they had arrived back at Berkeley Square, determined to relieve the peculiar tension in the air. ''I can't think when I had such an exciting afternoon! May we do it again, and perhaps you will take us to the British Museum too?''

''Jocie,'' said Honor, distracted, for Andrew's strong hand was assisting her to the ground, ''you must wait for your uncle to ask you himself.''

''Not at all,'' said Andrew curtly. ''I fully intend to see that my nieces enjoy themselves, even if it seems beyond your own capacity to do the same.'' He scooped Minerva, who was sound asleep, into his arms. Spencer appeared dolefully to open the door and Andrew carried her inside, where they were greeted by Arabella in her usual flutter.

"Oh, Andrew! How delightful that you should be here, for Phoebe was so upset that she might have missed you. We must sit down and plan the week's activities. Of course, you know about the dinner we are holding on Friday, but we really must go through the other invitations and decide which to accept. There are so many that my head is just spinning. I really don't know which are the most suitable . . ."

"I'll just take Minerva to her bed, and then I shall join you in the drawing room," said Andrew, ignoring Honor and starting up the stairs. Honor followed with an ignoble desire to kick his shins.

He put Minerva to bed, and spoke quietly with Jocie for a few moments. He then turned to Honor. His face was completely without expression.

"Good day, Miss Winslow. If it would be convenient, I should like to take Jocelyn to the British Museum tomorrow. I think it would be best to leave Minerva here with you."

"As you wish, my lord," said Honor stiffly, suddenly feeling completely miserable. Something of what she felt must have shown on her face, for Andrew's features softened. "Look here, Honor," he said gently. "We must make peace, you and I, if we are to rub along in each other's company. I meant no offense, you know."

She raised her eyes to his, and immediately dropped them again. "Nor did I, my lord. Thank you for driving us. It was kind of you."

"Kindness had nothing to do with it. I enjoy my nieces, and believe it or not, I actually enjoy your company as well. You know, you would find life much easier if you didn't fight against it so much. I can see that it is very difficult for you to adjust to living in the outside world, but it is really not such a bad place. You might take advantage of the time you have in London to learn a little about life and its pleasures."

Honor couldn't help her sudden grin. "I do hope, my lord, that you do not give such advice to all the young women of your acquaintance."

Andrew laughed. "That's more like the Honor I know.

And no, I am the soul of discretion—most of the time. And you know perfectly well what I meant, so don't try to use that one against me.''

"I wouldn't dream of it, my lord, for I am far too sheltered to know what you were referring to in the first place." Then, remembering herself, she said, "You'd better go. Miss Rutherford and her ladyship will be growing anxious.''

Andrew shook his head. "It seems that some things are simply not destined to change. Thank you for reminding me of my responsibilities, Miss Winslow. I shall come around tomorrow at two o'clock.''

He took his leave, but as he went down the stairs, his face was thoughtful as he recalled a conversation he'd had with Bryonny some months before. He would have a word with Arabella, he decided. Honor would have some pleasure whether she liked it or not.

The next afternoon, after Jocelyn had returned from her trip full of breathless excitement and chatter, Honor was summoned downstairs. She was sure it was another of Arabella's panics over the preparations for that evening and she was surprised to find Andrew with her. She had thought him long gone.

Honor curtsied. "You wished to see me?"

Andrew regarded her neutrally, but a small smile played at the corner of his mouth.

"My dear Honor," said Arabella, "I've run into the most terrible dilemma, and you could do me such a favor if you would oblige me.''

"Certainly, my lady," said Honor, wondering why Andrew suddenly looked so amused.

"You see, my dear, the small dinner we planned for tonight to give Phoebe some practice in society has suddenly been thrown off. Poor Mrs. Constantine is indisposed and has had to cancel, and I cannot think of anyone to make up the numbers at such short notice. If you would help me by joining us and evening out the numbers, I would be so terribly grateful.''

"My lady, I could not possibly . . ." Honor was horrified at the prospect of being thrown into the middle of thirty members of the *haut ton* for the evening. What if one of them should realize her true identity?

"Nonsense," said Andrew succinctly. "You, Miss Winslow, have the opportunity to serve, and serve you shall."

She glared at him, knowing this was all his doing, for Arabella would never have come up with the idea on her own, and Phoebe most certainly hadn't suggested it. "I cannot possibly come to dinner. I have nothing suitable to wear," she said firmly.

"Ah, but we have already thought of that! Phoebe's maid can alter one of my own dresses," said Arabella brightly. "All she needs are your measurements! So you see, Honor, dear, there is nothing to keep you from joining us!"

"But the children—"

"Will be in bed, fast asleep," said Andrew, his eyes dancing at her obvious discomfort. "I am most sincerely sorry, Miss Winslow, but it appears there is no way out."

"Really, dearest Honor," continued Arabella, "it would make all the difference in the world. Do say yes."

"Of course she will," said Andrew. "Won't you, Miss Winslow?"

She colored under his regard. "If it is that important, my lady," she said faintly, seeing no way out, "then yes, I would be happy to help."

"Good girl," said Andrew with satisfaction. "Off you go, then, to have your dress altered. Now, Arabella," he said, effectively dismissing Honor, "about this seating arrangement. I think it would be better if you placed . . ."

She crept out of the room, unable to believe the misfortune that had just befallen her.

Four hours later, Honor turned before the mirror, anxiously examining her reflection. Arabella had given her a dress of deep primrose silk with a demitrain, and a knot of ribbons fell from the high waist to the hem. Honor assessed herself. Betsy had arranged a ribbon through her curls, and now that her hair had grown out somewhat, it looked almost feminine.

Her skin was lightly flushed, a result of anxiety, Honor thought, and her gray eyes seemed to be unusually bright. She removed Andrew's cameo from her drawer and carefully attached it to her bodice. Then, taking one last look, she went next door to the nursery.

"Oh, Honor!" Jocelyn cried, running up to her and clasping her hands. "You look beautiful!"

"Beautiful," echoed Minerva solemnly.

Honor smiled. "Not beautiful, I think, but passable perhaps."

"No, miss, the girls be right," said Betsy shyly. "Them lords and ladies won't hold a candle to you, not even that Miss Phoebe, what with all her fine airs and graces. Don't you worry none, miss. You be a dream tonight, and that's God's truth."

Honor laughed. "Thank you, Betsy. You and the girls have given me the confidence I was lacking."

"But it's true, Honor," insisted Jocie. "Do you remember what you once said about being beautiful suddenly, and having admiring men around you? Well, up until now, you've been just Honor, our governess, but tonight you look like the very finest lady ever. It even makes me think that one day even I might be transformed, for it is my new goal in life," she said with as much dramatic intonation as the glorious Mrs. Simington could ever have hoped for.

"Oh, Jocie." Honor took her little face between her hands. "Of course you will be! Just look how you've begun to blossom already. Not too many more years, and you'll be going down the stairs instead of me, and far prettier, I assure you."

"And me too?" said Minerva.

Honor felt her eyes start with tears. "And you too, my darling," she said, kissing her forehead, wishing it could be true.

Minerva beamed and said, "Beautiful Honor."

"I completely agree with you, Minnie," said a deep voice from behind Honor, and she spun around, her breath catching in her throat.

"My . . . my lord," Honor said in a croak. It was he who was beautiful, she thought with a little shock. She had never before seen him in full evening clothes, and the black swallow-tailed coat, white watered-silk waistcoat, and black satin knee breeches did justice to his magnificent form. His calves were encased in white silk stockings, and he wore a pair of diamond-buckled slippers.

"Good evening, Miss Winslow," he said with a little smile. "The girls are quite right. You look lovely. I've come to take you downstairs, against the chance that you might have a sudden panic and flee the house altogether."

"You, my lord, should be that lucky," said Honor, recovering her composure.

Andrew grinned. "And you, ma'am, should be more polite to your fairy godmother."

"I did receive the impression that that was exactly the role you played in this, my lord, but I must confess, you're the oddest-looking fairy godmother I've ever seen."

"Oh, and have you seen a great many, then?"

Honor opened her mouth to reply, but she caught Betsy staring with her mouth open, and Jocie had a distinct smirk on her face. "I think we'd best go," she said quickly. "Good night, my loves. Be good, and I shall tell you all about it in the morning." She kissed them, and waited as Andrew did the same. He whispered something into Jocie's ear, and she giggled and gave Honor a wicked look. And then Andrew offered Honor his arm and she took it.

"What did you say to Jocie, my lord?" she asked suspiciously, once they were safely in the hallway.

"I told her to wait until midnight to see if you would turn into a pumpkin."

Honor laughed. "If you continue to goad me, my lord, I shall set out to prove you wrong. And then where would you be?"

Andrew glanced down at her. "I would be extremely satisfied, Miss Winslow. As you have pointed out on a number of occasions, I am extremely spoiled, and am accustomed to having my own way."

Honor bit the inside of her cheek in vexation, wishing she had never spoken. Andrew merely smiled. "I am pleased to see you wearing the brooch, Honor. I have never seen you do so before."

"I have not had an opportunity before, my lord."

"Then I am glad you have had one provided for you. It looks nice on you."

"Thank you, my lord." She flushed under the direction of his gaze, and he laughed.

"I beg your pardon. And I meant what I said: you look lovely. Shall we descend, Cendrillon?"

Andrew allowed her to go down by herself, which she said she felt more fitting, and he did not quibble, but he made a point of introducing her to various people, just as he did Phoebe. He kept a careful eye on them both, but Honor dealt more comfortably with the situation than even he had expected. She had an unconscious charm and natural poise with people, and that did not surprise him; what did surprise him was that for all her protestations about her lowly position in life, she exhibited absolutely no self-consciousness. In fact, dressed as she was—and it had given him a little shock to see her so—she looked to the manner born and behaved so. Phoebe, on the other hand, much to his dismay, seemed to have no inclination to leave his side for a moment. He decided to leave Honor to her own devices, and concentrated on steering Phoebe in the right direction.

He was seated next to Phoebe at dinner, and had to prompt her to speak with old Lord Kincaid on her left. Honor, who was across the table and five places down from him, had been seated next to Julian, at Andrew's own suggestion. She seemed to be involved in a deep discussion of politics with the group around her, led, as usual, by Julian, and he grinned, absently listening to Phoebe with one ear. Honor was quite the most amazing woman he had ever encountered, a genuine chameleon. He hoped that the evening would do a good deal to bolster her self-confidence. It was worth all the persuasion it had taken him to convince his old friend Anna Constantine, with whom he had enjoyed a long and diverting relationship, to cancel her acceptance.

Andrew was completely unaware of Bryonny's interested gaze upon him from across the table.

After dinner, someone suggested dancing, to Honor's complete dismay. The idea was taken up with enthusiasm, and they removed to the ballroom. One of the guests, unfortunately accomplished, sat down at the pianoforte and struck up a melody which seemed to please his compatriots, for they quickly chose partners and began the first of the patterns. Honor, who had not danced for years, slipped out onto the terrace and watched the festivities through the open window. The music drifted pleasantly out over the garden. Andrew led Phoebe out in the first dance, which she managed prettily. And after that Honor saw that Andrew was never without a partner. Indeed, it was clear to her that he had never had a problem attracting women, for there seemed to be a constant flutter around him, and she could hardly be surprised.

She turned away and leaned over the railing, looking down into the garden, feeling completely out of place. Dinner had been tolerable; in fact, Julian had gone out of his way to make it enjoyable and she had not once been in a position where she was forced to offer up social nonsense. It had been fascinating to listen to Sir Henry pompously carry on about politics from further on down the table, and she knew perfectly well what Julian had been doing when he had introduced the subject. And she had enjoyed the discussion with her own dinner companions. But she could not fully participate in the world to which she had been born, nor appear too much at ease. She could not for one moment allow herself to forget her position in Sir Henry's household. It was all so difficult, these layers upon layers of deception. She started at the sound of footsteps behind her, and quickly turned.

"There you are, Honor!" Andrew came up to her, looking amused. "What are you doing hiding out here? I've been looking everywhere for you! Could it be that you did not want to be found?"

"I felt in need of some fresh air, my lord," she said lamely.

"Ah," said Andrew. "Your lungs must be bursting with the stuff by now."

"I am perfectly content, my lord. Shouldn't you be inside looking after Miss Rutherford?"

"Miss Rutherford," he said, highly entertained, "will survive without me for a few minutes. As will I without her. But nevertheless I am bound and determined to achieve my end."

"And what end is that?" Honor asked tightly.

"I am going to see Phoebe Rutherford a married woman by the end of this Season if it kills me," he said. "Now, enough about that, for I have another end in mind, and this one is much more immediate. I don't suppose that this sudden need for fresh air has something to do with the fact that dancing was not taught at the convent?"

"That was a consideration, it is true," she said, wishing she hadn't brought up the subject of Phoebe at all. It had only forced her to hear the worst from his own lips.

"Then it's high time the situation was amended, and I am in the perfect position to do so." He bowed. "Miss Winslow, may I have this next dance?"

"Oh . . . no, my lord, I beg you! I will make a fool of myself!" She backed off in alarm as he stepped toward her.

"Not if no one can see you," he said, pulling her into his arms without giving her a chance to say anything else.

"But I do not dance," Honor protested, trying to break away. "Not at all!"

"That is the purpose of the exercise, Honor." He slipped an arm around her back and took her hand in his. "It is very simple. One, two, three. Follow me."

Honor's heart sank. There was nothing she could do short of creating a scene. Oh, why could he not leave her in peace? But he was already pulling her into the first of the movements. She had never felt so awkward in her life.

"Please, not on my toes, Miss Winslow. If you continue looking down, I shall suspect you of trampling them on purpose. Look into my eyes, and just relax. It is very difficult to dance with a broomstick."

Honor reluctantly smiled and looked up into his eyes. She forgot everything she had been trying so hard to remember. His arm tightened slightly on her back as she relaxed into his arms, and he drew her closer, spinning her around in circle after circle. She went with him, her body reading his every move as if she had been doing it all of her life.

"That is very much better, Miss Winslow," Andrew said, grinning down at her. "One would think you'd been at this for years!"

Honor laughed breathlessly. "It's very dizzying, isn't it? I'm surprised it's allowed after dinner."

"That, my dear Honor, is the only time it is allowed. And preferably after a large quantities of champagne have been consumed, but we shall have to wait for the end of the war for that. Have you ever had champagne, Honor?"

She shook her head and closed her eyes as the garden went around once again.

"Then that is another situation I shall have to remedy, and I hope in the near future." He looked down at her.

Her head was flung back and her eyes were closed, the dark lashes fanned out on cheeks that were flushed. Little wisps of curl clung to her forehead. She had a smile of sheer delight on her face. She looked radiant, almost a different person, relaxed, happy, and very, very beautiful.

Andrew's step slowed slightly, and he stared at her in amazement.

"Why, Honor," he finally said, his voice very low. "Can it be that I have actually given you some pleasure? Is this the woman you have been hiding from me all this time?"

Honor's eyes flew open, and in that unguarded moment they went to his and held them, filled with unspoken things. Andrew's step stopped completely, and Honor's breath caught in her throat at the expression on his face. He was still holding her, but his hands had tightened on her arms and his eyes seemed to search her very soul.

Terribly alarmed, she twisted away. "Please let me go, my lord. You're hurting me!"

He released her, but his eyes stayed locked on hers, and his breathing was fast and uneven. "Honor . . . What the devil . . . ?"

"I . . . I must go, my lord. It is late, and I must be up early with the children."

"What?" He ran a hand over his eyes. "Oh, yes, of course. It must be midnight, then—pumpkin time." But he did not smile.

"Well past, I should think. Good night, my lord, and . . . and thank you for teaching me the dance. I enjoyed it." She turned on her heel and fled.

Andrew stood looking after her, a dazed expression on his face.

* * *

He was still standing there five minutes later when Julian came out on the terrace.

"Ah, there you are, my friend. I was wondering where you'd gone to. Would you like to join me in a cheroot? . . . Andrew? What's the matter? You look as if you've been hit over the head."

"I think I have been," Andrew said slowly. "With a glass slipper, no less."

"Oh," said Julian, smiling. "Our dear Miss Winslow? I saw her flying up the stairs a few minutes ago. She looked as if she had five devils on her tail. You didn't do anything indelicate, did you, Andrew?"

"Indelicate? No, of course not. I danced with her, and stepped on her dress like a clod. She excused herself and went to repair it. Julian, how much do you know about the girl?"

Julian considered. "Oh, hardly anything. The connection was through her father, who lived not far from the Abbey before he died. Why do you ask?"

"No particular reason," Andrew said casually. "I just wondered what age she was when she entered the convent. She's not very accustomed to male company, is she?"

"I wouldn't say that. It seems that she took you straight in hand for that time you were laid up."

"Mm. Maybe it's just social ineptness. Why did she leave the convent?"

Julian looked at Andrew more carefully. "I hardly know the particulars. You'll have to ask her. She merely wrote to me and requested a post."

"I just wondered how close she'd come to taking vows."

"She must have hit you fairly hard with that slipper, my lad. I shouldn't play around with these convent girls, Andrew. It's not safe. That reminds me—have you heard what the Regent's latest doxy pulled?" He launched into an outrageous story and soon had Andrew laughing, but neither man's mind was on the joke.

This is the monstrosity in love, lady,
That the will is infinite, and the execution confined.

—William Shakespeare, *Troilus and Cressida*, I, iii

Honor, despite how tired she was, could not sleep; she finally gave up the effort. She shrugged herself into her robe and went to the window, staring out across the moon-washed grass. She saw only one thing: Andrew's face looking down into hers.

How much had he sensed? Too much, that was for certain from the look on his face. But perhaps he would think it was just the moonlight and the dance, and the effect of the claret at dinner.

That was absurd. If the situation had been reversed, she would have known perfectly well that something was extremely peculiar. One didn't look into someone's eyes and feel as if a keg of gunpowder had gone off. Nor have the full touch of another person's soul on one's own. There was only one thing to do, and that was to pretend that it had never happened. Let him think he was mad for once. She went back to bed.

The thought that he might be mad never crossed Andrew's mind. He was preoccupied with wondering what, exactly, had passed between Honor and himself. It was the most extraordinary thing that had ever happened to him, as if for one split second they had been the same person.

Morning broke, and he was still awake trying to puzzle it out. He had had two severe shocks: the first was the realization that he had fallen deeply in love with Honor Winslow. He could not pinpoint when or even how it had happened, only that it had always been there in some fashion and had simply grown stronger until it had come bursting into his mind last night, like the sun exploding over the horizon. The second was that there was something very wrong.

When he had locked eyes with her, it was as if a mask

had fallen away from her. He had suddenly seen clearly all the feelings she had so successfully been hiding from him. The strongest had been love: acute and overwhelming love. But then he had seen the hesitancy and guilt beneath, and finally deep unhappiness.

Andrew stared at the ceiling, his hands locked behind his head. He loved Honor. Marvelous. Now that he finally realized it, what in the name of heaven was he going to do about it? That was a fine question. He had sworn he would never marry without love; it hadn't occurred to him that the woman he loved might not want to marry him. It also hadn't occurred to him that once he found her, he might not be able to live without her. Honor. All this time and he had been falling in love with her, not aware of it. How stupid could a man be? The hell of it was that he knew without a doubt that she was equally in love with him and he hadn't realized that either. How long had that been going on? he wondered. And it must have caused her great unhappiness, thinking him to be indifferent, the lord amusing himself with the servant. He winced, thinking of some of their conversations. How was he going to convince Honor that their different stations made no difference to him?

If he could only find out more about her background, which he was sure was perfectly respectable, he could use that information to convince her that she was not beneath him. That *was* the argument, wasn't it? Or was it? He wasn't sure that he even knew anymore. What in sweet hell had gone on between them, anyway? It wasn't just a matter of realizing he loved her, and she him; this communication had gone far beyond the normal bounds of love as he understood it. It had felt so familiar, so right, somehow. And Honor knew it.

He thought of the first time he had seen her, of the stirring of something indefinable. It had been faint and simple in the beginning, but with time it had grown, becoming stronger and more complex between them. There had been his accident; that was when it had really begun. She had been the first thing in his mind when he had come around, and the last thing before the fever. There had been the sense of warmth and comfort, and ease and old friendship. And then Christmas Eve, when he had kissed her. Dear God. He flushed, remembering how powerful that had been. And Honor always after that pushing him away, shutting him out. . . .

And no wonder. It was certainly no surprise that last night had scared her. She knew him well enough to know what he would do. And as soon as it was decent to pay a morning call, he would do it.

Honor had just sent the girls off with Betsy for a walk and was organizing the day's lessons when she felt eyes on her and looked up, startled. Her hand froze. "My lord . . ." she said uncertainly, rising. "The girls are not here at the moment."

Andrew came through the door. "Simms informed me."

"Oh. Well, Miss Rutherford is not up yet."

"I am not interested in Miss Rutherford's whereabouts. I have come to see you, Honor."

"Me? Why me, my lord?" She could not read his face.

"Oh, I think you know the reason very well. In fact, I am sure you were expecting me."

Honor's heart sank. "I do not care for guessing games, my lord."

"Nor do I." He walked up to her and took the papers she was still holding from her hand. "I speak of last night, Honor."

"Last . . . last night?"

"Yes." He knew he had been right. He saw it on her face and in her eyes. He led her to a chair and drew another up next to it, sitting down opposite her and looking at her intently. "Last night when we were dancing, something happened, something interesting."

"Interesting, my lord? Do you mean that I enjoyed myself? I hope you have not come to start up on that again, because it is most unkind—"

"Honor, for pity's sake, leave it. You know what I am speaking of. Can you not tell me the truth even now?"

She colored. "You confuse me, my lord. I feel there is something urgent you are asking me, and I have no answer for you, because I do not understand the question."

Andrew's eyes raked her face and he saw her embarrassment, which he could well understand. He also saw that he would not get anything more from her, no matter how hard he pressed. He was quiet for a moment, then stood.

"As you will have it, Honor," he finally said. "But you know exactly what I am talking about. If you won't discuss it with me now, I shall wait until you will. I give you fair warning. And you of all people know that I do not give up until I get what I want."

She stood also, her face crimson. "Good day, my lord."

He didn't bother to answer. He turned on his heel and went out.

Honor sank back down on the chair, her entire body beginning to tremble. She did not move for a very long time.

Much to her amazement, Andrew left her alone. For the next fortnight she saw him only when he came to take the girls for a treat. She was never invited along, although he treated her cordially enough. But for the first time since she had known him, he made absolutely no effort toward her. He behaved exactly as any member of the aristocracy would behave toward a governess, and she found that, rather than relieving her, it distressed her deeply. He was brutally beating her down with her own weapon, and they were both aware of it.

The Season had arrived in earnest and Honor suffered silently as he arrived in the evenings to escort Phoebe and Arabella to the opera, the theater, and balls and routs when Sir Henry was unavailable, which was most of the time. It cut deeply to know that despite what had passed between them, he was still callously pursuing Phoebe. And Phoebe made it worse by constantly dropping little hints of what they had done together, and what they were going to do. That evening, she knew, the three Rutherfords were attending the Crawford ball, and Andrew was to be there. She had watched them leave, Phoebe beautifully dressed in light blue figured silk and lace. Honor felt like the gray little partridge left behind as ever, and she had to chastise herself for being absurd, and remind herself that it was she who had chosen it to be this way.

* * *

To her complete amazement, Betsy delivered a note to her at eight o'clock the next morning, the second week in April. It was addressed in Andrew's writing.

Dear Miss Winslow,
Please would you dress Jocie and yourself in riding habits and come directly down? I have horses saddled and waiting. I have decided it is time for a riding lesson. Please consider this an avuncular request, not a royal command.

> Your servant, etc.,
> Chesney

Honor read the missive four times before deciding that there was no possible way she could refuse, given the way he'd worded the thing. Clever devil, she thought. Now what was he up to? But her spirits cheered immeasurably as she sent the reply with Betsy and dressed. She and Jocie were downstairs within fifteen minutes.

"Good morning, Miss Winslow," said Andrew, who was casually lounging in the front hall. "Hello, Jocie, my dear. Come along now, let's not waste any more time. The park is fairly empty at this hour, and we want it to stay that way."

So saying, he went out the front door, leaving Honor to stare at his back suspiciously.

They mounted up and rode through the streets, Andrew chatting away about nothing in particular. Honor was still puzzling out what Andrew was up to when they went through the gates of the park and he turned to them and said, "Now. Pay attention, both of you. Miss Winslow, I have noticed that you have excellent hands, but your deportment is lamentable. You have an alarming tendency to list to starboard, and this matter really must be corrected. Jocie, you're not much better, and it's what comes of being allowed to ride astride. I told your father he should have put you on a sidesaddle from the time you were six and not left it so late. I've given the matter a certain amount of thought, and I believe I know what the problem is. The first principle of a sidesaddle is this . . ."

He talked for some time, and then put them through their paces, watching carefully and making suggestions, which Honor found were very helpful. He soon had them both in fits of laughter as he imitated their mistakes for them, and finally, after an hour of instruction, he declared the lesson finished.

"Let's have a peaceful walk up to the pond, shall we?" he said, setting off. People were beginning to trickle into the park, and every now and then Andrew would exchange a greeting, but he didn't stop for conversation until they came in sight of a young man who appeared to be a long-lost friend of Andrew's, and he excused himself and spurred his horse ahead, leaving Jocie and Honor to catch up to him in their own time. Honor paled as they approached.

" . . . heard you had been invalided out," Andrew was saying. "Where have you been keeping yourself?"

"I've been staying in the country," the fair-haired man said. "I had a long recovery to make."

"Sounds nasty. See here, you must meet my niece Jocelyn and her governess, Miss Winslow. They both take a great interest in the war." He turned in his saddle. "Ah, good, here you are. This is an old friend, Captain Lambert. He was with Wellington in the Peninsula, Jocie, with the Grenadiers."

"How thrilling," said Jocie rapturously.

"How do you do," said Captain Lambert with a smile. "Miss Winslow?" He bowed, and then gave her a puzzled look. "Have we met before?"

"I don't believe so, sir," Honor said with as much aplomb as she could gather. Her heart was pounding violently.

"As Miss Winslow has only just come out of a convent, I think it highly unlikely," Andrew said with a smile.

"Oh, I beg your pardon. But as I was saying, the campaign was well worth it. It seems that Boney is finally on the run and we should see an end to the war any day. I just heard that Soult is in fast retreat and Wellington is on his heels. I, for one, couldn't be more pleased. I'd stop a dozen bullets to see a British victory."

"I'm delighted that it appears you won't have to. When did you return to England?"

"Not until three months ago. I was fortunate to have made it out at all."

"I'm sorry to hear that. What happened, if you don't mind my asking."

"I took a bullet in the lung. I was lucky to have had a good surgeon, and the little soldier to take me off the field and keep me breathing till he got there, and then after, when they swore I was finished."

"The little soldier?" asked Andrew, puzzled.

Honor moved ahead with Jocie out of earshot, much to Jocie's extreme disappointment. But Honor could not bear to hear another word, for she well remembered nursing Stephen Lambert, and was thanking God that he'd been too ill to take in much of anything, including her own muddy appearance.

"The little soldier of the Peninsula, Caro Manleigh," said the captain. "Surely you've heard tell of her, General Lord Peninghurst's daughter? She had extraordinary healing skills."

"Ah, yes," said Andrew. "A distant cousin, as it happens. I met her once at Chesney when she was hardly out of leading strings. As I remember, I brought her late into tea covered in grass stains and received a scolding. What's become of her, I wonder? Is she still in the Peninsula?"

"I have no idea," said Captain Lambert. "But I'd like to be able to thank her one day for what she did. It was a shame about her father. By the way, my condolences on your brother's death."

"Thank you," said Andrew. "Speaking of my brother, my niece and her companion seem to have gone ahead. I should catch them up. I hope to see you soon, Lambert."

"Good-bye," said the captain, and rode off in the other direction.

"Why did you ride off, Miss Winslow?" Andrew asked curiously, posting up to her side. "I thought you thrived on discussions of the war."

"I did not think when the conversation turned to bullet wounds that the topic was any longer appropriate for Jocie's ears," she said stiffly, doing her best to appear unconcerned.

"Bloodthirsty little Jocie? But I suppose you're right. As you once pointed out to me, she shouldn't be encouraged. But it's hard on her, all of this business. My brother treated her as the son he never had, and she conformed admirably. And then poor George died, and Jocie had to deal with Sir Henry and a whole new life and expectations of her. It's no wonder she developed a religious mania, begging your pardon, of course, Miss Winslow. I am very keen, however, on encouraging this new idea of hers to become a lady. In truth, I thought it would never happen, and it seems very much thanks to you that it has. So I thought that perhaps if I helped her out a little in ways that I am able, she might blossom under the attention. I did not want you to think that your own seat was the reason for the lesson.''

"Naturally not, my lord. Although I am fully aware that it could use a great deal of improvement.''

"A certain amount of instruction would not go awry,'' Andrew said with a little smile. "But tell me, Miss Winslow, for I have wondered since the first day I saw you out. Where was it you did learn to ride?''

"I . . . I learned from my father, my lord.''

"I have to assume he taught you as my brother taught Jocie. You learned astride, did you not?''

Honor hesitated.

"Come, Miss Winslow. It was not hard to come to the deduction. I understood that you rode Cabal like the wind after I'd been injured, and he is not an easy animal to master, let alone one to allow a stranger on his back, especially after such a fright as he must have taken. As he wore my saddle, I only wonder how you maintained the skill after so many years with the nuns.''

Honor's eyes fastened on her mare's ears. "I suppose that I remembered when necessity struck. There was no time to think about it. And I did manage to ride at the convent, so I was not completely unused to horses when I left.''

"I see. Why *did* you leave the convent, Miss Winslow?'' Andrew looked across at her, a little frown between his eyebrows.

"I was not meant for a religious life, my lord.''

"Indeed, I should think not,'' he said dryly. "Were you happy there?''

"Happy enough. But it is a part of my life that is finished. I'd prefer to leave it behind me.''

"Mm,'' Andrew said noncommittally. "Well, I think I

must spend more time teaching Jocie her seat so that she does not leave that behind her. She is of an age when she may ride to hounds, and I should hate to see her sliding off sideways over the first fence. But I speak of autumn. To be more immediate, I thought that tomorrow we might attend to Minnie's desire. There is a fair in Reading. It is a drive, but if you wouldn't mind that, would you allow the girls the pleasure?''

''It would make Minnie very happy, my lord.''

''Good. We'll make a party of it. You will come with us, naturally. That is, of course, if the preparations for Miss Rutherford's ball the following week do not keep you. But I imagine you have it very much under control. Let us hope the weather holds, for there is nothing worse than rain to dampen the spirit, don't you agree? Jocie,'' he called, ''please remember to sit up straight; you look like a sack of potatoes. Just think what your father would have said. Of course, he would no doubt have had you in breeches, so who am I to complain?''

He carried on in this same light vein until they had reached the house, and then he took his leave. Honor spent the rest of the morning sewing up Jocie's hem, which she would later have to unpick and do again.

The next morning Honor dressed the girls with a certain amount of trepidation. She could not be pleased with having to spend the entire day in Andrew's company, but she could not be displeased either, for she had missed him. It was safe, she told herself as she tied Minnie's hair ribbons, for the door between them was not only shut but also locked. Hadn't yesterday proved it? And what harm was there in a day's outing?

She brought the children downstairs at the appointed hour, only to find Phoebe in pelisse and bonnet, ready to go out.

''Good morning, Miss Rutherford,'' Honor said as she helped Minnie into her coat. She was amazed to find Phoebe up at the early hour, and wondered what possible engagement she could have.

''Good morning, Miss Winslow,'' Phoebe said with a condescending smirk that made Honor grit her teeth. It was fortunate, she thought, that she and the girls saw so little of Phoebe, or by now they would surely have come to blows.

"I do hope you will keep the children contained, Miss Winslow, for Lord Chesney and I will not wish to be bothered on our excursion. You understand, of course."

Honor stared at her. "You are coming with us, Miss Rutherford?" she managed to say.

"Naturally," said Phoebe with what was apparently meant to be a sophisticated air. "Lord Chesney and I thought the outing an amusing diversion for the children. He is so patient with them; I believe he has a strong sense of responsibility for his brother's offspring." She walked over to the mirror and adjusted the angle of her hat, then looked over her shoulder at Honor in a pitying fashion. "When we are married," she continued, "I do hope that Lord Chesney sees fit to send the girls away to school. It is such an advantage in life to make early connections. I am sure I have found it so myself. Of course it will mean your seeking another position, Miss Winslow, but I should be very happy to offer you a reference."

Jocie came to Honor's side. Knowing that Jocie had heard and must be at the very limit of self-control, given the violent grip she now had on the back of Honor's dress, Honor turned to her and gently said, "Do see where your sister has wandered, won't you, Jocelyn? She might well have gone into the morning room for the remainder of your mother's chocolate."

Jocie gave Honor a look brimming with pent-up hostility, but obeyed, clearly signalling her resentment.

Honor drew in a long, controlled breath, and faced Phoebe. "Miss Rutherford," she said as calmly as she could manage, "let me speak plainly with you, as we are apparently to spend a full day together. I do not mind what you say to me, for I am more than capable of dealing with your barbs. But the children are another matter. Minerva needs kindness and gentleness, and Jocelyn no less, although she is better prepared to meet the world. If you must be with us today, please observe this simple request and try not to upset the girls."

Phoebe gasped. "How dare you!" she said, her lips going white. "How *dare* you speak to me in such a manner!

I shall see you on the street for your impertinence—I shall
see that you are dismissed! I shall speak to my father and I
shall tell Lord Chesney—"

"You have something to tell me, Miss Rutherford?"

Andrew came through the hallway, handing his hat to
Spencer, who was looking thoroughly appalled.

"Oh . . . oh, my lord," said Phoebe, horrified but sinking a pretty curtsy. "I was just saying how we were looking
forward to the outing you have arranged. Do we begin at
once?"

Andrew gave Honor a quick, assessing glance. Her head
was turned away, but he could feel her suppressed fury.
Good, he thought to himself. It's better than nothing at all.
"We do begin," he said with an ironic smile. "Miss Winslow, shall we fetch the children? Miss Rutherford, I shall
meet you in the carriage.'

Jocelyn emerged with Minerva just as Phoebe was sweeping out the door. Minerva took one look and went flying to
Andrew.

He swept Minnie up in his arms and kissed her soundly.
"Well-met, little one," he said, giving her a squeeze.
"Shall we go?"

Minerva did not reply. Instead she looked darkly at the
door through which Phoebe had just vanished.

"Ah," said Andrew in a whisper. "I shouldn't worry
much about that. Let's go to see a proper fair, shall we,
Minnie?"

Minerva nodded, and Andrew put her down and took her
little hand, leading her out to the carriage. Honor and Jocelyn followed behind.

It was a sight, that was certain, an incredible spread of
booths and tents and signs proclaiming the most extraordinary of exhibits inside, from the Fireproof Lady to the
Smallest Man in the World. The crowd flowed around them,
and the air was full of talk and laughter. They watched a
puppet show, which had Minerva giggling helplessly, and
then Andrew took Jocie and Phoebe, who kept her arm
tucked securely in Andrew's as if it were permanently attached to his sleeve, to see a few of the less alarming exhibits, while Honor helped Minerva, for whom the exhibits

would have been unsuitable, select a stick with bright red streamers of ribbon attached to it.

"Oh, how droll," said Phoebe when they emerged from the tent containing the Elephant Woman. "You should have seen her, Miss Winslow! She looked exactly like an elephant, did she not, Lord Chesney, all thick and gray, with a nose as long as a trunk. I'm only surprised that she did not have tusks as well. I cannot think when I have been so entertained! It's a pity little Minerva could not see."

Minerva cast wondering eyes at the tent. "I want to see."

"She's not really an elephant, Minnie," said Jocie quickly, looking at Phoebe scathingly. "Just a fat old lady. It was very silly, wasn't it, Uncle Andrew?"

"It was indeed," he agreed as Minerva's face crumpled with disappointment. "Come, I shall buy you all a sweet," Andrew said, leading them on.

They ate their sweets sitting on a bench, and watched the people parade by. And then there was suddenly a commotion and a great shriek rent the air.

"Stop, thief!" a voice screamed like a steam whistle. "My reticule, he stole my reticule! There he is—catch him!" Honor turned to the source of the noise and gaped with astonishment at the sight that met her eyes. There was no mistaking the enormous form and improbable red hair.

"Uncle Andrew, look, it's Mrs. Lipp, our housekeeper!" cried Jocie in the same moment.

Andrew shot Honor one amazed look, then jumped to his feet and started over to her, Jocie on his heels.

"Jocie, do come back!" cried Honor, but Jocie paid no attention. Honor quickly turned to Phoebe. "Stay here with Minerva," she said curtly, and ran off to where Jocie had disappeared into the quickly forming crowd. By the time she had managed to push herself through, Mrs. Lipp was sobbing hysterically, and neither Andrew nor Jocie was anywhere to be seen. Honor looked around desperately, pushed her way back out again, and finally saw Jocie shouting encouragement to Andrew, who had collared a scrawny little man and with one right hook to his jaw had laid him out on the ground. Two burly constables materialized out of nowhere. They congratulated Andrew, dragged the man to his feet, and Mrs. Lipp's reticule was duly returned, to her effusive thanks. The entertainment over, the crowd dissipated and Honor turned to Jocie.

"Jocelyn, I am absolutely furious with you! You know better than to go running off!"

"But, Honor, I saw the man running, and had to tell Uncle Andrew where he had gone! We caught him!"

"And you're a dear, sweet girl," sobbed Mrs. Lipp, her wig by now completely askew and in danger of falling off altogether, "and you are a true hero, my lord. Fancy your being here in my time of need!"

"But, Mrs. Lipp, what *are* you doing here? It is dangerous to be without an escort, as you have just seen!"

"Well, of course I have an escort," said Mrs. Lipp in injured tones. "He was buying tickets to the theater tent. We have friends in the next performance," she added grandly. "I was just going to rest my poor feet for a moment."

A man, for one could not call him a gentleman, as thin as Mrs. Lipp was fat, approached. "Here we are, Lavinia, my dear," he said solicitously. "I had to use influence, for it was all sold out, but . . . Have you met friends, my dear?" he added uncertainly, taking in Andrew and Honor.

"Lord Chesney, Miss Winslow, my fiancé, Mr. Pomphrey," said Mrs. Lipp in as close to an approximation of shyness as she could manage, the expression on her huge face extraordinarily bizarre as she batted very long, very black eyelashes.

"Your *fiancé?*" said Honor with difficulty, struggling not to laugh. It did not help that Andrew was making a slightly strangled noise next to her. "My . . . my felicitations . . . I had no idea."

"We have known each other these many years, but recently renewed our acquaintance with a happy result." As she spoke, she hastily rearranged her coiffure. "Lord Chesney rescued me, Hubert! A thief stole my reticule and he returned it!"

"Oh, my poor poppet! I am much obliged, your lordship," said Mr. Pomphrey, shuffling his feet.

Andrew bowed. "At your service. If you will excuse us, we must return to our party. Jocie?" He took her arm in an iron grip. As they walked back toward the benches, he said,

"Don't you ever do such a foolish thing again as chase after me. You have caused Miss Winslow no end of distress, and despite your penchant for adventure, you *will* learn to behave." Dismissing the subject, he turned to Honor with an expression of sheer delight. "Mrs. Lipp is everything you have told me, and more. And Mr. Pomphrey—how very well-suited they are! Jack Sprat and his . . . Honor? Honor, what is it?"

Honor's face had gone white. "Oh, no . . ." she whispered. Phoebe was deeply engaged in conversation with a group of her young friends, her back to the bench, which was empty. "Quickly, Andrew, it's Minerva! She's disappeared! I left her here with Phoebe, but she's gone!"

At that moment Phoebe turned and saw them, and came hurrying breathlessly over to Andrew. "Oh, my lord, you were magnificent—"

Andrew grabbed her by the arm and pulled her to one side. "Where is Minerva?" he demanded in a low hiss.

"Lord Chesney, you're hurting me! She's just there on the bench, for heaven's sake, where I left her . . . Oh," she finished in a small voice, seeing that it was empty and Honor and Jocie were glaring at her. "I told her to stay," she said plaintively.

"How could you be such a ninny-hammer! You know that Minerva cannot be left for a moment! Now, for the love of God, stay here with your friends, for I dare not leave you alone either. Jocie, you stay here with your stepsister. And do as you're told. Miss Winslow, come with me." He pulled her off.

"Where could she be?" Honor asked with a shaking voice, hurrying to keep up with his pace. "Poor Minnie, she might have gone with anyone! I should never have left her with Phoebe!"

"Phoebe is not capable of thinking of anyone but herself for more than two minutes, if that, but it wasn't your fault. Here, you take the booths to the left, and I'll go to the right. I'll meet you back here in fifteen minutes. At least I can trust you not to get lost." He moved quickly away and was soon lost in the crowds.

Honor asked at every booth, but no one had seen a little girl of Minerva's description. Her heart pounded in sickening panic, and she felt no compunction about stopping people of every walk of life in the street. But no one had seen Minerva. Feeling utterly hopeless, she finally returned to the spot where Andrew had left her. And then she saw him, coming toward her with Minerva held fast in his arms, the ribbons waving from the stick she held. His eyes found hers through the crowd, and he smiled, and it was as if a world of communication had passed between them in that one look.

Honor forgot everything in her flood of relief. She picked up her skirts and ran furiously toward him. "Andrew! Oh, Andrew, you found her!"

He laughed and held out one arm to catch her. Honor, oblivious of having crashed into him, took Minnie's face between her hands, laughing and crying at the same time as she kissed her cheeks and smoothed her hair, babbling in her relief, not even aware of Andrew's arm tight around her waist.

"Minnie, you scared me half to death," Honor said severely when she had recovered herself. "You mustn't ever, ever go off on your own!" She looked up at Andrew. "Where was she?"

"Minnie," he said with a smile, putting Minerva down and straightening again to meet Honor's eyes, "went to see the Elephant Woman for herself, didn't you, Minnie?"

Minerva nodded solemnly.

"And she found it to be just as we said. Thank God for the toy you bought her, Honor, or I might never have spotted her. It occurred to me that her curiosity might have gotten the better of her—isn't that right, sweeting?"

Minerva nodded again and smiled. "I saw her, Honor. I went under the tent."

"So you did, my darling, but you must promise me you will always stay close."

"Phoebe did not care."

"Perhaps not, Minerva, but you must think of the people who love you," said Andrew. "You do not like us to worry, do you?"

She shook her head and looked down at her shoes.

"All right, then. We'll forget about it now, for we're very happy to have you back safe and sound. But I think we have had quite enough excitement for one day. Let us collect the others and go home." He reached out for Honor's hand and placed it securely in the crook of his elbow, and took Minnie's hand in his own. "Hold on tightly, both of you, for I don't intend to let either of you go." He gave Honor a funny little smile that made her heart jump alarming. "Not today, not ever," he said softly, and headed off.

They returned home to see the Marquess of Hambledon's carriage outside. Spencer, at attention in the hall, indicated the drawing room, including Honor in the gesture with a doubtful expression, and, puzzled, she handed the children over to Betsy, who took them upstairs.

Sir Henry and Julian were inside, talking intently, but as they saw Phoebe, Honor, and Andrew, they both rose to their feet.

"Have you had a good day?" asked Sir Henry, smiling meaningfully at his daughter.

"Well enough, Papa," she lied. It had been a terrible day, and Lord Chesney had privately given her the coldest lecture of her life on the way to the carriage. She had sulked all the way home, internally swearing vengeance against Honor Winslow and the blasted children who had put her in such a position. It wasn't her fault that Minerva was addlebrained.

"We have had some wonderful news today," said Julian. "I came straight from the Ministry to inform Sir Henry, but I am sure you will all be pleased to hear it as well. Napoleon has fallen. The war is over."

"But this is marvelous!" cried Andrew. "We knew it was coming, but this is cause for celebration!"

Honor sank into a chair. "Over. Thank God." The nightmare had finally ended. All those years, all the lives lost. It was over.

Andrew gave her a quick look of concern. "Miss Winslow?" he asked gently, wishing he could take her in his arms then and there. "Perhaps you should go upstairs and rest now. It's been a strenuous day."

Honor smiled up at him. "I thank you for your concern, my lord, but I am very well. Indeed, I have experienced worse days than this one."

Julian raised an eyebrow. "Was your outing unusually invigorating?"

"If you consider Mrs. Lipp's reticule being stolen by a man of unfortunately low moral character, and first Jocie and then Minerva deciding to strike out on her own, I suppose you might call it invigorating," Andrew said smoothly.

"Mrs. Lipp? She went with you?" asked Sir Henry with an expression of horror, no doubt imagining the sight of his beautiful Phoebe strolling along in tandem with a woman who looked as good as a streetwalker.

"Not exactly," said Andrew. "We . . . ah, ran into her. It seems that Mrs. Lipp has been having a successful Season of her own; she has been offered for. She was with her fiancé, a Mr. Pomphrey, I believe?" His eyes danced at Honor.

"Yes, Mr. Hubert Pomphrey. I . . . I believe they had connections with the theater troupe."

Sir Henry flushed deep red. "That's gratitude for you! I take a poor relation practically off the streets, rescuing her from that disgraceful company, and what does she do—she goes running straight back the minute she sets foot in London! I should have known! And after giving her free room and board—"

"She looked very happy," said Andrew, grinning. "I believe she is in her element."

Honor smiled in return. "Yes. I think it is just how she must feel. It really was a . . . an interesting day," she said, standing. "Lord Chesney was responsible for returning both the reticule and Minerva. Thank you for taking us, my lord."

"It was indeed my pleasure."

"It is such good news you bring, Lord Hambledon. If you'll excuse me . . . ?"

"Certainly, Miss Winslow." Julian smiled at her, then turned his attention back to the company.

Andrew's eyes followed Honor out of the room.

Julian and Andrew left shortly thereafter, and Sir Henry demanded a private word with his daughter. "Well? *Well?*"

"Well, what, Papa?" asked Phoebe, a little startled by the intensity in her father's eyes.

"Have you made any progress? Has he given you any indication that he intends to offer for you?"

"Not yet, Papa," she said with a little pout. "He cannot be unaware of my feelings, for I have given him every attention, but he is so circumspect. I begin to despair he will ever offer, Papa!" She wasn't about to tell her father her part in the final debacle that afternoon.

"We cannot afford the delay, not now, with the war suddenly over." He paced the room. "If you don't marry him soon, we shall be ruined. Ruined, do you understand? There will be no more parties, no more pretty dresses, and you will never find a husband willing to marry you."

"But what more can I do, Papa? I have blushed and simpered and done all of the things you told me, and although he has been attentive, not one hint has passed his lips concerning marriage!"

Sir Henry looked at his daughter with disgust. "Then find some other game to play. You are a peahen, Phoebe. If you see that a tactic isn't working, then you must find another one that does."

"But what, Papa?" said Phoebe helplessly.

"I don't know, girl! He is a man, you are a woman. Think of something. I do not doubt his intentions, but I cannot wait until the end of the Season."

"Yes, Papa," said Phoebe, the light beginning to dawn.

"When do you next see him?" Sir Henry demanded, wondering how soon they could bring the matter to a close. His debts were closing in about him, and even the large sums of money he had been receiving from the French government had not been enough. And now that source had dried up overnight.

"Why, at my ball, Papa, three nights hence. Had you forgotten?"

"Ah, yes," said Sir Henry thoughtfully. "Yes, yes, indeed! That could be it, Phoebe. He is paying for it, after all. Perhaps he intends to speak with you then. You might indicate your willingness. Now, go, my dear. I have work to do."

Phoebe left him, her head full of plans. There had been a situation not unlike her own in *The Feckless Folly of Lady Lucinda*. The hero, Lord Rockinghurst, had not realized that Lady Lucinda was in love with him, although he nurtured a private passion for her in his breast. But he had not wanted to frighten her away, and so he had been proper and distant, although he contrived to be in her company as often as possible. Yes, that was it exactly! Her beloved Lord Chesney was protecting her from his own passion! She could scarcely wait until the night of her ball to unleash his desire. She scurried off.

Honor felt an odd tug at the corners of her consciousness that night, something insistent that pulled her up from the depths of sleep. She lay in bed for a moment, focusing, but it was gone, and she sighed and turned over, thinking of Andrew. And then she heard the sound of something hitting her window. There was a long pause and then it came again. She climbed out of bed and threw up the sash, looking out into the garden, one hand rubbing the sleep from her eyes. She could see nothing, and leaned out further, looking up to see if perhaps something was falling off the roof.

A low and familiar laugh floated up to her. "If you lean out any further, you shall fall straight into my arms, Honor. Won't you come down and accommodate me in a more conventional manner?"

She turned her head in sharp surprise and knocked it on the sill. "Andrew!" she whispered, rubbing her scalp. "What are you doing down there?"

He stepped out of the shadows into a pool of moonlight and grinned up at her. "Playing Romeo, my dear, what else? Dress and come down, Honor, before we wake up the household. I desire to speak with you."

"You're mad!" she said, but she drew her head back in and quickly pulled off her nightgown in favor of a warm dress. She tiptoed down the stairs, through the hushed house, and softly let herself out onto the terrace. Andrew appeared at her side as if by magic. His eyes were bright and his cheeks were lightly flushed. She thought he must have been drinking, but when he spoke, he seemed completely sober.

"I wondered if you'd heard me calling you. It took a very long time to wake you," he said softly. "You sleep deeply."

"I am not accustomed to having stones thrown at my window," Honor replied with an attempt at severity.

"Ah, but I'm becoming most adept at my aim. Come, we'll go to the end of the garden. I do not want to conduct this conversation in a whisper." He took her by the arm and led her down the steps to a stand of trees a good two hundred yards away, where there was a stone bench, and he pulled her down onto it.

"What is it that you want, my lord? I cannot think this is proper behavior for—"

"Honor, you shall call me Andrew if it kills you. And you have not a leg to stand on when it comes to proper behavior. Your halo is tarnished, my love. You have tried to mislead me—in a number of different directions, I might add—but you have failed."

"I . . . What do you mean, Andrew?" she said nervously, clutching her hands in her lap.

"Better. Much better," he said with satisfaction. "To begin with, I had a most interesting letter three days ago from St. Mary's Convent."

"A letter?" repeated Honor faintly.

"Indeed. I wrote to the mother superior concerning your time there. A simple inquiry regarding my nieces' governess. The mother superior was away, but her assistant, Sister Agnes, was more than happy to answer in her absence."

Honor shut her eyes and leaned her head back against the bench. It was all over.

"Why did you let me think you had been a novice, Honor? You're not even a Catholic, for God's sake—you're as Church of England as I am!"

Honor's eyes flew open in sheer astonishment.

"Sister Agnes kindly explained the circumstances to me."

"The . . . the circumstances?" Honor could hardly breathe through her relief. But *how* had Sister Agnes known what to say? It had been a private agreement between Julian, the mother superior, and herself that no one should know about Honor Winslow. There *was* no story! She had her answer in the next moment.

"Yes. Julian was not inclined to tell me about them himself when I asked, and referred me to you, but I knew perfectly well he would never have recommended you for the position of governess if he hadn't known something about you. I also knew perfectly well that I would get no answers from you myself. Why could you not tell me, Honor? There is no shame in impoverishment, is there?''

Honor put her head in her hands, overcome by a terrible desire to laugh. Julian had gone into action, no doubt spurred by his friend's curiosity and knowing him well enough to know that he was not a man inclined to let a matter rest. He had obviously given the story to Sister Agnes with just enough truth mixed in so that Andrew, with his acute perception, would not question it. ''It was not your concern,'' she finally said in a muffled voice.

''Not my *concern?*'' Andrew stared at her. ''For the love of God, Honor, it's more than my concern! You know that as well as I do! I have had enough of these games—I want an answer and I want it now, and you are damned well going to give it to me if I have to throttle it out of you!''

''What answer?'' she said helplessly. ''What answer can I possibly give you?''

''Honor,'' he said simply. ''Look me in the eye and deny that you love me.''

At that her head shot up, her entire body suddenly cold and then hot with shock.

He took her chin in his hand and forced her to meet his eyes. ''Lie to me now, Honor. You know you cannot.''

His eyes burned into hers, demanding, insistent, and she felt a physical urgency coming from him, an excitement she had never before encountered. She was not strong enough to push him away any longer, did not want to push him away . . .

''Oh, God!'' she cried, wrenching away from him. ''I cannot deny it, you know I cannot, but you must leave it, Andrew. For both our sakes, you must leave it!'' She closed herself against him, and felt as if she had cut off one of her own limbs.

He drew in his breath sharply, as if she had struck him. And she had, in the most brutal way possible. She only knew that she had to get away; she could not bear this terrible pain another moment. She rose and blindly stumbled toward the trees, tears streaming unbidden down her face.

But there was no escape. He was behind her and his hands

were on her shoulders, sharply turning her around. His face was stripped raw.

"I will never leave it, Honor," he said hoarsely. "Never. What is between us I will never let go. And whatever it is you are trying to keep from me, I will find it out. Do you understand? I *will* find it out. You cannot shut me out forever."

He abruptly let her go and disappeared into the darkness, the very air reverberating with his frustration and anger.

12

Framed to make women false.

—William Shakespeare, *Othello*, II, i

Honor went downstairs the next morning with a splitting headache. She was in no mood to deal with Arabella's vagaries but she had been summoned by Betsy, something about Arabella calling for the smelling salts.

"My lady, you called for me?" she said, entering the drawing room to find Arabella not swooning, but pacing frantically and looking as if she were about to tear her hair out.

"Oh, Honor, I did! The most appalling thing has happened and I simply don't know what I am to do!"

"Now, calm down, my lady, and whatever it is, we shall take care of it. Has there been trouble with Mrs. Spencer again about the ball?"

"No, no, you don't understand—it is Lord Chesney!"

Honor's hand went to her throat. "Lord Chesney—has something happened to him?" she asked sharply.

"Not that I know of," said Arabella, completely unaware of the shock she had just administered, and not seeming to

notice that Honor's face had paled, then flooded with color.
"But the ball is in two days' time and I have just had a note
from him. He's been called out of town on business! How
he could go when he knows I need him—he does say that I
have *carte blanche* concerning the cost, but what am I to do
about everything else? . . . Honor?"

"Yes, my lady," said Honor is an abstracted manner.
Andrew had gone out of town, but why? And where had he
gone?

"Honor, I declare you're not paying the least bit of attention to my problem! What am I going to do? There are
all the last-minute arrangements—and what is Phoebe going
to say when she hears? She'll have a collapse, and then
where will we be? Sir Henry is not going to be pleased!"

At that, Honor did focus. "Do you mean that Lord Chesney will not be back in time for the ball?"

"Naturally he will he here. He would never let me down
that badly. But that is not the point. Honor, *what* am I to
do?"

"Send a letter around to Lady Hambledon, my lady. I am
sure that she will know exactly what to do," said Honor
bleakly. Of course Andrew would never think of missing
Phoebe's ball.

"Oh, how absolutely inspired!" Arabella exclaimed, already fumbling for paper and pen. "I'll send a footman
around directly. What would we do without you, Honor!"

"I really don't know, my lady," said Honor, not thinking, and was relieved that Arabella appeared not to have
heard.

Bryonny duly arrived, and she, Honor, and Arabella spent
an hour discussing the finer details of the ball, Bryonny and
Honor both forestalling periodic attacks of hysterics with
diplomatic skill.

"But what am I to tell Phoebe?" Arabella finally said,
worrying at her skirt until the muslin was crushed under her
fingers.

"I don't see why Phoebe needs to be informed," said
Bryonny acerbically. "She hangs upon Andrew too much
as it is. It would do her good to spend more time with
people her own age."

Honor rose and went to the window, wishing she could escape altogether. And in the next moment, she wished she had.

"Yes," said Arabella sadly. "But she says she is in love with him, and Henry has so encouraged the match. He expects Andrew to offer on the night of the ball."

Bryonny stared at her as if she hadn't heard correctly. "Does he?" she said faintly.

"I suppose Andrew might well do so, too," said Arabella, "for aside from paying for it, he was very interested in seeing that she had the ball at the start of the Season. He really has been most attentive. I am surprised that he has decided on such a young girl, but the lands do run together, and there's the family connection, of course."

"Yes," said Bryonny, glancing over at Honor with a thoughtful expression. "Indeed. Well, then, everything seems to be decided. Now, is there anything else for today? Miss Winslow will see to the flowers, as we agreed. I do think that hanging baskets in the ballroom will do beautifully . . ."

Andrew returned to London in the late afternoon on the day of the infamous ball. He wearily descended from his carriage and was about to start up the front steps when, to his surprise and not particularly to his pleasure, the front door opened and Julian appeared.

"Just the man I was hoping to see," said Julian with a grin, coming down to him.

"And why is that?" said Andrew with a slight chill in his voice.

"My, my. Did your business not go well, then?"

"It did not go as I had hoped, no."

"It's a pity, because your sudden disappearance caused no end of a stir. Bryonny's been over sorting out the Rutherford mélange. Arabella has been threatening a swoon for three days now. Really, Andrew, your timing might have been better."

"My timing," said Andrew, "seems to have been impeccable."

"More impeccable than you realize. Congratulations, by the by. I hear you are to become affianced this evening."

Andrew's head snapped up, his eyes sharp. "I beg your pardon?"

Julian flicked a piece of lint from his coat. "Do you mean you are the last to hear? Ah, well, I understand it sometimes happens that way. I'm afraid I will be quite late, but I do so hope I don't miss the performance."

"To whom am I becoming affianced, if you don't mind my asking?"

"To Phoebe, of course. The entire household is in a stir about it, desperate to know if you have returned."

Andrew's eyes narrowed. "You jest, surely."

"Jest? I? Goodness, no. Bryonny heard it herself from Arabella, and Miss Winslow seems to concur. They are all quite sure of your intentions, with the exception of my wife, naturally. Young Phoebe is aquiver with excitement and Sir Henry is looking most anticipatory. You shall make a tasty meal, my friend."

Andrew drew a hand over his face. "I cannot believe it! How did such an absurd idea ever . . . ? Never mind. In that lunatic asylum anything could happen and apparently has . . ." He paused in mid-sentence. "Did you say that *Miss Winslow* thinks I have plans for Phoebe? That is too much to ask me to believe."

"Most assuredly. And Jocie has not wiped a scowl from her face since she heard the news from Phoebe. It seems that plans have been made in your absence, Andrew. You have returned just in time. I thought I might warn you."

"Thank you, Julian," said Andrew, frowning. "It would have been decidedly unpleasant to be unprepared."

"I owe you a few favors."

"About Miss Winslow, Julian. You said you knew her father."

"I said he lived nearby. I did not know him as such. You seem to have developed a keen interest in Miss Winslow's history, my friend."

"She is an odd girl. It sparks my curiosity to know why she lived in a convent until the age of twenty-two."

"Ah. I'm sure she would not want to have it known, but Harry Winslow was a drinker and a gambler. There was nothing left when he died. There was a bit of talk in the county and I don't recall any mention of relatives. Of course,

I was carousing up at Oxford at the time, so I'm not very well-informed. But the convent was preferable to the work-house, I suppose.''

"I suppose," said Andrew with an angry glint in his eyes. "If you'll excuse me, I must make ready for the evening's assaults.''

He turned on his heel and went quickly into the house, leaving Julian looking after him with a deeply concerned expression. He would have to have a word with Honor; Andrew was too persistent for safety. It was high time to end the charade in any case. He would simply have to make Honor see reason.

Honor put the children to bed, then went down to make certain that the last-minute preparations were proceeding smoothly. The flowers were all in place, huge amounts of food had appeared as if by magic, although Honor knew perfectly well what an effort that magic had required, and hired footmen milled about, preparing for the throngs of people. Satisfied, Honor took advantage of the half-hour before the first guests were due to arrive and went into the garden. Lanterns were hanging from every tree, but Honor passed them by and went down to the bottom, where it was quiet and dark, to the stone bench she and Andrew had sat upon only nights before. It seemed like a lifetime ago.

Despite everything that had happened that night, he was still set on a loveless marriage with Phoebe. But then, she thought dismally, he could never consider marrying the governess. The love, the flood of desire that had passed between them, could never again be denied; she knew he loved her, and that he wanted her. That should have been a comfort but it was the opposite. For if she had let him continue with what he had intended to say, what would have happened? No doubt he had thought to make her his mistress. And the horror of it was that if she really had been Honor Winslow, the governess, she might have sunk low enough to accept. This way, she had nothing at all, nothing but constant misery. And if she had allowed him to continue to quiz her, he would have known the truth, all of it: her deception, her treachery to his own family. And then how would she have explained herself? And how was she *ever* going to be able to look him in the face again after the other night, now that he knew—exactly—what he did about her feelings? She pushed her shawl aside, suddenly feeling uncomfortably warm.

It seemed that it was hopeless for anything between them. He would marry Phoebe, and she would leave to resume her true identity and pursue her life somewhere far away. It was time for her to leave, in any case. The war was over, and nothing, not one crumb of real evidence, had appeared to convict Sir Henry of her father's murder. China would be interesting. Yes, China. That would be far enough away. She would give her notice in the morning. Of course, she would miss the children dreadfully, but that could hardly be helped. And as for Andrew . . . well, one day she would recover. She had only to get through this one last night.

Her head lifted slightly as she caught the faint sound of voices coming from the rear gate. It sounded like Sir Henry, and there was a low-voiced, gutter-bred accent she couldn't place. Very quietly she rose and crept nearer, taking care to shield herself behind a tree.

"What do you mean, coming here like this, summoning me with a note as if you were halfway respectable!" hissed Sir Henry furiously. "I'm having a party tonight—half of society will be here! You must be mad!"

" 'Ere, 'ere, guv," said a little man whose clothes hung on him as if there were only bare bones holding them up. His head was covered by a cap, and the dark hid his face. "Just you mind who you's talking to. You owes me money, and well you knows it too, one thousand pounds' worth, and you said I was to collect me balance when the war ended. Well, it ended four days ago, and I ain't heard nuffink from you, and so 'ere I am, so yer better cough it up, or yous'll be the sorriest cove that ever was."

"Yes, yes, I'll give you your money, but you can't think for a minute that I have that kind at the ready! I'll have to go to the bank first thing in the morning. And I'll have it sent to you. I can't take the risk of having you seen around me, you fool!"

"You watch who you's calling a fool. I took care of yer problem, didn't I? All right and tight it was, just like you said, and his lordship dead as a doornail wiv nobbut the wiser. You just send me money to the White Horse Inn on the Brompton Road, care of Mr. George Tilton, tomorrow afternoon at the latest, or yous'll be as sorry and dead as that gentry cove Lord Peninghurst you had me quash, and no one the wiser about you, neither.''

Honor clutched at the tree in front of her. This was it! This was finally it. She felt almost ill. She would have to get word to Julian immediately. Thank God he was to attend the ball.

"You'll have it. Just get out of here!"

"Right, guv," said the little man. "Just you remember, no funny tricks. I've waited this long, and I ain't going to wait no longer for what's mine.'' He melted into the dark, and Honor quickly hurried back through the garden.

Sir Henry thought he heard a rustle from behind him and turned. He could see nothing, but his skin pricked as if someone had just been there. Slowly he walked across the grass, his eyes trying to penetrate through the dark. He was just about to dismiss his suspicions when his eye fell on the bench. There, lying on the stone, was a blue wool shawl, the very one he had given Miss Winslow for Christmas. He picked it up and ran it through his fingers, his little eyes narrowed.

"My lord, I have ordered your carriage for eight o'clock." Hobson offered forth a box of jewels.

"Thank you, Hobson," said Andrew, choosing among them. He withdrew a pin and, arranging the froth of cravat at his throat, tucked the sapphire securely into its folds. Another sapphire went onto one long, slim finger of his left hand. "That will be all, I think."

"Very good, my lord," said Hobson, his sharp eye flicking over his master with approval. "A glass of wine before you go?"

"That would do well. I'll take it up here." Hobson poured from the decanter and left with nary a bow. Sipping his wine, Andrew congratulated himself on how well he had brought Hobson around. He had become a most satisfactory valet.

Walking over to the window and looking out, he dismissed the thought of Hobson from his mind. He had one all-important, burning question. Honor. Honor, indeed, but most certainly not Honor Winslow. He had not wasted ten years of legal experience; his trip to Rutland had been explicitly for the purpose of finding out what Honor was trying so desperately to hide from him. And he had proven conclusively that there was something she was hiding, the least of which was her true name. There had indeed been a Mr. Harry Winslow who had lived near Hambledon, but he had died as quietly as he had lived, and without the tears of a child or a wife to ease his passage. There was no birth certificate for an Honor Winslow issued in the year of 1792, nor within fifteen years either side. It had not been a difficult conclusion to draw that Honor was not who she—or Julian—said she was. However, her presence at St. Mary's Convent was undeniable, for he had spoken with the gardener that very morning. The man had said that there had been a young woman of that description there, a pretty thing, although he could not say for how long, as he had only arrived less than a year ago himself. Andrew did not bother trying to speak with Sister Agnes, for she either knew nothing or was lying herself. But why, *why* had Julian lied to him just now? He had blatantly made up a story about poor Harry Winslow, but to what purpose? And what connection did Julian really have to Honor? He had to be protecting her from something. But what?

What any of it meant was beyond him, but if Honor was hiding a family skeleton, he was determined to find it out. Nothing was going to keep him from solving this riddle. And nothing was going to keep him from Honor.

As for the other business—his intentions toward Phoebe— that was a complication he didn't need. Phoebe he could take care of easily enough, but what could Honor have been thinking of him? Dear God, the other night . . . It was no wonder she had reacted as she had, given what he had made so clear to her. Had she thought he wanted Phoebe as a wife and her as a mistress?

It was insufferable, but at least it was one piece of the puzzle solved.

He put his glass down abruptly and went downstairs.

* * *

Betsy came in with the children's laundry and nonstop chatter about the guests and the dancing and the carryings-on belowstairs. Honor endured the chatter, but she could not bring herself to reply. For the last two hours she had sat unmoving in her chair, her mind completely occupied with the incredible conversation she had overheard. So many emotions crowded through her that every nerve ending seemed scraped raw. She could not bear to feel another thing. She only knew that somehow she would have to find a way to speak to Julian tonight. But how?

"And there be food, miss . . . oh, mounds of it!" continued Betsy blithely. "That's what Mrs. Lipp said, anyways. And bubbly wine and everything." She sighed and wrapped her arms around herself. "I'd give my right hand to be able to watch tonight, I'd be that pleased. But you could, miss! Why don't you go and have a peek, and then you could tell us!"

Honor smiled and shook her head. "I cannot go into the ballroom, Betsy. It's not my place."

"No, miss, of course not," said Betsy with a little grin. "But there's nothing stopping you from taking a turn in the garden. And maybe you could have a peek in through the window from the terrace, for who's to see you as long as you keep in the shadow?"

Honor was about to object when she suddenly realized that it was the perfect solution to her dilemma.

"Do you know, Betsy," she said slowly, "it's not such a terrible idea . . ."

Betsy giggled with delight, obviously having had the intention in mind from the first moment she entered. "You should wear the dress her ladyship gave you, miss, so's you'll fit in if anyone sees you. And that nice lace wrap would be just the thing to cover it. Here, I'll lay everything out for you, miss."

"Oh, Betsy," said Honor with a reluctant smile, "I suppose you're right: I cannot really go down like this. Very well, then, I shall do it. But not a word to anyone, do you promise?"

"Oh, yes, miss! Cross me heart and hope to die. Now, I have some nice hot water just waiting outside . . ."

* * *

Honor crept down the back way. She waited until there was a lull in the traffic between the kitchen and the door leading to the main hall, then slipped across the corridor and out the door to the garden, conveniently located past the servants' cloakroom.

The night was balmy, but despite that, there was not a soul to be seen. She could hear the music coming from the ballroom and it set off an echo of memory of a night in the not-so-distant past. She took a deep breath, pushing aside all thought of that night. Lightly she ran up the steps and over to the far end of the terrace, where the shadows wreathed her from sight. Through the long windows she could see quite clearly.

The ballroom was ablaze with light, and filled to overflowing. A country dance was in progress. Along the sides of the room clusters of people were gathered, and lines of matrons and their daughters sat against the wall anxiously waiting for dance cards to be filled. Fans fluttered, silks and satins rustled, and quizzing glasses were raised in inspection.

Honor searched the room for a sign of Julian but he was nowhere to be seen. Nor was Andrew, for her eyes had sought him out against her will. Her hand inadvertently went to the cameo that held her wrap closed.

And then she felt a hand on her shoulder and turned abruptly, stifling a cry of alarm.

"Why, Honor," said Andrew with a little laugh. "What are you doing skulking about out here? Are you indulging your penchant for fresh air again?"

Honor swallowed hard and looked away. Oddly, she felt nothing, only a peculiar numbness. "Y—yes, my lord."

"I see. And perhaps you might be checking on the fruits of your labor?"

"I . . . It is all very new to me, my lord, and I was curious. Just now I was looking to see if I could find a familiar face. But I saw no one other than Miss Rutherford that I recognized. I should go, my lord."

Andrew looked down at her. "It is a pity that this familiar face does not suit."

"No—I did not mean that. But it was impertinent of me to watch. I do not belong here."

"My dear girl, no matter where you think you do or do

not belong, you outshine every woman in that room, and that is the truth.''

She flushed under his bright gaze and a little stab of pain penetrated through her. "I think not, my lord. No one could outshine your . . . your protégée." Phoebe, her hair standing out like a flame, was in the center of the room, dressed in shining white satin and surrounded by a court of admirers.

"Mm," he said indifferently. "She does have a certain physical attractiveness if you like that sort of look. It's not really to my taste. But for once Miss Rutherford is occupied with someone other than myself. Or herself. I think I shall take advantage of the situation and give you your promised treat. I was going to bring it up to you later, but you have spared me the trip." He took hold of her arm and led her down the steps and into the garden, and she went with him, utterly powerless to resist.

"Sit here," he said, pointing to two chairs placed in a sheltered arbor. "And I forbid you to move. Have you eaten?"

"No, but I—"

"Then you must, for I am going to ply you with champagne and I am too much of a gentleman to do that to you with your stomach empty. I'll be back directly."

Honor realized that there was nothing to be done short of creating a scene, so she nodded her consent. She could not leave until she had located Julian, in any case.

Andrew was back in only moments with a plate laden with the most incredible assortment of food. Then he disappeared again, and when he came back this time, he was carrying two glasses and a bottle of champagne.

"Don't say a word, just eat," Andrew said as he poured out the pale, gently hissing liquid and placed a glass on the table next to her. "It's a fascinating process, the making of champagne. A monk by the name of Dom Pérignon refined the technique at the end of the seventeenth century, but he lost a good deal of his wine in his attempts to discover a way to keep the corks in and the bottles from bursting . . ."

Honor had no appetite, but she ate as best she could, as Andrew talked of inconsequential things. She had given up trying to work out what he was doing now. She could not fathom him. They had last parted on a note of pain and anger and he behaved now as if nothing had happened. But it no longer mattered. She felt almost indifferent, as if whatever was to happen was inevitable and she could only be swept along in the flow.

She drank her champagne and Andrew poured her another glass, and when she had finished, he took her plate from her.

"Better?"

She nodded.

"Good. Food does wonders for the body, but champagne feeds the soul. I can hardly believe you came with me so easily," he said with a little smile. "When I first came up, you looked at me as if I were the devil himself." He placed his hand on hers and felt her shudder. "Am I, Honor? Am I that much of an anathema to you?"

She mutely shook her head.

"Never mind, my love. It will keep. Tell me something, though. Do you mistrust my intentions?"

Honor looked over at him, coloring. She struggled for a reply. "I . . . I do not know how to answer."

"Then do not answer. I shall tell you myself that you can trust them without fail. They are entirely honorable—that I swear to you. And I would have thought you would understand that, knowing me as you do. I'll explain it all to you later, but for now, put aside that particular trouble from your mind, for you have been badly mistaken. I have not now, nor have ever had, any intention of marrying Phoebe Rutherford. You, however, are another matter entirely."

Honor was so surprised as to stare at him speechlessly.

Andrew laughed. "I wonder if the champagne has not affected your tongue. Or perhaps I have had a dizzying effect on you."

She shook her head, unable to believe it, but she could sense the truth of it. "Andrew . . ." she managed to say. "Andrew . . ."

Andrew sighed deeply at the telling expression in her eyes and looked up at the sky. "This is going to be a very long evening," he said with a groan. "A very, very long evening. And I must go back in, much to my regret." He stood and looked down at her. "Honor, we need to talk, you and

I. You know that. The time for deception and evasion is past. Will you meet me here after the guests have left?''

Honor did not take her eyes from his. She could feel it again, that sense of inevitability.

"Will you, Honor?" he asked again more softly.

She took a shaky breath. "Yes, Andrew, I will."

"Thank you," he said simply, and left her.

Honor covered her face with trembling hands. It was too much to absorb, all of it. And then she had another shock as a deep voice addressed her quietly.

"Honor? Are you ill?"

Her head flew up and she saw Julian standing in front of her, his face concerned. "I saw Andrew leave just now. You seemed to be having quite an intent discussion."

"Thank God you're here!" she said with relief, rising to her feet. "I thought I'd never find you!"

"What is it?" Julian asked quickly. "Has something happened?"

"Yes, something has happened, something important. I overheard a conversation Sir Henry had." She went on to tell him everything, as Julian listened carefully, interrupting her only to ask her to elaborate on a point here and there.

"I see . . ." he said when she had finished. "By God, I think you have done it! I had just decided to bring Sir Henry in without the final evidence we needed, but this is conclusive. And I'll tell you, Honor, there is no way Sir Henry can make that payment. He has been gambling heavily and losing badly. It's no wonder he wanted to bring Andrew to the point tonight."

"You *know* about that?" said Honor with great surprise.

"Hmm? Oh, yes, I heard about it a few days ago from Bryonny. Ridiculous. Even Andrew wasn't aware of the plans laid down for him until I told him earlier—you should have seen his face. But that's neither here nor there. The point is that the coffers are empty and there's no more coming in. Sir Henry's a desperate man."

"He's due to leave early this morning for the North. I believe it's political business, something to do with the election. Will you go after him?"

"No. I will wait for him to return. First I shall try to track down Mr. Tilton, which might not be as easy as it appears, but with a few days, I am sure we can bring him in.''

''But what about the inn?''

''If he has any sense, he's only going to use it as an address for receiving his money. But there are people to be spoken to and arms to twist if one knows how. I should leave immediately. You're quite sure that you're completely innocent in Sir Henry's eyes?''

''Quite sure. I think he's hardly aware of my existence. Please, do not worry yourself on that score.''

''Good, then. I shall go to the White Horse Inn and see what I can discover. It's as seedy a place as one could ever hope for, and crawling with vermin of Tilton's sort. I want you to stay here. Your absence would be noted. Does Jake know?''

''No. I'm sorry, I didn't dare try to go to the stables with so many people about.''

''Never mind. I'll contrive to let him know myself when I leave. He can come after me when his duties here are finished; I could use the extra help. You have done a good job, Honor; I am grateful. And do not worry. I will see that Sir Henry pays for his actions, and damn the consequences. Arabella and the children will be well off without him.''

''But the scandal? I should hate to see them touched by it.''

''There will be no scandal. That I will promise you, for they are innocent and should not have to go through life paying for Sir Henry's sins. I would not do that to Andrew in any case, for I know how deeply he cares about them. There are other ways.''

''Thank you,'' said Honor with relief, for it had been preying on her mind.

''It is time for us to end the game in any case.''

''About that, Julian—Andrew knows something. I do not know how much, but he does know that I have deceived him somehow.''

''Yes,'' said Julian with a smile. ''I thought as much. He's been making inquiries. Sister Agnes's letter wasn't quite enough, I'm afraid. I spun a yarn to him about dissolute old Harry Winslow and discovered after the fact from his groom that he's been up poking around near Hambledon for the last three days, looking in church records, that sort of thing. He's a persistent devil, I'll give him that. I should have known we couldn't pull the wool over his eyes for too long. I was going to warn you tonight, but obviously it is no longer necessary.''

"What would you have me do? He wants to speak to me later.''

"Refer him to me tomorrow; I would rather take any wrath that might be forthcoming. This does concern his family, after all, and it is really I who have fostered the deception on him. Please, do me this one favor, no matter how he might roar,'' he said, cutting off her objection. "It is still too dangerous for him to know the truth, most certainly tonight, for without me here to restrain him, he would be sure to charge after Sir Henry, if not George Tilton as well, and that would never do. I thank you, Honor. I thank you on a number of counts, for I know this has not been easy for you. But you have done us all a great service. Your father would be proud. I shall go inside now and shortly take my leave. I will keep you informed. And, Honor . . . good luck with my friend. Don't let him shake you.''

She flushed. "I shan't,'' she said, and left him.

13

You are one of those who would not serve God if the devil bid you.

—William Shakespeare, *Julius Caesar*, III, i

The ball had drawn to a close, and the last guests were trickling out the door. Andrew stepped out onto the terrace for a moment's respite, when a light step sounded behind him and he turned, wondering if it might not be Honor.

"Lord Chesney?" Phoebe said softly.

"Yes, my dear?" he replied, disappointed, and wishing he might have had just a few minutes' more peace.

"I was hoping for a moment alone." She moved closer and touched his arm. "I wanted to tell you how much I appreciate your efforts toward me. I fear I have not been very good at expressing myself."

Andrew's heart sank. "My dear child," he said, about to tell her that he knew of her mistaken assumption. "You have no need to be grateful, for I have been more than happy to see to my step-niece's coming-out. You did very well for yourself tonight, and I am sure you will have a productive Season and many beaus."

"But I do not care about beaus, Lord Chesney," said Phoebe, fluttering her eyelashes up at him. "Do you not understand? It is you I love, only you!" she said, quoting directly from *The Feckless Folly of Lady Lucinda* and then doing exactly what Lady Lucinda had done to Lord Rockinghurst, which had resulted in so successful a conclusion. She threw her arms around Andrew and, standing on tiptoe, kissed him passionately.

Andrew, utterly astonished, brought his arms up and caught at her wrists, pulling her away from him. "My dear Miss Rutherford," he said, putting her firmly to one side, "you flatter me indeed, but I am far too old for you. There are a number of young men who would be better suited to your attentions. You could make a very fine match this Season if you would put your mind to it. I believe you have fixed on the first male you chanced to meet, who just happened to be me, and I would not suit you, you know."

Phoebe stared up at him with disbelief. This was not the way the book went. "But I *love* you," she cried, forced to depart from the script. "You cannot mean this, for I *know* you love me in return! You have from the first! And even if you don't love me, there are my lands, and . . . and my beauty, and my youth, and the family connection! You could *learn* to love me!"

"I am deeply sorry if I have in any way misled you," he said, "but I could not. I could not, you see, for my affections are already engaged. I only hoped to help you make your come-out and see to a happy connection for you. I wish

I had foreseen your expectations, but surely now you must see that I could not marry you under any circumstances."

Phoebe's mouth opened, but nothing came out. She looked like a child who had fallen and for a moment was too stunned to react. But then her senses caught up with her and she drew in a deep breath and promptly burst into hysterical tears.

"No, no . . . oh, no," she shrieked. "It cannot be true! You were meant to marry me—my father promised you to me! I was to be a countess and wear jewels and . . . and I shall never, ever forgive you for this! I *hate* you, do you hear me? I *hate* you!" She beat her fists against his chest, tears of rage pouring down her cheeks.

Andrew, completely at a loss, looked to the door, but no help came from that direction. He took Phoebe's arms and held her flailing body away from him. "I think perhaps, Miss Rutherford, it would be better if you found your father and explained the circumstances to him. I cannot help but think it was unfair of him to promise me to you without having first consulted me in the matter. I can see how cruel and unfeeling you must think me, but I assure you, I was completely unaware of the situation."

"Yes," said Phoebe, sniffing. "Yes, I will go to my father. He will fix it. He *has to.*" She gave Andrew one last look, brimming with hurt and contempt, and rushed through the door.

Andrew ran a hand over his face and shook his head, but his hand fell away as he heard a smothered laugh coming from below. Slowly he walked over to the railing and leaned over, only to see Honor gazing up at him. It was obvious she had a perfect view of the terrace from where she stood.

"Honor," he said faintly, "I had not meant for you to witness that . . ."

"The kiss or the scene?" she said.

"You saw it all?"

"All. I imagine you now know how I felt on Christmas Eve."

Andrew gave her a quick grin. "I know exactly how you felt on Christmas Eve, and it wasn't anything like that. So you saw how it was?"

"I saw how it was. I would rather not have done, but to

be honest, I could not tear myself away. Oh, Andrew,'' she said, another laugh escaping, ''I would never have thought to see you brought down by a snip of a girl. I thought she was going to box your ears!''

''Honor, you are cruel, you know. But I begin to understand how you might have thought what you did. I only realized today, or I would have—''

''I know,'' Honor said simply.

''I'm sorry. Did Phoebe keep you abreast of the affair, then?''

''Every last detail when she could find a way to introduce it into the conversation.''

He sighed. ''Let me come down and we'll go to the end of the garden, where we can be private.''

They exchanged not a word as they walked, but a sharp current of anticipation ran between them, their senses heightened, no barrier left. And each carefully controlled the current, knowing it was not yet time to release it fully.

Andrew turned to her as they reached the dark shelter of the trees. ''Honor. There is so much—I hardly know where to start. But I do want you to know that I feel a fool for all the months I let go by without realizing how I felt. You have known all along, haven't you?''

She nodded, her throat tight.

''We'll talk about it later. And this misunderstanding about Phoebe—that was what held you away from me?''

''That, and other things.''

''Yes, and other things. Honor, I want to say something to you, and I want you to listen to me closely. I know you are not whom you have said. But it doesn't matter to me. It doesn't matter at all. Whoever your father was, whatever he did to make you hide yourself, it is insignificant. You could be the highest- or lowest-born person on this island, and it could not matter. Whichever is irrelevant. I meant what I said about the Queen of England that night at Croftsfield.''

Honor smiled. ''I know. I know that now. But although my father's identity and what he did is important, my being a governess was never really the issue. It was only an excuse I used to keep you away.''

Andrew groaned. ''All this time that I have been trying to beat down the point?''

"All this time."

"Will you tell me, Honor? I ask you now from humility. I . . . I know that I have been heavy-handed with you, and have trespassed where I had no right. But I know too that we have gone beyond that. You will not lie to me, I realize that, but you need not answer me if you cannot."

"I cannot, Andrew. Not tonight. And not because I don't want to, but because I have promised. Tomorrow I swear to you that you will know the rest."

Andrew was quiet for a long moment. Then he gently pulled her down onto the bench with him. "Julian knows something about this." It was a statement, not a question.

"Yes," said Honor calmly. "Julian knows everything about it. He wants to tell you himself tomorrow, and I agreed, because he is your friend and because it is his right. But he knows nothing about what is between us."

Andrew reached out and touched her curls with an odd, twisted little smile. "Yes. That is what I really wanted to talk about, this thing that is between us. Have you accepted it, Honor?"

"I know I love you," she said softly, and Andrew drew in a quick, almost painful breath. He took her hand, but said nothing, waiting.

"I have something to tell you, and I know that it will sound very odd. But it is the truth, and it is as important for you to know as the other." She paused, collecting her thoughts, wondering if Andrew would ever accept what she had to tell him. But she forced herself to continue. "I know of no other way to say this, and I pray you will trust me and not turn from me when I have finished. You see, I have been aware of you since we both were children, and loved you. I dreamt of you as a boy, Andrew, almost every night of my childhood. And years later I dreamt of you again, as a man, before you arrived at Croftsfield. As it is now between us."

He gave an involuntary start. "You dreamt . . . you dreamt of *that?*"

Honor could hardly believe his reaction, for it was the last thing she'd expected. She burst into laughter at the appalled expression on his face. "Heavens, Andrew, you show no surprise when I tell you of the rest, but when it comes to your body, your modesty knows no bounds! And no, I did not dream of *that,* as you so eloquently put it, for how could I? I know nothing about it.'' She fell into peals again.

Andrew grinned. ''I was merely ascertaining how far we had progressed in this relationship I knew nothing about. And then? Please do continue, Honor. You hold me enthralled.''

''And then you came to Chesney,'' she said. ''And you were . . . well, you were *you.* How else can I put it? But you didn't know me, you see, which made things very awkward on top of making me think I had quite lost my mind.''

''Hmm.''

''You're taking it very well, I must say.''

''What else can I do? I knew there was something odd almost from the beginning. You are not the only person who had a sense of familiarity, although I cannot confess to any dreams. Much to my regret, I might add, or things would have progressed a great deal further in them. My knowledge is not as limited as yours, you see, and I would surely have pressed my advantage. After all, a dream is a dream, and not restricted to the normal conventions of waking life.''

Honor shook her head. ''You are incorrigible.''

''No doubt. But then, I have no wish to be reformed.''

''Do you make light of me, Andrew? Do you not believe me?''

He smiled and squeezed her hand. ''In spite of the somewhat unconventional nature of this conversation, I would not think to doubt you, Honor. Tell me. What happened next? The accident, I suppose, as there wasn't time for much else.''

''That was the other strange thing. I remember waking that morning with a sense of uneasiness which I couldn't seem to dismiss. I almost leapt at the excuse to go into the copse for Minnie's scarf.''

''I see. And afterward?''

''Oh, that was when it became clear to me that whether I had lost my mind or not, it was of little importance. You were in trouble and you needed help and I could reach you, somehow, on some level. And so I did.''

''And so you did. In those days we had together, I think I began to realize something of it. And then came Christmas

Eve, when I kissed you. You were no blushing maiden until after the fact, and then you played a good game. I should have known something then, but I was so overwhelmed by my own reaction that I didn't think of yours until much later.''

Honor colored furiously, remembering.

It was Andrew's turn to laugh. ''Come now, Honor, it's not any different from any other indication on the subject I've given you.''

''No,'' she said in a whisper.

''Honor . . .'' Andrew slipped his hands through her hair, caressing her cheek with his thumb. ''You know how much I love you, even though I have never said it aloud. But you know it nonetheless. And you know that I desire you, although it scares me to death to think how that union might be. Death might be too close to the truth when I think what a simple kiss did to me. But I will have to wait to find out, for I would not do you wrong, even tonight, as much as I might wish to. Honor . . .'' He lifted her hand to his lips and kissed it, then met her eyes. ''I have never asked another woman this question, but I ask it of you now. Will you marry me? It is what is meant for us, I do believe that.''

She looked down at her hands. ''And what you learn tomorrow?''

''Could hardly matter. I only know that I need you with me, and that it would give me very great happiness if you would be my wife.''

Honor raised her eyes back to his, and she could hardly breathe, let alone speak, for the naked expression she found there. She released all the love and longing she had held in for so long. ''Yes,'' she whispered. ''Yes and yes.'' She saw him absorb it, and felt the impact.

He closed his eyes for a moment. ''Honor . . .'' he finally said. ''What am I to do with myself? I hardly dare kiss you for fear of what that might set off. Dear God, I love you. I love you, Honor.'' His hands tightened in her hair, and he drew her face to his. ''And I will kiss you, for if I don't, the wanting will kill me first.'' He lowered his mouth to hers, gently touching, testing. But at the first feel of her lips, all hesitancy was lost. There was nothing to stop the charge that exploded between them. Honor inhaled sharply against his mouth, her arms going around his neck, pulling him even closer.

"Andrew . . . oh, Andrew," she murmured against his lips, and he groaned and kissed her more deeply, his tongue touching hers, seeking more, his hands caressing her neck, her shoulders, stroking her back and sliding forward to cup her breasts, his thumbs playing over them, teasing her nipples until they were hard nubs.

Honor gasped at the feel of his hands on her flesh, the swelling of her breasts beneath his touch, the ache, the desire for him to continue, desire that set her entire body on fire. She would have lain down with him then and there, unable to think any longer, lost in the heat and languor and overwhelming need. It was Andrew who called her back, who abruptly cut her off and left her trembling and shaken.

He smiled down at her, gently kissing her temple and lightly stroking her arms. "You see, my love, it must be all or nothing," he said huskily. "There seems to be no in-between for us. I will speak with you tomorrow. We'll settle the rest of this. And by the time I see you tomorrow, I will have a special marriage license, courtesy of a bishop who owes me a favor. I don't think I can wait much longer, Honor." He grinned. "But then, nor can you."

Honor touched his face. "Nor can I," she said.

"Tomorrow, Honor. Tomorrow."

Andrew stood and walked away without looking back.

Sir Henry had had a most disquieting interview with his daughter. Not only had she been stupid enough to let the Earl of Chesney go, but, like the fool that she was, she had confronted him with her own misguided sense of love, thereby destroying any chance of a match in the future. That did away with any immediate source of income, he cursed. His entire world, so carefully constructed, was dissolving around him. Without the Chesney money behind him, he could no longer put off his creditors, let alone pay Tilton. And how much of *that* conversation had the girl overheard? Did she intend to blackmail him?

He chewed on his nail. Could he truly afford not to find out?

Sir Henry left Honor's room, perplexed. There was no

sign she had gone anywhere, for all her clothes appeared to be in her closet. He looked out of her window, puzzled and concerned, and then he caught a flash of movement in the lower garden. Perfect, he thought to himself. It was more than perfect! He was due to leave in the morning for the North; many people knew it. Perhaps he would leave just a little bit earlier than planned. Honor Winslow was proving to be a huge thorn in his side, and he did not need that along with the rest of it. And she was dispensable—truly dispensable.

Honor sat in the dark, unwilling to move and break the spell. Andrew . . . Tomorrow he would know it all. Tomorrow they would finally come home to each other in truth. In literal truth. And shortly her father's murder would be avenged. It was all coming full circle, and the months and months of unhappiness, of displacement, would be gone. Honor sighed and rubbed her eyes. She was tired, she suddenly realized. The day would come soon enough, and she needed to sleep. She stood and stretched. And as she did, something approached her from behind. She was just aware enough of the presence to begin to turn in surprise. And before she even had a chance to register what was happening, something struck her violently on the side of the head, and the world exploded and then dissolved into blackness.

It was past noon when Andrew pulled his carriage up in front of Grosvenor Square and jumped down. He had a short word with Julian's butler, then demanded to be taken to his lordship without another moment's delay.

"Good morning," Andrew said, entering the breakfast room, and suppressing his anxiety with an effort. "I presume Miss Winslow is here with you?"

Julian looked up from his piece of toast and regarded Andrew with mild curiosity. "Why would Miss Winslow be here?"

"Because she is not at the Rutherford house. Perhaps she had not yet arrived, then?"

"But I do not expect her. May I ask why you think she should be breakfasting with me?"

"Look, Julian, let us not beat around the bush. I know

you're involved in this thing, whatever it is, and I want to know what, exactly, Honor has been keeping from me. And furthermore, if Honor is not here, then I'd very much like to know where she is. Arabella is of the mind that she has run away from home, saying she has disappeared with no warning. Minerva is in uncontrollable tears and will not speak to anyone, and Arabella cannot deal with the situation. I said that most likely you had called her over here to attend to Bryonny, who, as she knows, left suddenly last night with the headache. My explanation was temporarily accepted. I did manage to ascertain, after receiving an incoherent reply from Arabella, that Honor's clothes are all in place. Therefore the only conclusion I can draw is that Honor might have decided to come here to speak with you."

Julian carefully put down his cup. "Honor had no plans to come here, to my knowledge. When did she leave the house?"

"No one seems to know, although in that household that would be the norm rather than the exception. But I cannot shake the feeling that something is wrong."

"Andrew, tell me. Did you speak with her last night after I'd left?"

"Yes," said Andrew, running a hand through his hair. "Yes, and she admitted that there was a deception and that you were somehow involved, and that I was to speak with you, at your own request. I would very much like that explanation—now."

"And indeed, you may have one," Julian said mildly. "Why don't you sit down, for there's a great deal to go through." His attention was distracted as Bryonny came through the door. Despite her new sprigged muslin and her bright smile, she was slightly pale and tired-looking. He took her hand. "Are you feeling better, darling?" he asked with concern.

"Oh, yes, I think so. I've just been too sociable and run myself down, Julian, so don't fuss." She kissed his cheek warmly, then gave Andrew a big smile. "Hello, Andrew! How nice to see you. Is this a social call, or should I leave you to your business?"

"It is certainly not a social call, my love. Here's a pretty fix: Honor seems to be temporarily misplaced and Andrew is in a taking.''

"Oh, Julian, no!" Bryonny's hand flew to her mouth. "What could have happened? I thought everything was going so well. You said so yourself this morning!"

"And so it is, as far as I know. I am of the opinion that Honor has gone out to do some chores. Or she might indeed be on her way here."

Andrew rubbed his forehead. "Please, may we dismiss with speculation and get down to the facts?"

Julian nodded. "I will try to make this as brief as possible, Andrew. The truth is that Honor has been working for me. I placed her as governess because I needed someone to gather evidence that Sir Henry was selling information to the French."

Andrew's fingers went quite white as he gripped the edge of the table in shock. But he did not interrupt; he didn't think he could have managed to speak if he'd tried

"Honor did a commendable job, and I was in a position to feed Sir Henry with false information, for which he was well-paid by the French. I'm afraid you came under Sir Henry's suspicions for a brief time, and ended up in bed for a few weeks, after a wire had been strung across the path from Chesney."

"It was not an accident?" Andrew asked, trying to take it in.

"Most certainly not an accident. Honor found and removed the evidence and had me summoned immediately. I decided to allay Sir Henry's suspicions, and gave him a thinly veiled warning concerning you. So it has gone on until a few days ago, with the war ending, and the cessation of Sir Henry's particular activities.

"However, there was one other task Honor was there to perform. She was to find proof that Sir Henry had been responsible for the death of General Lord Alexander Peninghurst. Lord Peninghurst had discovered Sir Henry's activities, you see, and threatened to expose him. He was deliberately murdered, although everyone thought his death had been caused by highwaymen. You might remember."

"Yes, of course I remember! Go on," he said impatiently.

"Last night, Honor brought me the evidence I needed. I spent the night waiting for a certain Mr. George Tilton to appear at the White Horse Inn on the Brompton Road. He never arrived, but I spent the time well, implying that I had need of his services, and gaining the confidence of his . . . ah, friends. My pockets are lighter for my trouble, but I expect to hear from him in the near future.''

"But who is Mr. Tilton?''

"The rather unsavory gentleman who actually arranged for Lord Peninghurst's demise. He hadn't been fully paid, and demanded the sum in full—by this afternoon. Honor overheard his conversation with Sir Henry and passed it on to me. As you probably know, Sir Henry left early this morning for the North. I am waiting for his return to London to charge him personally. There is no possibility that he will send the money to the White Horse, for he hasn't the funds, so I imagine he thinks he will lie low for a time where Mr. Tilton cannot find him.''

"Dear God . . .'' Andrew put his head in his hands for a moment, collecting himself, then looked up again. His face was white and strained. "I . . . I had no idea.''

"Yes, I know, for we took great care to keep you out of it. And I am sorry that it was necessary. But I felt that you could not be involved in any way.''

"And yet you had no qualms about involving Honor?''

"Oh, certainly I had qualms. But she convinced me herself that she could do the job.''

"Yes. How convenient for you to pluck Honor from her convent and place her at Croftsfield as governess.'' His voice was heavy with bitterness.

"Yes. Yes, it was convenient, although I had to go to a good deal of trouble over it. First I had to bribe the Duke of Bedford's governess to leave her job, then I had to place Miss Torch in that position so that Honor could take over for Miss Torch at Croftsfield. And then there was the matter of the groom to be removed. Fortunately he was quite happy to go to the Abbey.''

"And now, due to all of your machinations, Honor is missing.''

"My dear friend, I understand that you are upset by all

of this, but again, is it not possible she went out for a brief time?"

Andrew shook his head. "I do not think so. She would have left a message of some sort. I should . . . I should tell you. Last night Honor agreed to marry me." He dug into the pocket of his coat and pulled out a slip of paper. "This is how I spent my morning. You of all people should recognize a special license when you see one."

"My apologies, Andrew—and my congratulations, naturally," said Julian, now looking equally strained. "I had no idea you'd come this far . . ."

"Oh, were you keeping track of my personal life as well?" Andrew asked acidly.

"Indeed not, Andrew," Bryonny said gently. "But Honor confided her feelings to me some months ago."

Andrew looked at her carefully. "Did she? Exactly how *much* did she confide to you, I wonder."

"All of it," said Bryonny, meeting his eyes evenly.

"Then perhaps you'll understand why I am so concerned. I cannot explain it, but I *know* there is something wrong, very wrong."

Julian thought for a moment. "All right. Mr. Tilton will have to wait. We go to Berkeley Square. Will you come, my love?"

"I wouldn't let you leave me behind!"

"Good. We'll take your carriage, Andrew, as I've just had my horses put up. We'll leave immediately. If you are right, and I pray to God you are not, then there is no time to lose."

"Julian, wait. One thing. Who is Honor, really, and what was it that her father did?"

Julian paused. "I think that under the circumstances, that is one piece of information that can wait."

Andrew gave him a long look, then went out the door.

"Arabella, calm yourself," said Bryonny gently, sitting down next to her and taking her hand. "This is no time for hysteria. We are all here now, and we shall discuss what is to be done."

"When did you realize that Honor was not here?" asked Julian tersely.

"Not until late this morning," said Arabella, sniffing into her handkerchief, then looking up at him through swimming eyes. "I had left orders that she was not to be disturbed before ten because of the late night before. Betsy was looking after the children, and when she went to wake Honor, Honor was gone!"

"And had her bed been slept in?" asked Julian.

"Oh, well, Betsy said Honor always makes it herself, so who is to know? But her shawl is missing, because Betsy says that she keeps it over the back of the chair, and her evening dress is gone too! And Betsy said she was acting very oddly last night, looking as if it were the end of the world."

Andrew turned from the mantelpiece. "Is anything else gone, Arabella, anything at all?"

"Oh, Betsy said something about a pin of some kind."

Andrew drew in a deep breath. "That is more than enough."

"Oh, but, Andrew," continued Arabella without really hearing, "Jocie is preaching gloom and doom, and Minerva is in a terrible state and won't stop crying! She insists something terrible has happened!"

"Does she?" said Bryonny, frowning. "I wonder, could we try to speak with her?"

"Well, yes, but I don't know that you will get anything from her. Honor was always so good when she became like this." She burst into a fresh flood of tears.

"Perhaps you might help Arabella bring her down, Bryonny," said Julian, looking at his wife curiously, for he could not imagine what help poor little Minerva could be. But Bryonny usually had her reasons, so he did not question her. He opened the door for them and saw that Jake, whom he had summoned, was waiting in the hall. "Jake, would you come in now, please?"

"Yes, my lord." He entered, and Julian closed the door. "Andrew, may I present Captain Renard of the Grenadier Guards? Captain, I believe you already are acquainted with Lord Chesney."

"Quite well, my lord," said the captain with a smile. His thick Yorkshire accent was gone, and in its place were the well-bred tones of a gentleman.

Andrew shook his head. "I cease to be surprised. How do you do, captain."

"Captain Renard was Lord Peninghurst's aide. I placed him to assist Honor and protect her."

"My lord, I wish I were able to tell you something, but I only returned late this morning myself, and I have not been able to discover anything from any member of the staff."

They spoke quietly for the next few minutes, going back over various details, and then Bryonny and Arabella reappeared with Minerva and Jocie, who had insisted on coming as well.

Minerva took one look at her uncle and flew across the room, flinging herself into Andrew's arms and burying her face in his coat. He felt her little body shaking, and gently stroked her back, murmuring soothing words into her hair.

"No, don't leave," Julian said to the captain, who was tactfully about to withdraw. "The time for all of that is past. But keep your peace, just for the moment."

"Hello, Minnie, my sweet," said Andrew casually, sitting her up as soon as he sensed she had calmed. "Isn't this a fine how-do-you-do, with Miss Winslow getting us all worried? I'm sure she's just gone out for a quiet turn in the park after yesterday's excitement."

"She didn't," said Jocie obstinately. "She never would without saying! And Minnie says something bad has happened, and Honor told me we should listen to her when she says so."

"What's this?" said Andrew slowly.

Bryonny knelt down and took Minerva's small hand in hers. "Tell me, little one, do you know something about Honor? Where she is?"

Minerva look up at her with wide tear-filled yes. "She went away."

"Yes?" said Julian, wondering if they were going to get anywhere.

Minerva gulped and put her thumb in her mouth.

"Minnie?" said Jocie, crossing over and putting her arm around her. "You can tell, you know, for you won't be in trouble. Honor said you were clever about these things, remember?"

Minerva nodded. "I am c-clever. Honor said."

"That's right, Minerva," said Bryonny gently. "And now you can help us to find her. Where did she go?"

"The bad man, he hurt her!" cried Minerva. "He hit her! And he took her to his house. He will kill her! He will!"

Arabella smiled sadly. "Her nightmares," she said. "Honor said she dreams about a bad man."

"Never mind," said Julian with a sigh. "Thank you, Minerva. Jocelyn, take your sister upstairs, please. I must talk to your mama."

For once Jocie did not argue, and quickly left the room with Minerva in tow.

Julian waited for the door to close, then turned back to the room. "It is no more than I had thought. Bryonny, what did you think you could possibly get from the child?" he asked impatiently.

"Honor told me once that she had some kind of second sight. Apparently she knew when Andrew had been hurt, and knew her father was going to die."

Andrew stood. "Wait . . . There is something here. There *is* a kind of second sight which runs in the family. I gather it goes back quite a way. My grandmother was supposed to have had it, and her grandmother before her. Perhaps Minnie has inherited it."

Julian sighed. "As strange as it seems, there might be some truth in it. I have heard of things like this running in a family . . . but then, if we are to give any credence to this, where does it take us? How can it help us find Honor?"

"We start with what Minerva said about a bad man," said Andrew. "Henry seems a logical choice to me, given what you've said, Julian."

"Henry?" asked Arabella, by this time completely lost.

"Yes. We know that Minerva has never liked Sir Henry. Perhaps he is the bad man of whom she dreamed. Did she ever have nightmares before coming to Croftsfield?"

"No, but then, Minerva was badly upset when George died," said Arabella.

"Even so," said Julian slowly, "it is possible that Sir Henry is the man of whom she spoke, which makes her statement all the more compelling. It is just possible that

Sir Henry might somehow have realized that Honor overheard him, and waited for her after the ball—*after* you left Honor, Andrew. He could not have acted before then, not with the number of people around.''

"I don't understand!'' whispered Arabella. "What would Henry want with Honor? What did she overhear?''

"Arabella, you must be strong,'' said Andrew. "We haven't much time. Julian has a very unpleasant story to tell you concerning your husband, and I beg you to listen carefully.''

Once again Julian quickly ran through the sordid tale, and to everyone's surprise, Arabella neither succumbed to hysterics nor swooned. Instead, she sat up a little straighter and actually smiled when Julian had finished.

"I always liked Honor,'' she said. "And you too, Jake. I have thought and thought how to get away from Henry, but I could think of nothing that wouldn't bring disgrace on the children through me. I cannot be sorry for his own disgrace, for he is an evil man, and whatever is coming to him he deserves. I have been very unhappy,'' she finished simply.

"Yes, I know. Arabella,'' said Andrew sympathetically. "But it is nearly at an end. If Minerva is right, it must be Henry who abducted Honor. Then Minerva said he took her to his house. That would have to be Croftsfield.''

"Yes,'' said Julian. "Logically speaking, it makes sense. He would want to find out what she knows, and where better than a conveniently closed house, with no one to hear, and no one to question his presence should he be spotted in the area. And he already had an alibi that he was out of town.''

"Yes,'' said Andrew, "it make perfect sense. I think we should go immediately. Now the question is how to apprehend Henry without harm coming to Honor.''

"I will help in any way I can,'' offered Arabella.

"I don't think—'' Julian started to say, but Bryonny interrupted.

"Wait. I have an idea, and Arabella is instrumental. Listen . . .''

Phoebe did not wake until nearly two o'clock, having spent most of the night pacing her room in a passionate temper, swearing revenge on everyone she could think of, including her father, who not only had had no sympathy for her plight, after he had sworn she was to have Lord Chesney, but also had had such lack of feeling that he had actually slapped her. She called for her maid, and was astonished to discover what had been happening while she slept. She dressed in a fury and ran straight downstairs. The hall was empty, but she heard voices coming faintly from behind the closed doors of the drawing room. She put her ear to the keyhole and listened.

"I cannot agree, Bryonny," said a deep voice. "You have not been well of late, and I do not think you need further strain. In any case, it is too dangerous."

"Absolute nonsense, darling," she replied. "It only makes sense that I need the country air and peace and quiet in which to recover. I think I shall be in a delicate condition. Croftsfield is ideal and far closer that the Abbey, which would be too far to drive, don't you see? Arabella has kindly offered to accommodate me, and Captain Renard will drive us. I can hardly refuse her hospitality, can I?"

"She is right, Julian," murmured another deep voice, similar, but she knew it well. Lord Chesney, thought Phoebe, wondering furiously what it was all about. She had her answer a moment later.

"The argument is sound, Julian, and allows for the element of surprise, with the distraction Bryonny and Arabella can offer. She has to be there somewhere if we've put it together correctly, and I'll be damned if I waste another minute. For God's sake, man, we are talking about Honor! I love her! Surely you remember how you felt when you almost lost Bryonny?"

"Yes . . . I remember," he said heavily. "Very well, you have persuaded me. Come, then, we leave directly."

Phoebe picked up her skirts and hurried around the corner, her heart pounding. She waited until the front door had closed and she heard the clatter of a carriage departing. She could hardly believe what she had heard! *Her* Lord Chesney thought himself in love with Honor Winslow? That was the person to whom his affections were attached? It exceeded all bounds! No doubt he had offered her a *carte blanche* and she had fled, cleverly hoping to push him into marriage! And now he was going after her like a love-struck pup.

Phoebe thought carefully. Had there not been a situation in that story about the governess gone wrong—what had it been called? Oh, yes—*The Duke's Dalliance*. But in that, the wronged Lady Iris had taken a gun, and by holding it on the governess, who had deceived the duke into believing her to be something quite different, she had forced the woman to admit her ploys in front of a roomful of witnesses. He had turned back to his first and true love, kissing her feet and begging for forgiveness, which of course Lady Iris gave. Yes, it was perfect! She could not have ordered up the setting better herself. Phoebe went into the library. There behind the Bible was her father's secret drawer, where she knew he kept a hidden sum of money and a pistol. She first pulled out the money, only a slim purse, she saw with disappointment, but enough for her purposes. And then her fingers wrapped around the cold steel of the gun barrel. She slowly pulled it out and looked at it uncertainly. She had never handled a gun before, but then, nor had Lady Iris. And anyway, she did not intend to use it. She slipped it into the pocket of her skirt and, running downstairs, she had the kitchen girl go out and order her a hansom, for there seemed to be no one else to do it.

14

I am all the daughters of my father's house,
And all the brothers, too.

—William Shakespeare, *Twelfth Night*, II, iv

The sun was lowering in its afternoon arc when Honor regained consciousness. She opened her eyes to find herself in a strange room lying on a narrow bed. A chair creaked and she turned her head, wincing with pain.

"So, Miss Winslow. You are finally with me." Sir Henry glowered down at her menacingly.

Honor's heart leapt, and she struggled to sit up.

"Sir Henry," she said weakly. "I . . . I don't understand. What do you want with me? Where am I?" How much did he know? she wondered frantically.

Sir Henry held up her blue shawl. "This was careless of you, Miss Winslow. If you are going to eavesdrop on private conversations, you ought to take care not to leave such glaring clues behind."

"I don't know what you mean."

"Don't bother to lie. Why, I wonder, did you listen in? Did you think to blackmail me, Miss Winslow?"

"No, Sir Henry," said Honor desperately, wondering if there was any way to salvage the situation. "I did hear, I confess it, but it was quite by accident, and I didn't understand, only that you owed the man some money. I left, realizing I had intruded. I wasn't going to say anything, I swear it!"

"I don't believe you," he said, leering at her nastily. "I have had time to think, you see. I have thought how you arrived in my house, all full of sweet innocence. I have thought of how quickly you drew my family and my staff under your influence, how you encouraged my wife to stand against me, even how you insinuated yourself into Lord Chesney's good graces. I wouldn't even be surprised if you didn't have something to do with his rejection of my daughter last night. I saw him in the garden, you see, just before he left, taking his favors. I think I understand you very well, Miss Winslow. You are a fortune seeker. You lust for social connection, for money, for influence. You thought to find it at Croftsfield by any means you could!"

Honor thought furiously. She had to protect the truth at all cost, until Julian could bring Sir Henry in, for if he had any inkling of what they had been doing, Sir Henry would disappear completely.

"I admit you have seen through my act," she said, changing her tone of voice. "I can see now it was foolish, for you have discovered me. But you need not hold me prisoner. It is not worth my life—or yours.''

"What do you mean by that!" he said, suddenly looking nervous.

"Just that. You will kill me for what I know, but if you do, you will be exposed. Last night, I gave a letter into the hands of Lord Chesney, with whom I have had some dealings of an . . . an intimate nature, I admit. I was afraid that you might have discovered my presence, and I took the precaution of writing down everything I heard. I told Lord Chesney that if anything should happen to me, he was to open the letter and reveal the contents. Of course, I led him to understand that what was inside was of a personal nature, for he is a man of lofty ideals, and had he had any idea, he would have acted on it straightaway.''

"I don't believe you," said Sir Henry uncertainly. "Chesney has no interest in anything to do with you, other than how you can sweeten him. At least I now know how you spent all that time locked away with him in his bedroom. You and your winsome ways. It's a disgrace! You will pay for this, Miss Winslow, and pay dearly.''

"Oh, please, you must understand!" Honor said on a sob. "He . . . he offered me money and jewels if I would . . . I would . . .'' She broke down altogether, praying she was being convincing. "I have nothing of my own, Sir Henry. I only wanted to better my life. But I can see how foolish I have been. I will keep my silence—I will go away and you will never hear of me again!" She rose to her feet, reached out an imploring hand, swayed, and pretended to faint.

"Bah . . . women!" he said with a sneer. He looked down at her inert body. "I will learn the truth, Miss Winslow," he muttered, and left, locking the door behind him.

Honor waited for his footsteps to fade away. She cautiously opened her eyes and took in her surroundings. She was in a small room, bare of furniture with the exception of an iron bedstead and mattress, upon which she was lying, a small bureau which held a cracked jug and flowered china basin, and the wooden chair.

It was dark, and she managed to stand up on the bed and reach for the window. She pushed at it, but it would only open an inch or so. Still, it was enough, and she wriggled her hand through and managed to unlatch the shutters, freeing one side. The faint light filtered in through the grimy window, and she could see the line of a rooftop and a lifeless chimney. Croftsfield! she suddenly realized. Of course—she must be in the living quarters above the stables. Poor Jake, she thought inconsequentially. Then she sank back on the bed and prayed for Julian and Andrew to work it out between them.

Andrew's carriage flew at a breakneck pace. Village after village flashed by, and they stopped once at a posting house to change horses, for after an hour at that speed the animals were exhausted. The change was accomplished in record time and they were on their way again. In a little over two hours Andrew, who had insisted on driving the full distance, reined the horses up just short of the Croftsfield drive.

"Captain Renard, you take the carriage in," he said shortly. "Lord Hambledon and I will walk from here, and go in the back way. Make sure you assist Lady Hambledon in, and keep watch while we cover the house." He reached into a compartment next to him and withdrew a pistol.

As he did so, Julian was inside giving Bryonny and Arabella final instructions.

"Do whatever you need to, Bryonny, but you must convince Sir Henry you are in earnest. We need as much time as possible to cover the house, so any distraction, no matter how foolish, is to our advantage. Are you *sure*, my love, that you are up to this?"

Bryonny grinned. "This is just what I need to restore my spirits, Julian! You know how I love adventure. Now, don't you worry; Arabella and I will do very well, and I am very happy to play my part."

Julian smiled, and kissed her lightly. "I cannot be surprised. I shall see you shortly. But if there is any sign of trouble, you are to remove yourselves immediately."

"Yes, my lord," said Bryonny, her eyes dancing with anticipation. "Now, go! We are quite capable, I assure you."

Julian gave her a questioning look, his doubts only slightly quelled. But he knew that Bryonny never panicked, and that lent him reassurance despite his reservations. Arabella was another matter.

"Arabella, I thank you," he said, taking her hand. "Whatever happens, keep your head, and follow my wife's lead."

"I will. My only thought is to see Henry brought down. Do not concern yourself with me."

Julian examined her face, and was pleased by the determination he saw. He nodded, then kissed his wife again and alighted.

"Let's go," he said to Andrew as the carriage started off at a leisurely pace, then smiled broadly when he saw what Andrew was tucking into the pocket of his coat. "The very thing. I always knew you were a man of foresight."

"When dealing with your affairs, my dear Julian," said Andrew dryly, "one never knows when one might have need of a gun."

"So, Miss Winslow." Sir Henry finished tying Honor's ankles to the chair with the rope he had found in the stable beneath. Her hands had already been bound, although she had struggled all the way, and he was breathless with his efforts to subdue her, and out of patience. But it made no difference. He had already decided what was to be done.

Honor glared at him furiously. "You are loathsome! I have told you that I am willing to cooperate with you! You know very well that the only danger you are in comes if I disappear! I think you are a very stupid man to risk yourself so."

"Stupid, you say? No, my dear Miss Winslow, I think not. If I were stupid, I would never have come as far as I have. It is you who are stupid, for I don't believe a word of your story. I don't think there was any letter. I think you intended to blackmail me. Well, you were very wrong. You see, I intend to kill you, and I shall dispose of you in a way that no one will discover. I shall concoct a perfectly plausible story to account for your disappearance. It is very simple."

He smiled, and as he did, his hand reached out and ripped the lace shawl from her shoulders. Andrew's cameo fell to the ground with a little clatter, but he didn't notice it. He was winding the lace between his hands into a tight, thin rope. And then he advanced on her.

"Sit here, Bryonny," said Arabella loudly, actually enjoying herself despite her nerves. She drew up a chair in the great hall. "I know the house is a shambles, with everything under holland covers, but Jake can air out the morning room, and I shall go directly upstairs and prepare a bedroom for you."

"Thank you, Arabella," said Bryonny weakly. "You have been so very kind to me."

The captain moved away from the staircase where he had been listening. "He's coming," he whispered, then took up his post next to the front door.

Arabella swallowed hard, and Bryonny gave her a reassuring smile. "My husband is so grateful to you for offering the use of your house."

"It is nothing! You shall feel better in no time, with the country air and rest, you shall see."

Sir Henry started down the stairs in astonishment. He had heard a carriage, to be sure, and with tremendous foreboding had crept across the lawn and through the back way to the upstairs landing.

There he had hidden in the shadows, his heart pounding with fear and a cold sweat clamming his skin. But it was not the law, only silly Arabella and Lady Hambledon of all people! He decided to brazen it out. No doubt they had come in search of Honor Winslow, and it would be best to allay their suspicions.

"What are you doing here!" he demanded as he descended the rest of the way. "You should be in London with the children!"

"Why, Henry!" said Arabella, evidently extremely surprised to see him, which relieved his mind considerably. "I might ask you the same question. I had thought you had gone up North!"

"Well, of course," he said impatiently, irritation with his wife growing. "I am on my way, but stopped off to collect some papers. But I ask you again, why are you here, and Lady Hambledon as well?"

"Good day, Sir Henry," said Bryonny. "I hope our unexpected arrival has not inconvenienced you."

"Lady Hambledon has not been well, Henry," said Arabella, flustered as usual, he observed sourly. "Her husband particularly desired her to rest in the country, and I offered Croftsfield, as it is close to London. You need not worry about the staff, for Lord Hambledon will provide his own. I expect him shortly."

"I . . . see. Would you not have been better off in your own home, Lady Hambledon? I am sure it would be more comfortable."

"Hambledon Abbey is much too far for Lady Hambledon to travel, Henry. She is in a delicate condition, you see."

"A delicate condition?" asked Sir Henry suspiciously. Lady Hambledon enjoyed perfect health. It all seemed far too coincidental to him; if they were looking for Honor, why not say so? But he could not challenge his wife on the subject, for he would not know Honor was missing, if his story were to remain straight.

"Henry, dear, you must not be so obtuse. Lady Hambledon is in the family way. I am sure I felt just as ill when I carried my own children."

Sir Henry colored, for looking at the girl closely, he could see that she did indeed look paler than usual. "I see. I beg your pardon, Lady Hambledon. I had not meant to be indelicate. But surely Lord Chesney would have offered Chesney hall? It is far more suitable than Croftsfield."

"Henry, I do not know why you are being so difficult! As it happens, Chesney is about to undergo extensive renovations, which is exactly what Lady Hambledon does not need to be exposed to, all that noise and dust. Now I shall go prepare your chambers, Bryonny, my dear."

Bryonny nodded gratefully, and delicately pressed a handkerchief to her brow.

"No!" said Sir Henry quickly. "That is, it would take far too long to make a room comfortable. I think it would be best if you took Lady Hambledon to the King's Arms for the night, Arabella. It is very well-appointed, and accustomed to Quality. There you could have a hot meal and a private parlor until the house can be made more presentable. I could not allow you to stay here under such deplorable

conditions.'' He moved to the door. ''Jake, see their lady-
ships to the carriage.''

The captain did not move.

''Henry, you are being quite nonsensical, and inhospita-
ble as well. Can you not see that Lady Hambledon has had
enough traveling?''

''Indeed, Arabella,'' said Bryonny faintly. ''I would not
think to put your husband out any more. Thank you for your
efforts, but it is clear he would rather I went elsewhere.''
She struggled to her feet, and, to Sir Henry's alarm, and
apparently in the habit of all women, she fell into a swoon.

Andrew was about to push open the kitchen door when a
noise coming from across the courtyard caught his attention. A shutter from one of the upstairs stable windows had
come loose and was banging against the outside wall. The
window itself was open a crack.

Andrew frowned. ''That's odd,'' he murmured to Julian,
pointing. ''All the others are fastened shut. I think I'll go
and have a look. Why don't you go inside and see what you
can find? I'll meet you back here.''

Julian nodded his assent and Andrew ran across the
courtyard to the grooms' entrance, where the door opened
easily enough, its hinges squeaking only slightly. In moments he was up the stairs and on through to the passage.
He went directly to the second door on the right side and
pushed it open.

Honor was slumped in a chair, her head bowed over her
chest. Around her neck was tied the twisted cord of lace.

Andrew did not pause. He rushed to her side, and with
fingers that felt clumsy and useless, he managed to loosen
and pull the material away. Where it had dug into her tender
throat the flesh was mottled with purple and red.

Andrew dropped to his knees and picked up her cold
hand. ''Oh, dear God . . . Honor?''

He instantly started to work at the knots at her feet and
hands, and as soon as she was free, he picked her up in his
arms and laid her on the narrow bed, holding her close to
him. ''Honor . . . Honor, my love!''

He held her tightly and rocked her, desperately bringing
his will to bear, calling Honor back to him. He could not

lose her now, not now. And in that moment he felt Honor stir and cough, and she drew in little gasps of breath. A semblance of color crept back into her face.

"Oh, thank God . . ." Andrew loosened his hold on her and gently laid her back on the bed.

Her eyes opened, and her hands went shakily to her throat. "Andrew?" she whispered. "Oh, Andrew." Her hand went to his face to see if he was real.

"And who else?" he managed to say, covering the hand against his cheek with his own, suddenly weak with relief.

Honor coughed again and struggled to sit up, and Andrew helped her.

Julian appeared in the doorway, and his face darkened as he took in the scene. "What happened here?" he demanded.

Andrew met his eyes. "Henry," he said in a tone of restrained fury, "attempted to strangle her."

Honor shuddered. "I thought . . . the lace went around my neck, and then . . ." She shuddered and bit her lip, trying not to cry.

"I know, my love," said Andrew gently. "I know."

"It's all right, Honor," said Julian. "Sir Henry is in the house with Bryonny and Arabella and Jake. He must have left you when he heard the carriage, thinking the job was done. And thank heaven for that timing. He doesn't know that Andrew and I are here." He glanced at Andrew. "All goes according to plan, my friend."

"Excellent," said Andrew. "Do not worry, Honor. Sir Henry cannot hurt you now."

Julian nodded. "We have him just where we want him. I suppose he thought you would expose him?"

"Yes." Honor swallowed painfully. "But I told him nothing. He thinks I was trying to advance my position in the world. And that Andrew and I had an . . . an arrangement."

"The low, filthy—" Andrew bit off the epithet and stood, his fists clenched.

"I let him think it. And the other."

"It is just as well," said Julian, smiling at Andrew's expression. "It will be easier this way to lead him into the net. And Honor is accustomed to playing roles, you must remember. Sir Henry's assumptions should count for little.''

"He left Honor for dead," said Andrew softly. "I will see him in his grave for that, never mind the rest. No more of these games, Julian!''

"Only one last one, my friend. Patience. You will have him before the night is out. I go now. I have just arrived, you see, to attend to my so-frail wife. You go in the back way and wait by the upstairs landing. Sir Henry obviously thinks you are safely dead, you see, Honor, and all proof of his complicity dead with you. We shall prove him wrong, yes?''

"Yes," said Honor.

"Julian!" protested Andrew. "You cannot expect Honor to confront him in her condition! Have a little heart!''

"It is not my heart, Andrew, that you should be addressing. Honor, do you think you can manage?''

"I would not miss this moment for the world." She looked at Andrew questioningly, then back to Julian.

"Andrew knows most of the story. Not quite all. I neglected the personal details for reasons of my own. All will be revealed shortly.''

She smiled. "I understand. What would you like me to do?''

"If it is not too repellent, tuck the lace around your neck, for I do not want your bruises to be immediately apparent. Then wait on the upstairs landing with Andrew. You have an entrance to make, my dear. I will give you your cue. Andrew, you stay back. It would be best if Sir Henry thinks he has only me to deal with. But keep him in your aim.''

Andrew nodded his agreement, but his eyes were dark with worry. "I trust you will let no harm come to Honor?''

"No harm. We must play out this last act, Andrew. And then we will have an ending to our story.''

Andrew waited until Julian had left. "Honor," he said, sitting down and stroking her hair and holding her to him, "I did not know. Julian told me most of it. I am sorry, for I misunderstood so much . . . And today I was frantic, knowing there was something wrong—" His voice choked.

"But you came," she whispered.

He stroked her face, his fingers tracing the curve of her

cheekbones. "I love you, Honor. I cannot believe I came so close to losing you. . . . ''

"No closer than I did to losing you all those months ago. And this time you brought me back." She smiled. "Although in truth I think I must only have fainted from fright and lack of air, or I doubt I would have recovered so readily. But you may consider the debt that so worried you canceled."

He buried his mouth in her hair with a little laugh. "Honor. What am I to do with you?"

"Andrew . . . About Julian and Sir Henry—there is not time now to talk about it, although I promise you we will. But I must go back to the house. I have a very private debt to settle with Sir Henry."

"I can imagine," he said savagely.

"No, not just that. I want you to promise me that no matter what transpires, you will understand that the things I have done I have done from necessity. I never wanted to have to deceive you."

"Honor, I have told you. Whatever it is, it can make no difference. If you are ready to confront this, I would not think to stand in your way. But are you quite sure you can manage it, my love?"

"Oh, yes," she said with a gentle smile. "I am very sure. I have waited nearly a year for this day to come."

"Then we go."

"Wait! Wait, Andrew, my cameo—it came off earlier. Please, could you find it? It rolled onto the floor somewhere."

Andrew smiled. "I am touched by your priorities, my love. Look, here it is." He retrieved it from the floor and carefully pinned it back on her bodice. "Come, let Henry receive the full force of your wrath."

He helped her to her feet, arranged the lace around her throat, and took her back to the house.

It had taken Julian only a few minutes to reach the front door. He adjusted his clothes, then knocked.

Captain Renard answered the door with a confirming nod. "My lord," he said solemnly, returning to his Yorkshire accent. "It is good to see you have arrived, for Lady Hambledon has taken most ill."

"Thank you," said Julian, striding into the hall, and, ignoring Arabella and Sir Henry, he went directly to Bryonny's side.

"Bryonny?" he said gently. "My sweet?"

Bryonny's eyes, which had been glued shut by sheer force of will, fluttered open and he helped her to sit up. "Julian . . ."

"It appears you swooned, my love. I should never have let you undertake the journey!" As he spoke, he squeezed her fingers reassuringly and smiled.

"I am better now," said Bryonny, understanding and giving him a smile in return. "You know I often swooned when carrying Andrew. It is nothing, really. But, Julian, Sir Henry doesn't want us here. We should leave."

Julian looked up at Sir Henry, his eyes cold. "I think not. My wife must rest. She has had enough strain for one day."

"Yes . . . of course. I had not realized," Sir Henry replied, seeing no way out. He would have to dispose of the girl's body later, somehow. At least it was safely away in the stables. "You are welcome, naturally. I had only thought Lady Hambledon might be more comfortable at an inn while the house was prepared."

"How considerate," said Julian. "Come, my love, let me help you to a chair." As he did so, he addressed Arabella. "I do not mean to distress you, my dear, but as I was leaving, I had a visit from Andrew. It seems that Miss Winslow has gone missing from the house. Do you know anything of it? Andrew is most concerned."

"Honor . . . gone? How terrible!" Arabella cried. "Where could she be?"

"I believe I know what might have happened," said Sir Henry with more composure than he felt. "We had words yesterday. Miss Winslow came to me confessing that she was in trouble. I am sorry to tell you that she had been indiscreet and was with child as a result. I told her that she would have to find another position, for I could not keep her under my roof in such a condition. I am sure you understand. She was very upset, but I did not expect her to leave quite so suddenly. Naturally, I was going to speak to you of this, Chesney, as you had recommended the girl, but it did not seem urgent at the time . . .'' He trailed off as he found four pairs of eyes staring at him.

"My dear Sir Henry," said Julian very quietly, but each word rang clear in the deep silence of the hall. "Surely you cannot expect us to believe such a ridiculous story."

"But it is the truth!" Sir Henry said vehemently, feeling an inexplicable sense of foreboding. "Why would I fabricate such a thing?"

"Perhaps because you abducted her yourself."

Sir Henry looked at Julian with astonishment, his face turning bright red. "Ab—abducted her! What fustian! What would I want with her? Surely you do not think that I had any interest in seducing a child like that?"

"No," said Julian pleasantly. "I think you had something quite different in mind."

"This is absurd! I haven't laid eyes on the girl since early yesterday!"

"Really, Sir Henry?" said Julian, looking up over his shoulder. "How extraordinary. What say you now?"

He spun around and gaped as if he had seen a ghost. Honor stood alone on the stairs.

"You!" he spluttered. "It . . . it can't be!"

"In the flesh," said Honor in a whisper, which the soreness in her neck had little to do with; she could barely speak through her loathing.

"So." He gave her a calculating look, thinking swiftly through his shock. Sir Henry had never been one to panic unduly. "I would have thought that you would have had the sense to keep to your room, Miss Winslow," he said coolly. "You seem to have even less of a sense of self-preservation than I thought—do you want the entire world to know the truth? I tried to protect you, you fool! One does not flaunt trysts of this nature, at least not in polite society. That you could do such a thing in front of my wife is beyond all bounds! Arabella, darling," he said, turning to her, "it was a moment of madness. I swear to you it will never happen again! I am not without blame, but she made it so tempting, surely you can understand?"

Arabella said nothing, only looking at him with hatred.

Sir Henry looked about him, satisfied by the quiet. He had shocked them. And Honor had obviously decided to keep silent. She had more intelligence than he had credited her with.

"I can understand why you all look at me so," he murmured with an attempt at humility. "I am at fault, as I have said. But can we not leave it now, and forget my foolish indiscretion? It is not the first time a man has been taken in. We all make mistakes!"

Julian inclined his head. "Indeed, but your mistakes, Sir Henry, have been manifold. Surely you did not think that any of us would believe your preposterous story? You see, I know that you attempted to murder Miss Winslow."

"*Murder* her?" Sir Henry laughed. "Why would I do such a thing?"

"Because you knew that she had damning evidence on you," said Julian evenly.

"Evidence . . . What? How dare you, sir?" Sir Henry blustered, frantically looking for an avenue of escape, and then started toward Honor as if to grab her.

In a matter of a split second, he found himself staring into the barrel of a pistol.

"I wouldn't, if I were you," said Andrew, who had appeared as if by magic. "Honor, move next to Bryonny. I don't think Sir Henry is feeling particularly charitable toward you." In fact, Sir Henry was staring at her murderously, but he saw no need to dramatize the fact.

"Thank you, Andrew." Julian folded his arms and leaned against the balustrade. "It's really such an ugly tale."

Sir Henry turned to Honor, his little piggish eyes glittering. "You will stop at nothing, will you? And what story will you tell now, I wonder. Not the truth, of course, that I took you away because I had discovered your treachery in my own house, your filthy efforts to insinuate yourself into Chesney's affections! And now you say that I tried to kill you." He turned to the others. "Well, let me tell you, it is lies she gave you, all lies, designed to protect herself! It is true, I took her away, but only to protect my daughter, for I discovered what Miss Winslow was plotting. She thought that by conspiring against my daughter's happiness she would rise in the world. I only intended to frighten her, I swear it! You cannot believe a word of what she says. Damning evidence, indeed! It's laughable!''

"Laughable, Sir Henry?" said Julian calmly. "Is it laughable that you conspired to kill Lord Peninghurst—"

"*What*, man? You must be insane!"

"—because he had stumbled onto your nasty secret. And that secret was that you have been feeding confidential government information to the French all this while to cover your enormous gambling debts."

Sir Henry went white.

"You see, Honor and Jake, here, have been keeping track of your movements and your correspondence. It has been most illuminating."

Sir Henry wiped his mouth with a trembling hand. "Spies—spies in my own house?"

"I would be very careful whom you call a spy, Sir Henry," said Julian.

"This is absurd!" spat Sir Henry, recovering himself. "A governess and a groom? It's ridiculous that you would trust any information from either of them. They are probably in league with each other! How much did they charge you for this supposed information? A small fortune, I shouldn't wonder!"

"Not a penny, Sir Henry, for both were in the service of their country. You see, we've known about you for some time. Shall I tell you how? It is such an interesting story, much of which you might know, but I guarantee that there is a great deal which you, and the others gathered here, with the exception of my wife and my two . . . accomplices, do not."

"I don't know what you are talking about!" cried Sir Henry. "This is preposterous!"

"Preposterous, yes. But I believe you and the others will find it most enlightening. Shall I begin?" He looked around the hushed room. He had their complete attention. "Good. It begins many years ago, when General Lord Alexander Peninghurst was summoned from Constantinople to the Peninsula by Wellington. He prepared to go, intending to send his wife with their daughter back to England. But within days his wife was dead of a fever. His daughter refused to leave him, and so Lord Peninghurst took the girl to the Peninsula instead. From then until last year, Caroline Manleigh was at her father's side almost constantly. Perhaps you heard tell of her, 'the little soldier of the Peninsula,' of how she attended the wounded on the battlefield with the skill of a physician, with no thought of her own safety.''

Andrew looked over at Honor with a sudden sharp question in his eyes, but her gaze was fixed on Sir Henry, and she appeared oblivious of him.

"So they lived," continued Julian, "for five long years. Until Wellington became aware that there had been a bad breach of security in the government. Lord Peninghurst was sent home with his daughter and his aide, Captain Renard, most recently your groom.''

Sir Henry's eyes flicked to the door, and Jake Renard inclined his head. Sir Henry licked his lips nervously, his wary gaze returning to Julian.

"And then Lord Peninghurst died, only weeks after his return. I went to visit the bereaved daughter. She told me that her father's death had been deliberate murder, and she told me why. In fact, she told me a good many interesting things. And she asked for my help in apprehending the man responsible. Naturally, I gave it to her.

"I arranged for Honor Winslow and Jake Renard to become attached to your household, for I was quite sure this was where the leaks were coming from. I fed you false information with just enough truth to convince the French that your source was infallible. And I have waited until I could find proof that you were responsible for Lord Peninghurst's murder.''

"And now you think you have found it because of what this stupid girl has told you? It is lies, I say! She is nothing but a scheming hussy! She admitted as much to me herself, that she would do anything for money and position!''

Honor's eyes flashed. She pulled the lace from her neck, exposing the ugly welts, and Arabella stifled a cry against her hand at the sight. Honor stepped forward, facing him defiantly. "Unlike you, Sir Henry, I would rather die than betray my country. I would never sell out her secrets for any reason, most certainly not money or position. That's what truly disgusts me about you. You did not even act from a political conviciton—it was sheer greed that provoked you to do what you did, not caring how many lives might be lost by your treachery. And to protect yourself from discovery, you took the one life that mattered more to me that any other in the world. You murdered my father, Sir Henry, as surely as if you had shot him yourself.''

Sir Henry stared at Honor.

"You look surprised," said Julian to Sir Henry. "I fear I neglected to mention a relevant part of the story. I found Lady Caroline in a convent, where she was recovering from the death of her father. It was a sister order to the one that had taught her nursing in the Peninsula. Allow me to present to you Lady Caroline Manleigh, only child of the late Earl of Peninghurst.''

"Caroline . . ." Andrew whispered.

Her eyes went to his, and she smiled slightly. He shook his head in disbelief, then grinned. There were a thousand thoughts that crowded through his mind, and a thousand questions.

"What do you have to say now, Sir Henry?" Julian demanded.

Sir Henry mutely shook his head. His pale face was covered by small beads of sweat, sweat that had also soaked through his coat.

"Put the gun down, Lord Chesney." Phoebe advanced into the room from behind the stairs. She had arrived only at the very end of the conversation, but lost not a moment, for it was the perfect time to make her entrance. She held the pistol before her, waving it at Honor. "Put it down and push it over here to me." She was exceedingly pleased with the way the command had sounded.

Andrew complied, watching her very carefully. Then he moved toward Honor.

"Stay away from her!" ordered Phoebe.

Andrew halted, regarding her warily. He mistrusted not only her intent but also her rationality, which complicated the situation considerably. "What do you want with Miss Winslow, Phoebe? Your argument should not be with her."

"You are so wrong, my beloved. You still do not see how you have been taken in? It is even worse than I thought! I knew from the beginning that she had designs on you. Here, tonight, you have heard that she has deceived you all into thinking that she is this . . . this lady, because she wants to entrap you! Who would believe such a story! Not I, I tell you that!''

"Give me the gun, Phoebe, dearest," said Sir Henry coaxingly. "You're a good girl to come to the aid of your father."

"Your aid, Papa? I cannot think what aid you require other than money, and I was supposed to bring it to you by offering up my beauty and my body." She threw her head back in what she had read was a noble gesture. "You never took my heart into consideration. You promised me Lord Chesney, thinking only of yourself and how your pockets were to let, without thinking how my heart might break if I could not have him."

"No, Phoebe . . . no!" said Sir Henry, wiping the sweat from his brow. "I did it for you, so that you would have a fine husband and a good future!"

"And you took Miss Winslow into our house," Phoebe continued, ignoring him, "and let her scheme to take away the only man I could ever love. Admit it, Miss Winslow! Admit you conspired from the very beginning to capture Lord Chesney!"

Phoebe by this point was so caught up in her performance that she had completely forgotten that the gun in her hand was not a prop. "Relinquish him now," she said, gesturing at Andrew, "and all will be forgotten." And so saying, she squeezed her hand into an impassioned fist.

The gun went off with a great crack.

"Oh, no," gasped Phoebe, dropping the pistol in horror. "Not again!"

Andrew swayed for a moment, then fell slowly to the floor.

Chaos ensued, punctuated by Arabella's screams, and Sir Henry took advantage of the moment to run out the back way. Captain Renard did not hesitate, running across the hall and scooping up Andrew's gun from the floor in one swift movement, and took off after him.

Honor immediately fell to her knees, her heart in her throat at the sight of the blood covering his chest. "Andrew?" she whispered. "Oh, Andrew, no!"

He managed to open his eyes and smile. "It is not an easy road to marriage, it seems."

She laughed shakily, at the same time tearing the coat and shirt from his chest to expose a long gash through the muscle of his armpit. Sighing deeply, she looked up at Julian.

"Bad?" he asked anxiously.

"A flesh wound," she said with relief, prodding gently with exploring fingers. "The bullet passed cleanly through."

"Ouch—easy there," said Andrew, trying to sit up, but giving up the effort. "This is becoming a bad habit, my love."

Honor smiled, and bound up the cloth of his shirt into a pad and pressed it closely against the torn skin.

"Ah, well," said Julian with a smile. "Although the road to marriage is fraught with peril, it appears you will survive it."

"Fair is fair," murmured Andrew, and promptly fainted.

Julian went straight to Phoebe, who had not moved, pocketed the pistol, and took her roughly by the shoulders. "I should thrash you, you little fool. You might have killed him!"

Phoebe burst into tears. "I didn't mean it! I didn't mean to shoot him, I swear it!"

"That is the one thing I do believe. And just what did you mean by 'not again,' may I ask?"

"Nothing," sniffed Phoebe. "I didn't mean anything."

Honor looked up from her administrations to Andrew, her eyes narrowed. "I think," she said slowly, "that we have the answer to Andrew's last 'accident.' You placed the wire across the path, did you not, Phoebe? You read about it in your novel, the one that went missing. Jocie confessed to me only a few days ago that she had taken it. She told me the story. I wondered then, but could not believe it. Why, Phoebe? Why would you do such a thing?"

Phoebe glared at her, seeing that there was no point in denying it at this late date. "All right, I admit it. But the wire was meant for you! I knew you always rode that way in the mornings. And I had seen you with him in the copse the night before, carrying on! Even then you were trying to steal him from me! Nothing goes right for me," she said, bursting into tears. "Nothing at all."

Julian shook his head. "I cannot stay and listen to this now. Remain here, Phoebe. I will deal with you later."

He started out the front door.

Sir Henry ran as fast as he could, and given his bulk, it was not easy. He kept to the bushes, dodging and darting, and finally rounded the corner of the house. Lord Chesney's carriage stood there, the horses still attached, and with a last surge of energy, generated by relief that escape was so close at hand, he dashed forward.

A small figure moved from the shadow of the great elm on the lawn. "I warned yer, ye thievin' cove!" a voice cried, and a shot rang out in the night.

Sir Henry halted in his steps, his hand going to his heart. It came away covered in blood and he looked down at it in surprise, then toppled slowly to his knees and fell onto his face, dead.

Epilogue

But this denoted a foregone conclusion.

—William Shakespeare, *Othello*, III, ii

Andrew opened his eyes the next morning, fuzzy-headed, stiff, and sore. His upper arm was bound by a thick white bandage. For a moment he thought it was still winter, but the trees outside were in leaf, and the vague pain in his arm was on the opposite side. And he was most certainly in his bed at Chesney. But as he slowly rose into full consciousness, it all came flooding back. Honor! he thought with a start. What had happened to her?

Hobson knocked softly and came through the door carrying a tray. "Good morning, my lord. I am pleased to see you are looking better. I have a nice bowl of gruel for you here."

"Oh, no," said Andrew dangerously. "No gruel. Not now, not ever again!"

"But Miss Winslow . . . I mean, Lady Caroline, sent it up, my lord," said Hobson, impervious to his master's mutinous expression.

"Where is she, Hobson?" he demanded impatiently.

"Downstairs with his lordship, the marquess, and her ladyship, the marchioness," replied Hobson grandly.

Andrew smiled. Some things would never change, and one of them was Hobson, no matter how he tried. The other was Honor.

"Send for her, then, at her convenience, Hobson. And remove the gruel before I throw it at your head."

"Yes, my lord," said Hobson happily. "May I say how shocked we all are at the turn of events, but how very pleased at the outcome, my lord?"

"Yes, you may, and have. Now, out with you! And fetch Miss . . . ah, Lady Caroline."

"My lord." Hobson bowed, and left with a great show of dignity, but when he had closed the door behind him, he grinned and danced a little jig.

Hobson wasted no time.

Only a minute later Caroline stood at the threshold of the room, her heart pounding. It was here, finally, the end of it. All the lies, all the subterfuges were gone. She took a deep breath and opened the door.

He was sitting up in bed, his chest bare and his hair tumbled. She was thrilled to see that his color was good and he looked perfectly well. "Andrew?" she said softly. "You wanted to see me?"

"Honor! Don't just stand there, come in. I need to talk to you and it will not wait another minute. Come, sit down." He indicated the side of the bed.

She moved forward, trying to appear calm, and then her composure was lost as Andrew's hand reached out and took her hand, pulling her down next to him.

"You are not to think for a moment that I am chained

here in this bed, for I am not. I have only just woken and have not had time to collect myself.''

''Yes, my lord,'' said Caroline with a smile.

''I am delighted we are in accord on the point. Are you well? No ill effects from yesterday?'' he asked with concern, looking at the bruises on her throat.

''None.''

''It is all right, then?''

''For me, at least, it is wonderful! Oh, Andrew, you have no idea what a relief it is! We have not discussed it, but I know it doesn't matter to you—at least it shouldn't, given how many speeches you've produced on the subject, and . . . Oh, Andrew, how are you? I haven't even asked!''

He laughed, and grasped her hands. ''I am well enough. But I confess I do not know what to call you. It goes through my mind that I should say 'Caroline,' but I am not yet accustomed to it.''

''It doesn't matter what you call me. 'Caro' or 'Caroline,' or even 'harridan' if you wish. Andrew . . . I can hardly believe it is over.''

''Over and yet just beginning.'' He shifted in the bed, turning to face her. ''There is something you need to know which explains much about us. I only realized yesterday, when I finally learned who you truly are. I met you once, you know, years and years ago when you were hardly more than a baby. You came to Chesney with your parents. I remember it well: I took you out to play, and we ended climbing the hill and tumbling down it a number of times. I thought you were a marvelous little girl. But more important, you and I are second cousins through our mothers.''

''Andrew . . .'' Caroline gazed at him in delight. ''We are cousins? And I met you as a baby?''

''Well, not quite a baby. Three, I think. But you were certainly too young for me to entertain any romantic thoughts about you. Come to that, I was too young to have romantic thoughts at all. I think I was—''

''Eleven or twelve! At least that is how old I always thought of you in my dreams. Until this last year,'' she added with a smile. ''It all makes sense, the dreams, everything . . . well, almost everything.''

''Yes, and there's something else. Our mutual great-great-grandmother was well-known for her extraordinary intuitions. The trait popped up now and again in other members of the family, which explains a little about Minnie. And perhaps in an odd way, about us. I must say, I'm rather taken with the fact that you've loved me since you were three. You are a loyal one, aren't you, Caroline? But speaking of that, what about the rest? I'm so sorry about your father. Will you tell me . . . ?''

They talked for a long time, and when they had finally said everything that was necessary to say, Andrew took her hand.

"I feel very stupid, you know. I should have put things together much sooner. In the park that day, Stephen Lambert practically handed you to me on a platter with all the trimmings. But you never let on a thing. And all the business about riding Cabal as you did, and your extraordinary aim—''

"I never bore weapons, Andrew, but I did have to know how to shoot. And how to ride astride on any mount.''

He smiled. "Indeed. And there was the fact that naked men did not put you to the blush, nor even impress you. It cut, indeed it did.''

"Well, really, Andrew, what could you possibly expect? That was the last thing from my mind, although Hobson blushed enough for all three of us. Julian was the only person of any use . . . oh, and Captain Renard, who brought you in and helped me strip you. But he has done that before, so he was quite accustomed.''

Andrew shook his head. "You are a remarkable woman, Caroline Manleigh.''

"I do love you, Andrew. And . . . and thank you.''

"For what?''

"For understanding.''

Andrew pulled her to him and held her close against his chest. "How could I not?'' he said softly against her cheek. Then, sitting her up, he said, "Caroline, I haven't even asked—what about Sir Henry and Phoebe? What an inconvenient time to lose consciousness!''

"Sir Henry is dead. It is the most extraordinary thing, but Mr. Tilton came straight to Croftsfield to make good his threat. He shot Sir Henry and disappeared. Julian and Captain Renard laid chase, but as far as anyone knows, he's vanished off the face of the earth.''

"It is astonishing that he should show up just at that time," said Andrew. "But it cannot be all bad, for he effected a very simple solution to the problem."

"That is exactly what Julian said when he finally returned. You should have seen him, Andrew. He was magnificent! He lit into Phoebe with a vengeance, until he had her shaking in her shoes. And when he was finished, Bryonny had her say."

"I am gratified. I don't take kindly to being shot, but being shot on a misfire is an insult to my pride. How is she dealing with her father's death?"

"The usual hysterics. I think she is truly very upset, but to be brutal, I think she is mourning the loss of her glittering future more. But there is something I haven't yet told you, which is another reason Bryonny and Julian were so furious. It wasn't Sir Henry who strung the wire across the path, Andrew. It was Phoebe."

"What!" he roared. "The blasted girl not only shot me, she brought my horse to his knees? It's beyond belief!"

"Yes, and a misfire of another sort," said Caroline with a smile. "She meant it for me. She mistook you for Julian in the woods the night before. You are very similar in looks, you see, and she thought I was trying to take you from her."

Andrew mutely shook his head. "Unbelievable. The child should be locked up where she can do no further harm."

"But she will be, in a way," said Caroline, her smile broadening. "She is getting her just deserts. She is being sent to Italy for a year. To a convent," she said unsteadily, and then burst into laughter. "It seems so . . . so appropriate."

Andrew grinned. "It is indeed. I assume this was Bryonny and Julian's idea?"

"It was. But Arabella came up with the idea of Italy. In fact, it is a good one, for Phoebe will be away from any possible talk." She smiled. "Arabella is a great deal stronger than you might think. As it happens, she could not be more pleased that Sir Henry is dead, and has no qualms about saying so. On top of all the rest of it, did you know he beat her?''

Andrew frowned. "I suspected it. Poor Arabella. But at least she is free of him now.''

"But what of that, Andrew? I cannot like to think of her alone at Croftsfield with the children. You know how much she needs companionship, and there are the girls to think of. Jocie and Minerva hate it there.''

"But that's very simple, my love. We'll have them with us at Chesney—if you don't mind, that is.''

"Mind? Oh, Andrew, I didn't like to ask, as it is your house, but nothing would make me happier!''

"It's your house as well, my love, or will be shortly, and I doubt Minerva or Jocie would take kindly to my removing you from them. As for Arabella, I think she will welcome the suggestion.''

"But what a lovely wedding present! If you only knew the awful things Jocie said months ago about your having to marry and how it would take Chesney away from her forever, even before we thought it was Phoebe—''

Andrew looked at her severely. "It hurts, you know, that you ever thought such a terrible thing of me. It really rubs bitterly . . .''

Caroline raised an eyebrow. "I hope you are not looking for sympathy, my good lord. For you know perfectly well you might have disabused me of the notion anytime after Phoebe's first loving appearance in your bedroom.''

Andrew laughed. "I would have done had I been privy to your thoughts, but you were bent on keeping them from me, my lady. Oh, Caroline, what a shrew you are. Here I can call you that with perfect right, and yet you put me through such torture for so many months. The earl and the governess indeed. And I should strangle Julian and Bryonny both for their parts in the piece.''

"It was my own doing, as I have told you, and you are only unhappy because you were left out. But speaking of your friends, there is something else astonishing, Andrew. When I left them, they were engaged in a heated discussion concerning Bryonny's impetuosity.''

"Oh?'' he said with great interest. "Which particular aspect of Bryonny's impetuosity?''

"Well . . . it seems there was more truth in her story than she let on."

Andrew's eyes danced. "Surely not . . ."

"Indeed, yes. She is with child, and her husband cannot decide whether he is beside himself with joy or rage at her lack of concern for her health."

"Most typical," Andrew said with delight. "Never fear, Bryonny shall have him wrapped around her finger in a moment."

"She seemed well on her way. There was some matter of a carriage ride between Croftsfield and Chesney, for which Bryonny seemed to feel Julian was entirely responsible. Or so it was as I made my exit."

Andrew threw his head back and roared with laughter. "Oh, dear!" he managed to say. "Do you suppose you'll have me in the same state in a year from now?"

"Do you mean in the blessed state of matrimony, at point in a carriage, or about to become a father?"

"I plan on the first and third most certainly, my love. The second I had not thought of, but it sounds most intriguing. But we do need to discuss our plans, Caroline," he said, his eyes growing serious. "I have a marriage license burning in my pocket, you know, and I should like to put it to good use."

"Yes, I know, and Julian charged me to tell you that if you're not downstairs in an hour, you'll be married in your bed. He has a minister, you see."

Andrew laughed softly. "Trust Julian. Does it suit you, Caroline?"

"It suits me well, my lord. Oh, and Captain Renard was kind enough to fetch the children from London, so they are here as well."

"Good. Then send in Hobson and tell him he is to attire his master for his wedding. And, Caroline, would you like to wear the dress my mother wore on her marriage to my father? You are much the same size. Nugent will know where it is. You shall have her ring as well, if you would like it."

"It would honor me to wear them both, Andrew," she said, her eyes shining.

Andrew squeezed her hand. "Go, before I have an impulse to kiss you. I swore to myself I wouldn't do that again until after we were married, and I think I can manage to wait one more hour.''

They were married in the Chesney chapel, which was just off the main hall. Louisa Montague's wedding dress of deep gold silk and Brussels lace fit Caroline as if it had been made for her. Andrew drew in a deep breath when she appeared, and Caroline laughed out loud as she interpreted the look he gave her, which had very little to do with the wedding at hand and a great deal more to do with the event's aftermath.

Bryonny and Julian, Arabella, and Jake Renard acted as witnesses, with Jocie and Minnie serving as impromptu and very excited flower girls. In the hall outside, Hobson and Nugent tried hard to restrain their tears. Flowers were carried up to adorn the master bedroom, and celebrations had already begun in the servants' quarters, where they were in the throes of preparing a wedding breakfast.

Finally, after what seemed like hours of eating and drinking, congratulatory speeches and general festivity, Andrew gently detached Minerva from his lap and turned her over to Caroline. He excused Jocie, Arabella, and himself, and they had a private but brief talk that left Arabella in transports and Jocie in tears of happiness. When they reentered, Jocie ran up to Caroline and hugged her.

"I love you, Honor," she whispered. "Tomorrow I'll remember to call you Caroline. And I was wrong about everything. I am so happy you have married Uncle Andrew. And I am so happy about coming home to Chesney."

Jocie lightly ran out before Caroline could respond.

She turned helplessly to Andrew, tears in her eyes.

"Thank you all for being here," he said, taking her hand, which now bore the family wedding ring, and addressed the company. "I am a shot man. I think it is time to retire."

"Shot by Cupid," said Julian with a laugh, but he rose, and with hugs and kisses and more words of congratulation, the wedding guests took their leave.

"Thank God," said Andrew, having finally achieved the safety of the bedroom, for they had been waylaid by the entire Chesney staff, who had gathered to toast their happiness. He took Caroline into his arms. "I know it is not yet evening, nor close to it by a long time, my love, but I have been a patient man. And I am your husband. Would you reward this imperfect flesh?"

"Andrew," said Caroline with a smile, "it is no good to throw my old remark up in my face time and time again when you know exactly what I think of your flesh and always have. But I must ask you if you do feel well enough for that sort of exertion."

"Harridan," he said huskily, stroking her neck.

"I shouldn't want you to faint at a crucial moment."

"Which particular crucial moment?" inquired Andrew, drawing the dress from her shoulders and kissing the flesh beneath, then moving his mouth to the lobe of her ear.

"I do not know, my lord," she said weakly into his hair. "As I have told you, I know nothing about the activity."

"Then it is time you learned. And God help us both, my love."

He led her to the bed.

Many hours later, Andrew managed to raise his head and lift himself up on his elbow. "I have something I must say to you, Caro, my sweet."

She opened her eyes and gazed up at him. " 'Words, words, mere words,' " she quoted dreamily.

"And very much from the heart when it comes to that. Caro, I am depleted in body, no matter how full I am in mind and spirit. No man could be fuller and not be in the kingdom of heaven. But now, my love, mundane as it may seem, it is well past the dinner hour. Shall we have something to eat? And let it *not* be gruel."

Caroline burst into laughter. "For a man of your physical appetites, my dearest, we'll call up a feast for kings. And let us pledge our troth in champagne. Hobson will be most gratified to know you still live."

"I am most gratified myself, Caro. There were a few moments I questioned the matter."

He bent down to kiss her, and was lost in the question yet again.

SIGNET REGENCY ROMANCE
COMING IN SEPTEMBER 1988

Sandra Heath
An Impossible Confession

Laura Matthews
Miss Ryder's Memoirs

Caroline Brooks
Regency Rose

The New Super Regency
Mary Jo Putney
Lady of Fortune